I0684558

Sean O'Mordha

Man With No Name

Celtic
Publications

Copyright © 2011 Sean O'Mordha
All rights reserved.

ISBN-13: 978-0-9829842-8-4
ISBN-10: 0982984286

DEDICATION

To Christopher B. and Christopher N. Moore,
for their special day:
May 11, 2012, and being the kind of persons
you are.

CONTENTS

ACKNOWLEDGMENTS

An author does not write in a vacuum and many people contribute to a story without them, or sometimes even the author, knowing that they do so. Of course, family are major contributors with encouragement and sometimes technical assistance. Educators and friends also contribute by the things they say or do.

I do wish to give special thanks to Benjamin Suyematsu, a student at my alma mater, the University of Wyoming in Laramie, and fellow Wyomingite. It has been many years since walking to classes on that campus and Benjamin was gracious to take time from his schedule to bring me up to date on changes and procedures. Thank you and best wishes for your future.

—Sean O'Mordha

Sean O'Mordha

Chapter 1

Triton and the Hermit

Philippe struggled to hear the radio weather updates about the storm as the thunderous cannonade booms of the bow battling for survival against the wind and mountainous waves. Catching only bits and pieces, he really didn't need to hear someone tell him about the storm. It was his only connection to life as thick, black clouds boiled up behind. He wasn't making the progress hoped for. The typhoon was gaining.

Fatigued after piloting the sail boat through increasing heavy seas all night, by his calculations Vanuatu and safe harbor at Port Vila should be within his grasp with morning light. By 0800 hours the weakest of light revealed no land fore and aft. A sinking feeling knotted his gut. Piloting the boat prevented him from checking the GPS below, but the wind and waves ahead of the storm obviously had pushed him much further north. He was a good sailor; conditions deteriorated way beyond his abilities. His last hope was to round the long finger on the north end of Vanuatu and swing into Big Bay and shelter from the storm. He could put into any one of several fishing villages there. When he tried turning the wind and waves herded him steadily north and beyond land, tossed at the mercy of the storm and fate into the open ocean.

A few months ago he would have sought help by praying. That was no longer an option since God was punishing him. That left riding out the storm, but despite the *Catherine*'s great open ocean design, he gravely doubted that would be possible. Nearing complete exhaustion, a volcanic peak and lagoon rose out of the black, churning waters directly ahead. He felt some hope return until spotting the boiling water directly in his path. A reef!

◆　　◆　　◆

The Olympian gods amassed their army along the horizon. The tiny island would not escape the brunt of the assault. Aeolus, ruler of the winds, preceded the attack, first as a deceptive breeze, steadily crescendoing to a hideous shriek. Zeus, astride a chariot of seething, black clouds, ravaged the advancing line with fiery bolts. Aello, the whirlwind, and Calaeno, the blackness, moved ahead of the attack. Triton called forth upon his conch, raising up the ocean to overwhelm the main island's first line of defense, crashing over the reef with the roar of a blinded Polyphemus to surge through the lagoon as a thick, ugly froth and assail the beach.

The worst was yet to come. This was only the

advancing edge of the typhoon bearing down upon the cluster of tiny islands, mostly deposits of coral supporting a few palms and some low vegetation. They would be punished severely, the main island as well, but that volcanic remnant was firmly seated to the ocean floor. High above the raging attack a lone man stood upon a parapet of the lava-born fortress rising defiantly against the Olympians.

The observer was unconcerned. He and the island had withstood other attacks. This storm, like all the others, was not the worry, only a passing inconvenience. No, the worry was the little boat fighting to make its way into the lagoon that lay between the remaining halves of the old caldera. Whoever piloted that craft through the brutalizing swells would find no haven. It was a doomed bath toy tossed out of control.

Rain began splattering the man's face, droplets rippling down the weathered face to drip off the tip of a gray Vandyke. He watched with apprehension as a pang of remorse slipped through his breast. He disliked people, though that was probably not exactly right. Loathed was a better description. That's what brought him to this lonely island in the middle of the Pacific Ocean. That's why he seldom ventured into civilization except for supplies every few months, crafting the visit so as to have as little human contact possible. Those other trips were a necessity part of work. Despite the pain, and bitterness, and hatred of the past, he didn't enjoy watching some hapless, innocent fool die, even if logged as collateral damage.

Aeolus' breath, like a great scythe, sheared the tops of the waves creating a horizontal wall of water as Zeus' army pursued the small boat toward its death. The smooth, gray tip of a waterspout materialized from a black cloud, snaking to the surface, slashing back and forth like a whip herding the Olympians' victim forward.

Shoving weathered hands deeper into his pockets, the man hunched broad shoulders as the boat made a pitifully desperate run for the lagoon. Mostly likely the pilot was unaware what lay ahead. It would be difficult to see what was coming. The lagoon would appear the alternative to avoid the volcanic rocks and cliffs of either island. Unseen until the last moment were Kahuna's Teeth. In any case, a few hundred meters more and it would be all over. The man hated feeling so helpless.

Something happened eons ago, probably a crack in the wall separating the ocean from the hot belly of the volcano. Water poured through the fissure and into its bowels. The old caldera erupted in a fragmenting explosion. Two sides of the vent disappeared and the ocean buried the fire. What remained were a smaller, elongated, half-moon island, the much larger main island upon which the man stood, and the old caldera, now a lagoon between the two remnants. The western end of the large, elliptical lagoon had filled with coral sand, but the eastern side, the side where the boat headed, was a jagged, rock reef hiding just below the surface.

Contacting that barrier, the boat lurched awkwardly sideways, the bottom gone in that instant. Triton's victorious blast from the conch created a wave that lifted it high in the palm of its frothed hand, carrying it well onto the submerged rocks and smashing it into oblivion.

The scene reminded the man of a professional wrestling match he watched as a little boy. The 'villain' lifted his opponent high overhead, slamming him to the canvas, and then throwing his hulking torso onto the stunned opponent. That's what the ocean did, pick the small boat high up on its watery shoulders, slam it onto the reef, breaking it like a crystal bowl, before burying the remains beneath a huge wave.

Piece by piece the masticated remains were tossed and mixed with foam, relentlessly reduced in size by the canine-like teeth of the reef as the man watched with forced detachment until spotting a bright orange object bobbing amid the foaming breakers coming ashore. Whipping water from the lenses he focused the binoculars. It appeared to be a dog in a life vest, struggling as it towed another orange object.

Picking his way down treacherously slippery rocks to the beach, he battled along the shore, occasionally knocked down by watery fists, their fingers tenaciously trying to lock him into their deadly clutches, and drag him under. The little light available was gobbled up by ocean spray so one couldn't be sure where the animal came ashore, and then his foot struck something soft. Lurching forward he fell onto the sand, immediately hammered by a wave that clawed and pulled him seaward. Awash, the man was struck by something — a body! A human body!

Latching onto the life preserver, he dug bare feet into the shifting sand and struggled toward shore. A wave hit, carrying them both against the cliff, then tried dragging them out. Frantically, he fought off the attack aided by some large boulders standing away from the cliff, acting like football linesmen to break the ocean's brutal charge. Able to stand, he easily slung the light body over his shoulder and retreat back to the only breech in the cliff. Another wave slammed ashore, but with feet well planted, he stood against it. A few more strides and he began clamoring up the drenched, mossy rocks to higher ground just as a big, orange lifevested dog shot passed, nearly knocking off him off the rocks.

The Olympians roared with rage at having lost their victim as he lay the body down. The man had no interest toting a corpse all the way up the mountain, besides he needed to let his heart slow down. Despite being in good, physical condition, this was too much exertion for someone of any age. Expecting an adult, he was surprise to see a boy, mid-teens, and judging from the coughing, still alive. Rolling him onto one side kept the now torrential rain and any vomit from finishing the drowning. After resting a time, he cut the life vest free and heft the boy over his shoulder once more to complete the steep climb to the fortress-house.

Gaining a small, level shelf and rounding a tall, basaltic slab leaning against a sheer cliff, the rescuer pushed through a heavy door set in the mountain. At that moment the dog suddenly reappeared and bolt passed into the dark, cavernous interior. Closing the heavy, steel door was difficult as Aeolus' breathe pommeled viciously at the surface, but leaning a free shoulder into it and pushing with powerful legs the man managed to secure the latch though feet slipped repeatedly on the wet floor. A heavy steel beam dropped into place spanning the frame reducing the storm's furry to muffled wails. Thick, rock and concrete walls made the cave structure impregnable.

Gently depositing the body on the floor, the man slumped exhausted into a wicker chair, resting for some time before disappearing down a tunnel. The dog, panting, and obviously overjoyed at being inside, sat near the boy, dripping water into a pool of water. Returning, the rescuer threw some towels down and began drying the boy while checking for injuries. Other than a few bruises, superficial cuts, and abrasions, the only damage seemed to be a large bump on the side of his head. That was a worry. Medical help for more than simple fractures was impossible until after the storm—a couple days from now according to the radio warning.

The dog, a Golden Setter, looking every bit the drowned rat, didn't seem to have any serious injuries, either, which was amazing, considering the pounding both must have received while being tossed ashore. The man cut the dog's life vest free and dried it, then himself, tossing the remaining towels on the Teak floor to soak up the puddles. Lifting the boy into his arms, he carried the limp body to a room deeper inside, gently placing the lifeless form on a cot before turning up the yellow light of an oil lamp for a closer inspection of damage.

The boy appeared the same height as his own five-eight and gratefully lighter, maybe 130 pounds. Where the man had been raised, the cowboys characterized such people a long drink of water. Locks of fine, straight hair lay plastered over an elongated face. Very gently, almost lovingly, the man lifted the ginger-colored strands from the boy's eyes, re-depositing them behind the ears. Several centimeters or so above the roots the hair was darker. Sun bleaching was not uncommon for someone exposed to the tropical sun, however, the lad obviously was blond. Smooth, golden bronze skin indicated he spent a good share of time outside. He guessed the lad had Scandinavian heritage although the face held European features, reminiscent of French.

Certainly, he had undergone a similar transition. His own thick crop of dark brown hair suffered similar bleaching upon arriving in the islands, although what remained were ever diminishing locks touched with mousy gray. Over time, his own skin became burnt a swarthy brown.

The boy's shredded lava-lava barely clung to the slender waist exposing the outside of his left thigh, which bore a nasty abrasion from hip to just above the knee, fortunately not deep enough to draw blood. Some minor cuts still seeped blood. There were other abrasions and bruises scattered from head to foot. These he treated with gentle, fresh water sponging and a smear of an oily substance concocted from native plants. However, he needed to check for more pressing damage.

Beginning with the legs and arms, he used practiced fingers to check for serious damage. There was a modicum of consciousness so that he watched the boy's face for any reaction. There didn't appear to be anything significant and moved to the torso, checking the ribs. Lesser damage would not be known until the boy became more fully awake. Likewise, checking the abdomen failed to detect any signs of internal damage. Confirmation of that, too, would have to wait.

Draping a wool blanket over the body to respect his privacy, the man removed the soggy remnant of the island kilt and the one remaining deck shoe before adding a second blanket to ward off the cave's natural chill. The dog curled up on a rug next to the bed, shivering. The smell of wet dog rankled the man's nose as it received a blanket and reassuring pat on the damp head. An almost imperceptible smile turned the corners of the man's mouth when a memory flashed to mind, escaping from a stifled vault. A pleasant one for a change.

After stoking the belly of a wood stove, the man settled into a padded rocking chair and opened a book, but read little, instead staring at the visitor. A grandson would be near this age, if things had been different. Suddenly his attention shifted to a small desk tucked against a dark wall. Most of the time he managed to avoid eye contact with the thing. It was a shadow lurking on the fringes, like the memories it contained, but this time there was a tugging urge to visit that receptacle of pain.

Slowly, reluctantly, he stood and shuffled toward it. Enveloped by shadows, his hand reached down to slide the center drawer open. There it was, exactly as left so many years before—the Ruger automatic, small, compact, simply designed, efficiently destructive. Behind, buried deeper in the drawer the pictures—a woman holding an infant, a man beaming proudly, another of a small boy, smiling impishly while seated on his father's lap. A tear welled up and cascaded down a roughened cheek.

The gods-driven storm lashed and pounded with aberrant fury, to no avail. They would have to sink the island to ferret the humans out of its rock fortress. For that, they were weak. With the storm's cannibalistic energy spent, the third day dawned bright and warm as if nothing happened. The boy stirred occasionally during those hours, never fully waking until toward the end of that sun-filled day when he began moving more vigorously. Suddenly his eyes opened wide to stare at the ceiling.

"Hello," the man said softly from his chair next to the stove.

The boy didn't respond, just looking at the ceiling, rocking his head slowly to either side while gazing about the darkened room.

"Do you speak English?"

The boy's head snapped sideways to glare at the man. It was as if eyes saw, but the mind couldn't sort out the images.

"Où suis-je?" he said, blinking rapidly, obviously trying to get eye and mind working together.

The man's smile was faint. *Ah, French,* he thought. *New Caledonia?* "On an island, a rock really," the man replied, using his native English. "So, what were you doing on that boat on this big ocean?"

"Boat? What boat?" the boy asked, still using French, but obviously spoke English.

The man leaned forward, the look of concern etching his face. "A relatively small boat heading for a reef barely ahead of a very large storm."

"Storm?"

"So, what's your name?"

"Philippe." the boy replied quickly, then expressive, green eyes went blank, obviously struggling to remember a last name.

"Don't strain yourself. You took a nasty hit to the head. If you can't remember everything right now, it will come back in time."

Obviously fluent in both languages, they continued talking, but responses to selective inquiries alternated between French, English, a smattering of Islander, and a confusing mix. The man's grasp of French and the general Island dialect were respectable, but despite which language used his guest had great difficulty remembering more than a first name. Lengthy silence preceded responses to carefully phrased questions before answered in slow, simple sentences. After taking some fresh, chicken soup, the boy drifted off to sleep.

Awaking late the following morning, Philippe wished his heart would stop. Every beat slammed his head as if being hit with a mallet behind the left ear. He wanted to massage the pain, but a very tender bump covered the spot. The man said he'd been shipwrecked and tossed ashore during a typhoon. He didn't remember. There was a lot he couldn't remember. His mind seemed as empty as the ocean, but inexplicably felt safe here. Was this how a new baby felt? Was he a newborn in a teenager's body?

Philippe's first recollections were distant, fuzzy, dark, frustratingly slippery, offering little to anchor to. He forced his eyes to focus. The man's beard encompassed lean lips, the skin a deep cinnamon, the eyes dark, foreboding, penetrating, as if capable of burrowing deep into one's core. Heavy lines at the corners of those eyes creased deeply on a concerned face. It was often hard to understand the man's words. The man didn't always follow Philippe, either, something about him mixing French, English, and Islander.

The man looked over the top of a book. "Good morning."

The boy struggled, but the words came slowly. The man spoke English. Philippe's grasp of English was good, but felt more comfortable with French.

The man's voice was scratchy and sometimes gruff, yet patient. Philippe moved to rise, groaned and fell back. The man came to his side.

"Now that you're more alert I want to check you for more serious injuries."

"I hurt."

"Where?"

"All over."

"Let's see if there's something more specific."

Since the first day, he repeatedly checked for swelling and discoloration. Nothing appeared more serious than bruising. Further examination had to wait until the lad was conscious. Starting with the shoulders, he felt along each clavicle, pressed along the arms, bent the elbow and wrist joints, and then rotated the shoulder. When there was no response, he moved along the right rib cage. That seemed alright as well. Because of some abrasion to the skin on the left side, he anticipated a problem and tried to be extra gentle. Touching the third and fourth rib from the bottom drew a gasp and pained response. He gently checked those two carefully.

"They don't appear broken. Might be cracked. Still painful," the man reported.

From there he pressed on the boy's belly, thankful there was no show of swelling or discomfort.

"Why do my legs feel funny?"

"What do you mean?"

"They tingle."

He took the left thigh in both hands and squeezed. "Feel that?"

"I can feel you squeezing," the boy said, staring at the false ceiling.

He check the right thigh with the same response, and then the calves. Nothing in the boy's face indicated pain. Taking each leg above the ankle, he flexed that joint, bent the knees, and lifted the legs to check the hips. No problem.

"I want you to bend your left knee."

The boy looked down. After a couple seconds it became obvious something was wrong. He could bend each knee only following concerted effort. Panic began to spread over the boy's eyes.

"What do you feel?"

"A tingling feeling, like the time I sat too long and they went to sleep."

The man methodically massaged each leg from thigh to ankle, lifting and carefully bending each joint again, paying special attention to the hip. Except for a light smattering of adolescent hair on the lower legs the skin was smooth, the muscles strong, and well developed.

"You swim a lot?"

"Yes. I love taking the guests through the reef."

"Where you live must be a beautiful place."

"Oh, yes. So many colors, and so many pretty fish. The guests are always surprised."

"Where is that?"

The question was answered with silence as the boy's eyes glazed over and furrows appeared along his brow. "I . . . I can't remember?"

"There are many such places here, too."

A mask of confusion and concern covered Philippe's face. "I should remember, but I can't remember. Why?"

"Probably too much water got in your ears causing a short circuit." The man forced a smile. "That's easily solved. I'll take you outside and hang you upside down in the sun for a few hours to dry." It was meant as a joke, but his patient panicked.

"I can't go outside."

"Why?"

"They might see me."

"Who?"

Again the look of confusion clouded his face. "I . . . I don't know?"

A gray plastic, tackle box sat on the bedside table containing First Aid supplies. The Man reached in, withdrew a small, clear envelope, and opened it. Repositioning himself at the boy's feet he said, "This is a pin. I'm going to prick you with it. Tell me if you feel anything."

Lifting the left foot he could see his visitor rarely wore shoes. The bottoms were tough. He touched the heel of the boy's left foot. Nothing. Then the ball and a couple toes. Nothing. The calf and upper leg produced some results. The same held for the right leg. Satisfied that the hip was undamaged, and that he had some feeling, the man turned the lad onto his side. There was some bruising on his lower back and hips, but careful fingering didn't reveal anything serious.

Returned to a face up position, he asked, "Feel like sitting on the edge of the bed?"

"Yes," the boy replied, reverting to French,

crying out with pain. "I hurt."

"The ribs?"

"Yes."

"Move slowly. The ocean beat you up pretty good," he replied, helping him up. "I'm going to tape those ribs. It's not going to be pleasant, but they will feel a little better when you move.

This was a job he had performed far more than once, on others and himself. Securing the wrap, Philippe took in some air and smiled faintly. "I can breathe without it hurting so bad. Thank you. "I'm feeling dizzy." His face paled.

Quickly fluffing pillows against the headboard, he helped the boy lean back, wanting to keep his head elevated. Once reasonably comfortable, he went to the wood stove, returning with a blue-enameled, metal cup filled with a steaming brew.

"Here, try some soup. Actually doesn't taste too bad once you get used to it."

"I have had this before," Philippe said after taking a sip. "My mother gives this to me when I am sick. It always makes me feel better."

"Not much left of your clothes. I've got a lava-lava you can have," the man said, handing Philippe a brightly colored piece of cloth. "Anything else wouldn't fit."

"Thank you. This is all I usually wear anyway, when I must wear something."

Philippe fell asleep after a second cup of soup, waking with a start three hours later. Turning his head from side to side, he obviously was trying to place himself again, relaxing a little upon spying the man seated in a chair next to the stove, Ellie curled on a rug next to his bed.

"What is that noise?" he asked with a hint of panic.

"Just the typhoon knocking on the door trying to sell some rain and wind. I'm not interested."

"It cann't hurt us?"

"Can't make a typhoon strong enough to blow down a mountain. How are you feeling?"

"Sore, but not so much as before." He tried sitting on the edge of the bed.

The legs continued to move sluggishly. He tried standing, but fell back with a cry of pain thanks to the damaged ribs.

"My legs. What is wrong with my legs?" his voice was filled with fear.

Scooping the visitor up and gently cradling him like a small child, he said, "Judging by a bruise on your back, you took a pretty good shot to the spine. I've seen this before. What you need is a treatment."

Exiting the low-ceilinged room, they entered into a twisting corridor of bare rock dimly lit by a series of short-handled, electric Tiki torches angled upward off the wall.

"This looks like a cave."

"It is. We're inside a dormant volcano. At least for now. The halls and rooms are the result of gases and magma flows. The previous owners did extensive remodeling, but I've dressed it up some to make it a bit more homey."

When they arrived at an intersection Philippe asked, "Where does that go?" indicating a passage to the right slanting steeply upward.

"Outside. A nice, quiet, sunny place. Very private. We'll go there later."

Gradually the corridor widened as the smooth, rock path skirted a miniature waterfall drizzling into a large, elliptical pool of clear water.

"Water is good therapy. Soak those bruises. Try moving those pegs around. Once you get strength back you can try walking," the man explained carrying his charge into the steaming pool, setting him on a submerged ledge so his head, shoulders, and upper chest were above the surface. Since their arrival, the dog steadfastly refused to leave the boy's side, but here was content to lie on the damp ground and watch closely. It obviously had its fill of water for a while.

The pool was hot, but bearable. Bubbles rising from the smooth pebble floor felt like a masseuse's fingers kneading away the hurt and soreness. As long as Philippe didn't move his head quickly, the pounding subsided to a dull throb. The man gently helped Philippe repeatedly flex one leg then the other. They moved reluctantly and then only when concentrating on the action. Time became meaningless as the youth gradually felt stronger and limbs responded more willingly, and the pain lessened.

"It's time to go."

"Pooh!" the boy retorted, pursing his lips in an impish pout.

"How about riding piggy back?" the man asked, turning his back to the boy and squatting low in the water.

"Papa carried me this way when I was little," Philippe replied, wrapping his arms about the man's neck, long legs about the man's waist. "Go, horsey," Philippe said with a slight, playful laugh.

They returned to the pool later that day and three times every day that following week, each visit promoting rapid progress so that Philippe cautiously leaned back to float about the surface and moving strengthening legs while the man watched, waiting in anticipation. Then, with one strong stroke, the boy propelled himself under the waterfall. Instantly he began thrashing and screaming as the man leaned back and laughed as he had not done for years— since long before coming to the island.

"It's freezing!" Philippe gasped in a high-pitched soprano, splashing a rapid withdrawal. The dog, called Ellie, sat up and barked happily, displaying a big, sloppy tongue grin.

The man continued laughing before rising and walking away. "I'll round up something to eat. Don't drown."

Philippe listened to the man's hearty voice cackle long after disappearing down the tunnel until a profound silence enveloped the little domain. Every move seemed amplified as it reverberated from off the smooth, shiny, black and gray rock to harmonize with the trickle of water entering the pool. The sudden exertion had renewed the pounding in his head. Philippe moved to sit near the edge and leaned back, concentrating on relaxing until it settled to its usual, dull groan. Ellie approached, dark eyes alight with happiness, mouth curled into a smile, tongue eagerly licking Philippe's face several times. The boy responded by scratching his friend's ear.

However, Philippe's energy level was too high

after so much sleep and physical restraint and soon returned to floating about the pool again. Now aware of the icy waterfall, he toyed with it by slipping beneath the surface to pop up directly under its trickle, then down again. The sudden temperature contrasts were invigorating. Engrossed in the game he didn't notice the man return with a large, woven basket of fruit.

"Hungry?" he said, taking a slurping bite out of a mango.

"How long have you lived here?" Philippe asked, swimming over and taking some fruit.

"Thirty-seven years."

"There is no one else?"

"People aren't welcome here."

"I am people."

"I'm not sure what you are. If you are people, I'll reserve judgment whether to keep you or toss you back in the ocean." He sounded gruff, but there was a twinkle in his eyes.

Chapter 2

The Intruder

⊕ime being of no concern, man and boy had no idea how long they lingered in the grotto, swimming and talking. To Philippe, it was pleasant, light-hearted chitchat. For the man, the conversation was laced with carefully couched questions as he continued probing the damaged memory for clues to who this visitor was.

"I'd like to go outside, if it is safe," Philippe said, stepping out of the pool and walking toward the path leading upward.

"Here," the man said, handing him the lava-lava, haphazardly tossed aside before entering the pool. Philippe laid it over his shoulder, continuing completely unconcerned about his nakedness.

The tunnel opened from a sheer cliff perhaps twenty meters high onto a small, palm-dotted plateau that fell in a long glide to the northern shoreline and an endless, unblemished sea beyond. Coming from the cave's darkness, the brightness was overwhelming so they remained just inside the tunnel for a time that their eyes might adjust. Philippe relished the sun's warmth. The man loved the womb-like feeling of the cave, but often found pleasure outside, sitting on a rock outcrop or under a palm to simply watch frigates soar high overhead or listen to the orchestral symphony of ocean and jungle.

Philippe quickly found a large, flat slab of lava, spread the rectangular piece of clothing, and stretched out on his stomach using his arms as a pillow. The man found a favorite sitting rock under a shady coconut tree, settled in, and studied his visitor over the top of a novel. As the right question or situation jarred loose a fragment of the boy's memories to rise from the depths of their prison, so did suppressed memories from the man's past surface at unexpected moments.

He smiled a little as the boy started to purr softly, so like the little child he had nurtured long ago. He judged Philippe about fourteen and well on his way to becoming a head turner among the ladies. Aside from the mischievous sparkle in those bright, green eyes and warm, effervescent smile, Philippe was emerging from childhood athletically built. Wide, well-muscled shoulders tapered to a narrow swell at the hip and long, strong legs. He definitely was a swimmer and that may have been his salvation bringing him ashore. However, it was the boy's bottom mounding up like the hill on the adjacent island that led the man's mind back through time to a vision of diapers and a boy not yet a year old.

The new father was amazed that such a little kid could poop so much. The sight of the greenish goo provoked rumblings of nausea. The smell was another contention. How could such a sweet thing offer such disgusting rewards?

Once again, in his mind, the man lovingly sponged the little, round butt, powdering, and diapering it with pride, reflecting on the child's promised future. Some day that little tot would produce his own baby and grandpa would have the privilege of doing this all over again. Turning his head, the man spit in wounded disgust! Would have —if things had been different.

The boy's arm twitched. The man looked up. The boy's leg jerked, then his body seemed to writhe in spasms. The man tossed his book aside just as Philippe lurched into a sitting position crying out, "Papa! Mamma!" Then in a heart-wrenching whisper, "Papa? Mamma?"

As the man approached, he noticed the boy's translucent eyes were glazed as they stared into the vaulted sky, tears cascading down brown cheeks. Sitting next to the boy he instinctively encircled quaking shoulders with a firm arm. In response, Philippe buried his head on the man's chest and sobbed so hard to tear the veils of heaven. Eventually lifting his head, the boy turned away as if embarrassed.

"Every day I prayed to God to forgive me. I confessed to Father Josteau, but he said my penitence would be hard."

"What could one so young do to be so condemned?" the man asked gently, a hand still resting gently on Philippe's quivering shoulder.

"Whenever Papa flew away he passed very low

along the beach and waved the wingtips before heading out to sea. Jean-Peter said it was alright, that Father Josteau was stupid to say such things were bad. I told Jean-Peter we shouldn't. He only laughed." Philippe's words poured out in an almost unfollowable slurry, shivering as if in a Wyoming blizzard without a coat.

"What happened?" the man asked, trying to get the story into some logical order.

"We were heading to the beach for a moonlight swim and heard something in the bushes. It sounded like giggling and groaning. We crept up very quietly. A woman was sitting on top of a man. I couldn't believe what they were doing. Papa would send them away if he knew. Papa was very strict. Such things were not allowed away from one's cabin. I watched. I couldn't help it. Then I looked at Jean-Peter. He was rubbing himself. He saw me staring at him. He motioned that we should leave. We were very quiet and careful to make no sound. At the beach, we ran until coming to our secret spot. A shallow cave. We laughed and talked about what we saw then he began doing that again. Rubbing. I went to confession when we went to Noumea. I told Jean-Peter what Father Josteau said, but he laughed.

"Papa said he had business with his brother on the big island. Jean-Peter was returning to school in Queensland, so Papa flew him to the airport. Mamma went along to shop for some things. Fr. Josteau said God took them away to punish me. Why? I was doing penitence."

"If that's what the priest said he's very wrong. Something I learned a long time ago, God doesn't get that involved in our lives. He gave us an instruction manual on how to live with one another, but other than that we are on our own and whatever happens is a consequence from our own doing. So what happened to your parents and friend?"

A long pause told the man Philippe couldn't remember. Eventually he said, "A woman came and said I had to live with Papa's brother. I don't like him. Papa didn't like him either. It is not a good place."

The man looked down at the top of the boy's head snuggling once more against his chest. There was something in that exchange, more than remorse and bitterness. He couldn't quite put his finger on it.

"What's that over there," Philippe asked, sitting up and pointing toward the opposite side of the clearing, inside heavy brush. He had changed the subject, but they would come back to it, in time.

"A communications dish."

"Why is it covered by netting?"

"To keep the flies off," the man answered curtly, then softening, explained, "It affords me a link to the outside world—for what I do. I may have to work with people, but I don't have to live around them."

Instantly the man's eyes narrowed, crow's feet deeply etching the skin beside each eye as his ears tuned to an unmistakable throbbing. The two climbed the steep incline along one side of the wall where they could scan the southern horizon.

Across the wide lagoon lay the other part of the island, not so wide, but quite a long arc with a rocky hill dominating its spine. A dense growth of trees covered the whole of it. Flying very low along its shore, a helicopter skimmed the palm fronds.

"They're looking for something . . . or someone," the man said turning toward Philippe.

"But how could they know I would be here?"

Again, a piece of the past suddenly surface like a little boy peeking out from under his bed covers during a lightning storm to see if it would flash, and when it did, dive beneath their protective surface.

"They'll be over here next. They must be here to rescue you," he said, but the boy was all but falling down the incline to disappear into the cave. "Then, maybe, you don't want to be rescued." He returned to the entrance more casually, grabbing up the bright lava-lava, and stepping inside moments before the chopper floated overhead.

Whoever they were, it was an unwanted intrusion, but wouldn't see anything of his occupancy. The small satellite dish was well camouflaged within the jungle, the doors and windows, anything indicating habitation well concealed. His Japanese predecessors did a fine job of that. He and the jungle greatly improved upon their work.

As Philippe squat in a black recess not far from the entrance, curled into a tight ball, holding his pounding head, the chopper passed on to the north until the throbbing rotors were no longer heard. Peering down at the huddled child, the man knelt behind him and massaged the shoulders at the base of his neck. After a time, he stood, reached out a hand, and pulled the boy up. As if nothing happened, the pair returned to the mountain's depths, only the slap of bare feet on the smooth stone floor breaking the silence as they moved through the passageway.

Finally, the man said in a matter-of-fact tone, "You don't like helicopters?"

"It made me afraid."

"Why?"

There was a long silence before Philippe answered. "I don't know."

The man could tell it was an honest answer. Entering a room with many shelves of books, and where he spent time working on a computer, he said, "Like to read?"

"Yes."

"Try this. Horatio Hornblower. It's about a kid who goes to sea. Find a comfortable spot for a while. I've work to do."

During the ensuing days, Philippe settled into a routine of reading, surfing the hot pool, and lying in the sun, constantly alert for any unwanted sounds. The bruises and soreness disappeared; the headaches persisted, occurring with less frequency, but no lessening severity. The memory continued to retain gaping holes. Since the helicopter, the boy displayed no desire to venture far from the cave.

Three weeks after his watery arrival, they went to the beach where he had come ashore. He expressed fear going so far from the cave, but the man convinced him there would be no unexpected visitors. More relaxed about the outing, Ellie romped as the boy explored the rocky shoreline. The man sat and watched, thinking.

There had been a plethora of emergency messages throughout the storm area, but strangely silent about a lone boy on a rather expensive boat. Why the absence of concern? Like the inquisitive cat, the man became hooked on the investigation. During the first days, he didn't leave Philippe unattended, instead moving a laptop computer into the bedroom to work and search for answers.

There was absolutely nothing to go on except for a couple hints. The boy mentioned "guests," and a reef. That suggested an island resort. Also, he was deeply tanned—with no tan lines, and seemed completely at home wearing nothing at all. The first Google search was for nudist resorts. From the list of thirty-nine entries, the man zeroed in on the Australian Naturists Federation's web site and their listing of resorts and camps. From there he brought up the web page for the New Zealand Nudists Society. Maybe, but that was a long way for a boy to have sailed. A gut feeling told him to look closer. Gut feelings were important. They kept him alive all these years, something to be trusted and heeded. Back to the list. Perhaps the World Naturists Federation? On the second page his eyes settled on one entry—Pacific Holiday Tours.

Accessing the site, he used their search engine to specify nudist resorts in the southwest Pacific region and a list of recommendations. As the final entry scrolled into view, a slight smile pursed the man's lips. Up came a very exclusive resort, not on the general lists, located on a small island 185 kilometers NE of Nuemea. That was three days sail from where the boy crash landed.

More questions. Why would he start out? It was no secret the storm was headed for the area over four days before arriving. Granted, a short hop might be contemplated, to one of the neighboring islands, but this chunk of rock was a long way from nowhere and the last outpost before lots of uninterrupted water.

There was a link to the New Caledonia resort. He clicked and waited. The screen went blank before lines slowly began to form images. A light, lime green background appeared with an oval photo of a pristine, coral beach superimposed in the middle, a long, sickle-shaped beach cupping a turquoise ocean, pearl white-capped waves lapping gently ashore. At the far end, a rock dome jutted into the water. Along the shore, a manicured jungle edged the pale salmon-colored beach. Across the top appeared the simple greeting, "Welcome to Paradise." From the photo, he would agree. The strains of a Pacific love song by one of the many Isander groups began to flow from the speaker. They were good musicians with angelic voices. As the mouse arrow rested on the photo, it instantly changed to a hand with one pointing digit. There was a link. He left clicked the mouse.

The music continued as a montage of photos appeared. Within an elongated oval each various-sized photo depicted a wide assortment of activities —sunbathing, fishing, horseback riding, tennis, an Olympic swimming pool, several hot tubs, dining, round, thatched bungalows, dancing, trails. As he passed the arrow over the montage, it instantly changed to that ubiquitous digit. Initiating a left click, an enlargement popped up of that particular picture with a brief description. It really looked like a quality place to relax. The participants were naked although not in compromising poses.

One simple picture had a dollar sign leading to a rate chart of boat charters or flights to the private airstrip from Australia, New Zealand, and New Caledonia. He was impressed. All these amenities and the rates were quite reasonable. Obviously a popular spot for those who enjoyed such things, the reservation list was booked solid for the next thirty-five months, even December and January, which weren't particularly congenial to laying on the beach. That inconvenience was resolved with a battery of indoor tanning beds.

Back to the montage, he visited other activities. A picture of young a couple were introduced as the proprietors, their well-tanned faces beaming a warm smile. He was dressed in a white shirt opened at the collar; she was in a brightly printed dress indigenous to the islands. He was dark, handsome. She was stunning with long, blonde hair cascading over shoulders onto the multi-hued dress.

The man studied the picture before tipping his head to look at the boy asleep on the bed. The resemblance was unmistakable. He had acquired all the best qualities, light ginger hair framing a handsome face with a straight, but not overly large nose and wide cheekbones from his father. A lot of his mother was present with those enchanting, green eyes, and thin lips. Yes, Philippe was destined to be a lady-killer.

Returning to the main montage, he looked over more of the activities, and then spotted a small picture tucked in one corner. It appeared to be a boy running along the beach with a kite. He clicked on it. What materialized brought a lump to his throat. There on the screen was a bust portrait of his guest surrounded by smaller photos, the unmistakable story of a son's life from infancy to adolescence. "Our beloved Philippe." They obviously dotted on the boy; a boy running, playing, cradled in his father's lap while having a story read to him. He focused on that one picture for a long time as a single tear stained his sunburned cheek before reluctantly withdrawing from the bookmarked page.

As he exited the album, his blurred vision came to rest on the personalized invitation. "Charles and

Danielle Bonnét cordially . . ..” The names struck a chord. With practiced speed, he shot to another bookmark to access the Melbourne News Service, typing Charles Bonnét in the query box. Within seconds, a story popped onto the screen. The lump in his throat nearly strangled him.

> **New Caledonia** - *Local Businessman and Wife Missing. Charles Bonnét, his wife, Danielle, and a resort guest are reported missing. Charred debris identified as belonging to an aeroplane owned by Bonnét were found in the ocean seven kilometers from his resort island of Tanufu northeast of New Caledonia. So far, no sign of the occupants has been found.*

The article continued with an eulogy befitting a prince. Charles and Danielle were obviously well thought of. The article concluded:

They are survived by a son, Philippe.

A quick e-Mail to an acquaintance in Port Mosby brought an unsettling replay several hours later. In the absence of a will, the uncle quickly partitioned the court to declare him executor of the estate. While he managed the extremely valuable property, Philippe would receive a generous allowance from its income until turning twenty-one at which time the boy would assume full control. In the event of the boy's death, the property reverted to the uncle. That was the piece of information so disturbing. The boy's uncle was the founder of a notoriously illusive crime syndicate!

The man had a nagging feeling that all was not well on New Caledonia. The Bonnét's sudden and somewhat mysterious death seemed convenient, but why did a fourteen-year-old sail into a well-publicized storm? If Philippe had run away why wasn't something public put out? And, how did anyone know to look this far north let alone this particular direction? Why was the uncle moving so quickly to declare the boy dead and thus cement claim to the property? How could the man protect the boy's interests in such a way so not to reveal his location? And, what did the contents of the waterproof pouch found on the beach have to do with all this?

Chapter 3

Revelations

Standing on the mountain ledge where the man first watched his visitor attempt to outrun the storm, no one would guess a door lay behind the leaning slab of rock until stepping behind it. What he casually referred to as the front door was not a door in the normal sense, but an incredibly thick, steel plate solidly set into dense basalt. Skillfully concealed, this well-fortified entrance protected what was now a home, a marvelous creation of nature and man.

Naturally created by gases and lava flows when the mountain was cast, the tunnels and rooms were renovated to garrison a Japanese naval detachment during the big war, and then again by its current occupant. From outside, it seemed very natural, a volcanic peak rising precipitously above the ocean swells. Inside, it was an expansive home made comfortable with rich combinations of the natural rock and imported woods. The floor was a mixture of soft carpet, Teak wood, and smoothed rock. Enlarged natural fissures camouflaged windows affording hypnotic panoramas of ocean and the neighboring island in their ever-changing moods. Discrete screening kept unwanted things out while granting the sweet ocean breeze to permeate the cool interior. During inclement weather, like the typhoon, they were sealed.

The rock shelf serving as a porch extended some six meters from the cliff before beginning a rather steep decline scared by a narrow, zigzag trail terminating at the beach where Philippe and Ellie washed ashore. Along the east side of the porch another large rock blocked further travel in that direction like a railing as the mountain made a precipitous drop into the foaming ocean several hundred meters below. Back leaning against this rock, Philippe quietly basked in the sun, alternating between reading another book about Horatio Hornblower, gazing at the idyllic panorama spread out before him, or as at this moment, fighting another nauseous wave of pain in his head.

Ellie, lying at his side, head resting on his thigh, lifted her large head when the heavy door opened and closed and the man appeared. The pain had brought tears to the boy's eyes. Kneeling on the ground, he turned Philippe sideways so to slowly message his shoulders and neck. The muscles had knotted hard, part of a viscous cycle.

At first, the man thought the bouts of pounding, throbbing pain, frequently attended by nausea, were the result of the head injury resulting in seizures. Certainly, the loss of memory might indicate such and this was worrisome. However, the attacks did not last more than an hour or so. Native herbs and relaxing in the hot pool seemed effective at relieving the severity, although the boy said a dull, but manageable pounding often lasted several hours.

After the muscles recouped from the punishment endured coming ashore, and the bruised ribs no longer complained, the natural inclination to activity to release accumulating energy failed to trigger any episodes. The headaches suddenly appeared for no apparent reason.

The beginnings of an episode caused tension, tightening of the neck, shoulder and back muscles, which in turn caused increased head pain until spiraling to the point Philippe become physically ill, and one time, blacked out. Massaging helped unknit the balled muscles, followed by the rest of his body. The knots smoothed, the pain slowly retreated to a mere annoyance.

"What triggered this one?" he asked softly.

"I was just looking out at the ocean and remembered something, from the before time."

"What did you remember?"

"I . . . it's gone. Why can't . . .?" Philippe became frustrated, tensed, re-flaring the headache.

"Don't worry so. It'll come back. Relax," the man said as he fought down the knotting muscles. Philippe sighed. "Better?"

"Yes, thank you."

"Want to go for a walk?"

"Will it make my head hurt again?"

"We'll go easy."

That was his way. A self-imposed hermit of thirty-seven years, he tended to be gruff, sometimes abrupt. He hated people, or so he said, but treated the boy with the gentle care of a grandfather. Islanders call such a person *Akanche,* one who speaks and acts gently. He understood Philippe's need to move about sensibly, working the deeper bruises to keep the blood flowing and prevent clotting. Healing was progressing well. The taping about the chest was actually to restrict movement and allow the ribs to repair themselves. Removed a week after arriving, he experienced no discomfort. The problem was the head.

With the mind-shearing pain pushed down to a dull throb, the boy could better appreciate the adventure as they entered the dense, emerald wall of vegetation sweeping up from the black beach to envelop the mountain and cloak all but its most severe parts. Although broken here and there by jagged rocks, the turquoise waters of the lagoon gently caressed the shoreline. On the eastern end lay the reef, some of its jagged rocks barely protruding from frothy water like enormous teeth. These had eaten his boat according to the man.

That portion of the island they visited first when the boy could travel. The man wanted Philippe to see close up what he and Ellie survived. There was some hope it might jog his memory. It didn't. Ellie was so excited to be outside again she could care less this was where she almost died.

At first, Philippe thought they were returning to that portion of beach, but half way down his guide veered right onto a trail angling toward the western end of the lagoon. This was the polar opposite of the east end. There was another reef, a broad, submerged crescent of white linking the other island three-quarters of a kilometer distant. From a small plateau, Philippe glimpsed nearly a dozen little islands sprinkled amid the multi-hued sea along the western side. These were too small to accommodate more than a few trees and birds.

Slowly descending the zigzag trail, the cooling canopy of flora abruptly yielded as Philippe's bare feet sank into pillow-soft sand. Its gentle caress magnetically drew him to the water as he went ahead to embrace the gentle waves. The man called out something, but Philippe didn't hear.

As the waves sloshed up around his ankles Philippe heard a crackling noise that brought his attention back to shore. His heart struck a resounding thump as he screamed and fell backward into the water, arms flailing to take him into deeper water.

"Steady, lad. They're not real," the man said over a muffled laugh. "Just scare crows of sorts."

Philippe stared wild-eyed at a series of maniacal statues of beastly manifestations, combinations of human skulls, palm fronds, and woven grass skirts. Twenty or thirty specters stood scattered along the beach in both directions as if creating a defensive arc. Philippe's head began to throb murderously.

"What are they?" he groaned grabbing his head with both hands.

The man waded into the water, immediately massaging the boy's neck and shoulders again as he explained. "That white line connecting these two islands is like an underwater road. At low tide, you can actually walk over there. The water's not much more than twenty centimeters deep at most. At high tide, it's often less than a meter. When I came here, the Islanders warned me that a creature lived on the other island and came across on moonlit nights in search of human heads. According to some things I've read, it raised a lot of havoc with the Japanese stationed here during the war. They put up these things to scare it away. I think the Islanders did the head hunting, although I hear an animal scream over there now and then—like a tiger. I maintain them. Haven't had any moonlight visitations, so guess they must work."

"But, the skulls?"

"Some are coconuts. Carved them myself. Not bad for a non-artist. Adds a realistic touch. There are few real skulls, from the occupation era, but nothing fresh since I arrived."

Philippe's pain subsided, a residual hurt lingering until slipping deeper into the placid, warm waters of the lagoon to stretch out on his back. Lying motionless in the water, bobbing like a cork was soothing and relaxing, but he periodically lifted his head to eye the grotesque creatures.

"That rocky reef and this sand barrier create a pretty nice lagoon. Feel like a swim?"

Philippe pushed his feet to the sandy bottom to stand, whipped off the lava-lava, tossing it ashore, then stretched onto the water. For the first time Ellie entered the water in pursuit. The man watched as the two played for a time. As much as he disliked people, he didn't mind having this one around. The tiny stinging slipped back into Philippe's head, but not enough to stop from having fun with the dog. Not thinking of the past and the water helped Philippe to remain relaxed.

The man was impressed how easily the lad could glide through the water, like a two-legged dolphin. He joined them for a time. Tiring long before the boy, he retired to sit on the submerged, sand reef and watch. Philippe began swimming back. Ten meters out he suddenly stopped, took a big gulp of air, and dove. The man stood up. Apparently spotting something on the floor, he easily dove the five or six meters, seized it, stirring up a cloud of sand, and surfaced. Oblivious of the headache spurred by the activity, Philippe hurried to the man's side excitedly holding the encrusted treasure.

"I'd say, by the shape, it's a sword. Samurai. Probably from the occupation," he said, again massaging the boy's shoulders.

Seated cross-legged on the beach, Philippe began carefully flaking away the coral crust using the man's Buck knife. Slowly the hammered, steel blade came to view. Regrettably, it's once beautiful inlaid handle had dissolved and crumbled away, but the overall blade and tang were in surprisingly good condition.

"Quite a prize. Well, let's head for home."

Standing, the boy stopped abruptly, taking admiring eyes off the treasure held reverently in outstretched hands to cast about for his lava-lava. There were footprints in the sand, obviously ascribed to him and that of the man, but there was another set of prints coming from the trees to where his garment had been, turning, and going back. He searched the jungle as an unseen smile fluttered briefly across the man's face.

Ellie went on point, issuing a low growl as all eyes focused on one of the effigies setting in deep shade. Each was grotesque, but this one was different, seeming to have two heads. It divided and became two figures. Immediately Philippe spread his feet, planting them firmly in the sand, turned slightly sideways to the intruder with knees bent, the curved, two-handed sword held menacingly from the hip. The man's brow furrowed. That was one of the defensive stances of a martial arts swordsman.

Slowly, the second creature stepped from the shadows, a boy of similar age, stockier, not as muscular as Philippe, but much darker brown, almost black. A wide grin bared an ample view of stained teeth as he approached, waving Philippe's lava-lava teasingly over a thick pile of curly, bluish-black hair.

"Hello, Johnny," the man called out. "What brings you here?"

"Come trade," the boy chirped sing-song-fashion as he approached, seeming unimpressed by Philippe's posture as he draped the cloth over the sword point. "How much you give?" he continued, displaying a handful of pearls.

"Not much. No need for them around here," the man responded in an obviously toying tone.

The boy exaggerated a disappointed pout as dark brown eyes twinkled.

"They would be worth a lot in New Caledonia."

"Will Tangata take to New Caledonia when goes next time?"

"I usually do. Philippe, this is Johnny. He's a shrewd pest from the big island," the man said, introducing the Islander and pointing haphazardly toward the western ocean while inspecting the gems.

"What island?" Philippe asked, flipping the cloth off the point into his left hand and lowering the sword.

"See two little island there," Johnny said, pointing seaward before dropping to both knees to play with Ellie's ears. "Between can see Johnny's home."

Straining, Philippe barely made out something on the horizon, not more than a tiny white speck.

"That? How far is it?"

"By the map, about three leagues, about sixteen plus kilometers," the man answered. "Long way by outrigger, except for these fellas. Do it all the time. So what really brings you here?" he asked, seeming to have a second sense about things.

"Chief upset with Johnny. Father say I should go away until Chief cools down."

"And just which of the Chief's daughters did you make eyes at?"

A dark cast of blush came over the boy's face. "The one not so ugly. But she chase Johnny," he answered defensively.

"Yeah. In that case you're lucky to make the trip with all your parts attached. Let's go up to the house and have a bite to eat."

"Johnny have fish. Fix here?"

Philippe remained cool toward the Islander at first, but warmed to the irreverent, light-hearted character, as the three sat by a fire. The two friends talked. Actually, Johnny talked as the man, who he called Tangata, listened. It would have been difficult to wedge a word into the rambling oratory. Besides, Ellie liked Johnny as she lay at his side, but then Philippe thought the dog was a poor judge of character. She'd cozy up to anyone who scratched her ears—even Tomas.

Philippe startled at the sudden memory. Tomas was a gangster, his uncle's right hand man. Another revelation. More than that he couldn't ferret from the bank of suppressed memories. He kept this information quiet, but the man was staring at him. An expression, perhaps something in his eyes said he knew Philippe remembered something, but didn't pursue it. Not then.

Eventually, Johnny's oratory paused allowing Philippe to jump in with a question about something bothering him.

"He won't tell me his name," Philippe said. "You call him Tangata?"

"He always been that way. Never tell anyone name. Not real name anyway, so people call him

Tangata. That means man. It short for Tangata Aiwaiwa, mysterious man."

"Exchanging names implies establishing friendships. I don't want any," Tangata said gruffly.

"You Johnny's friend."

"That's your perception."

"What about me?" Philippe asked.

"The jury's still out."

A cold bucket of water tossed on the conversation put that line of discussion to rest, so Philippe sat with knees drawn to chest as the sun's immense, orange globe disappeared into the watery horizon. He could almost equate the lapping surf and crackling fire to the sizzle of where sun and water met. It was a pacific setting— the lingering aroma of fire-roasted fish, the waning moon-lite night filled with an array of brilliant stars attended by the subdued night chatter of the jungle behind them. Yet, an increasing uneasiness began to pervade the boy's thoughts.

"What about the creature over there?" Philippe had to ask.

"Bad," Johnny replied, shaking his head slowly from side to side. "Long time past, men from Johnny's island go there. Ceremony to become man."

"His people were headhunters," Tangata pitched in. "Took boys your age on a raid, captured some poor devil, and went to that island. The boy became a man by removing the victim's head. Stories say they roasted the remains and pigged out."

"No-o-o-o!" Johnny protested. "My people no cannibal. Catch fish. Eat fish. Only fish. Sometime wild pig."

Johnny's defense was so serious both Tangata and Philippe began to laugh. Realizing he was the victim of teasing, Johnny joined in. Just then, a high, shrieking wail drifted across the lagoon. Philippe leaped to his feet, sword raised horizontally overhead.

"Creature do not like laughter," Johnny remarked crossly.

"There really is something over there," Philippe spat, his heart pounding. The headache surged full-blown, bringing him to his knees.

"Relax. It doesn't come here," Tangata said, quickly rubbing the boy's shoulders and neck.

"What wrong with him?"

"His boat was driven onto the reef when the typhoon moved in. Tossed him and the dog ashore. Bumped his head pretty good. Still bothers him.

Johnny gently slid his fingers along Philippe's head.

"O-o-o. Not good."

The pain was intense. Philippe closed his eyes. Upon opening them, he found himself lying on his bed in the cave-house, Tangata and Johnny seated near the stove, talking softly.

"How'd I get here?"

"You passed out. Johnny carried you back."

"Thank you. I'm sorry. I don't mean to be trouble. It hurt so bad."

"No trouble," Johnny beamed. "You weigh like sea gull. Johnny hit head like that when fall out of coconut tree. Hurt long time."

"That explains a lot," Tangata said. "And I'll wager you were in the tree spying on girls."

The native boy lowered his head and blushed again.

Philippe sat up a little, moving slowly, afraid to escalate the pounding as Johnny brought a mug.

"Drink this. Make Philippe feel better."

"Whew! It stinks. What is it?"

"Go ahead and drink it. If it's one thing this character is good at, it's herbal remedies."

The jungle juice was palpable only by holding one's nose and swallowing fast. It warmed Philippe's throat, then stomach. The warmth radiated through his body until feeling as if floating on water. He lay back and closed his eyes to bathe in the soothing rapture. When he opened them, a shaft of sunlight was spilling through a window covering him like a warm blanket. As usual, Tangata was seated by the stove, reading.

"Good afternoon," he said, tossing a glance over the top of the book.

Philippe stretched slowly, feeling better than he had in weeks, but moved slowly so as not to encourage a return of the headache. He was pleasantly surprised to sit on the edge of the bed without problem. In fact, the ever-persistent, dull pounding was gone. Reaching up he felt for the bump. It was gone, too.

"Feeling better?"

"Yes, thank you. Did I sleep long?"

"Two days."

"Two days!"

"That concoction has that effect on people while it does its thing."

"Where's the native boy, Johnny?"

"Fishing."

"Johnny back," his animate voice chirped from the entry as he padded in to stand next to Philippe. "You take Johnny's arm."

Philippe was grateful for the steadying help as his head spun slightly, but no headache. After a few tentative steps he felt stronger, more confident.

"What was in that stuff?"

"You don't want to know," Tangata replied.

"Johnny have fish cooking on beach. We go and eat. Johnny hungry."

"I feel like eating a whale," Philippe added as Tangata smiled silently, but arriving on the beach Philippe commented, "I don't see a cooking fire."

"You stand on it."

"He's built a fire pit, wrapped the fish in palm leaves, tossed it in, and covered it over. How much longer, Johnny?"

The boy glanced at the sun. "Time for swim."

That suited Philippe who gladly tossed his lava-lava and raced Johnny into the water while Tangata found a comfortable spot to settle in and watch. A happy, panting Ellie lay at his side after tiring of a swim. Nearly an hour later two tired, laughing boys returned and flopped onto the sand.

"Johnny have surprise," he said, jumping up and running to one of the scarecrows, returning with something cradled in its arms. "Johnny fix."

It was the sword Philippe found, now polished with grip restored. Certainly not a majestic handle like the ones Philippe saw in books, but the highly polished wood and inlaid abalone shell was beautiful.

"Thank you," Philippe said, then began swinging the blade haphazardly until stepping into a series of formal moves.

"Where'd you learn that?" Tangata asked.

Philippe looked at him blankly, obviously searching for an answer. "I don't know."

"What is funny dance?" Johnny asked.

"It's called a kata, an exercise Samurai used while training with the sword," Tangata replied.

"I wouldn't just know that, would I?"

"No. You've had training. I'm curious. May I have the sword, Philippe? Now Johnny, wrestle

Philippe down."

"Johnny good wrestler," he beamed, reaching for Philippe then grunted, "What happen?" as he lay face up on the beach.

"I thought so. You've had martial arts training, and judging by the moves, quite a lot. Does that remind you of anything?"

Philippe's face went blank, searching the memory vault, but the door remained sealed. He shook his head negatively.

"Okay, I want you to attack Johnny."

"I can't do that. Master Yamamoto forbids it. Budō is for defense only." Philippe stopped short. "Master Yamamoto?"

"Kenta Yamamoto. He's a leading practitioner of Budō. Lives over New Zealand way. That means you've had the mental conditioning that goes with the physical, and that, my young intruder, may be a key to unlocking that stubborn memory. But that can wait. I'm hungry. Let's cannibalize those fish," Tangata said, drawing a scowl from Johnny.

The next morning Philippe went to the upper plateau, referred to as the back door, with his newfound treasure. Tangata sat off to the side and watched expectantly over the top of his book as the boy first just walked around swinging the blade haphazardly, until his feet began moving as if having a mind of their own. The Kendo training began working their way up from the subconscious. Over the next few days more and more surfaced until Philippe stepped trance-like through the rigorous routines for nearly an hour, sweat oozing from every pore until his body glistened.

Tangata watched and silently counted. There were five on-guard positions, some no longer taught because they were not used in competition. Philippe knew all five. To advance in rank a student must eventually master ten fundamental forms. The more one can demonstrate flawlessly, the higher the rank. Tangata at first judged Philippe to be in early to mid-ranking—a beginner. As practice continued, he revised that estimation upward as foot, body, and arm movements became synchronized, and the sword placement near perfect.

The peace and tranquility of the clearing became shattered when Philippe began to vocalize each strike. At first, it came as the high-pitched cry of a young teenager using pubescent vocal chords. That quickly changed as he expelled the air from his lungs with a guttural roar intensifying the strike.

Philippe's observer began counting the fundamentals. Upon finishing the fourth day, he counted all ten forms executed well. Besides knowledge, rank is earned dependent on the length of study and age. By this time Tangata had little doubt Philippe was at least a Shodan or 1st degree Black Belt. Himself a Shichidan or 7rd degree Black Belt, he felt the boy could easily be promoted upon turning sixteen. He'd speak to Master Yamamoto when next they met. It was interesting, however, he had not seen the boy at the martial arts compound, but then he did tend to keep to himself.

Sweating profusely, Philippe knelt in the middle of the clearing, lay the sword parallel to his left leg, placed hands on thighs, closed his eyes, and took deep, regulating breaths. Tangata finished a whole chapter and half of another before the boy moved another muscle. As Philippe stood, Tangata waited for that which he saw in the young man's eyes.

"I remember the storm," Philippe said vacantly. "It appeared like a movie. I'm in a boat. A really nice one. I think I stole it," he began, worry etching his innocent face. "The storm is coming faster than I had hoped. The wind drove me pass Vanuatu. I see an island and a lagoon. I'm thinking, just make the lagoon, it will provide some protection. Ellie's whimpering. She's frightened. I'm scared, too. We both have life vests on. I see the reef. I can't turn away. The storm has the boat. The keel is ripped off. The boat begins to break apart. We are lashed to her. I cut Ellie loose, then me. We are thrown into the water. The waves are horrible. I tell Ellie to swim for land. A wave hits me. I don't remember anything until waking up." Philippe looked at Tangata seated under the shade of a tree. "You are sitting in a chair looking at me." Philippe hesitated, his eyes going blank again. "That's all I remember."

"That's progress. You believe you stole the boat?"

"I don't know. I think so. When I was in the water, I remember thinking, destroy the boat, destroy the evidence, sink it, all of it, don't let them find any piece of it."

"Well, whoever 'they' are, won't. I burned anything washed ashore. There wasn't much."

Philippe sighed relief.

"Well, that's enough for now. You can meditate again tomorrow," Tangata suggested, but Philippe repeated the workout process again that afternoon followed by over an hour of meditation. If that helped rediscover anything more from his past it wasn't shared.

Chapter 4

The Enigma

The room was a long, rectangle lined with cherry-finished Teak wood to compliment the table and hand-carved chairs dominating the center. Large, raised squares of light gray carpet matching the floor were placed in frames on the walls. In the middle of each square, an expensive, one-of-a-kind painting illuminated by a bronze lamp. They were there for the personal enjoyment of their owner, not to be seen by outsiders. Some were purchased. Some were gifts. Some were neither.

Eight nervous men, four to a side, sat at the mirror-finished conference table hands folded in prosperous laps, each attired in expensive, dark, hand-tailored suits. All had beads of perspiration on their faces except a ninth seated at the far end. The opposite end of the table nearest the entrance was vacant.

Along the periphery stood eight dour men in

sunglasses, hands clasped in front, each behind their boss. The austere silence was occasionally marred by one director's occasional, nervous cough and another's asthmatic wheezing until the ornately, carved, double doors behind the empty seat slammed open with a thunderous explosion.

Except for the one at the end of the table who rose deliberately, each of those seated exploded from their chair as a slightly built man in tennis shorts and polo shirt with the arms of a cardigan loosely tied around his neck stormed into the room. Although darkly tanned, Philippe's Uncle Rousseau had a distinctive, reddish cast to his skin.

"Sit down," he snapped in Islander French. "Every one of you knows that our financial records somehow have been leaked to the police. My lawyers have them running in circles for now. We will weather this incident like all the others. Have you found Philippe?"

The man at the far end of the table was middle-sized, trim, darkly handsome. There was an air of confidence none of the others possessed—for good reason.

"We have found no trace of the boy or the boat so far. Calculating time and distance in relation to the storm, there are two islands northwest of here that would be the furthest he could have traveled. I chose to start the search there and work back.

"I made inquiries at a village on the north end of the main island. They are ignorant of Philippe's presence. There is a sizable lagoon at the island's southern end dividing the larger from the smaller of the two islands. According to the natives, the smaller one is uninhabited except by wild animals. It is a place they fear greatly and do not go near. Something about a creature. If Philippe attempted to steer for the lagoon and safety, a submerged reef there would have destroyed the boat. Likewise, attempting to land anywhere but on the north end would have resulted in disaster because of sheer cliffs, rocks, and coral reefs. A helicopter with two observers flew over the area carefully. They saw no wreckage on the shoreline; they did see something just inside the lagoon that could be a sunken ship. I had someone look at photos they took. It is too large to be the *Catherine*. The next landfall working back in this direction is Vanuatu. My men checked every port and continue to check outlaying fishing villages. At this time, there is no sign of Philippe or the *Catherine*."

"You believe the boy is dead, Tomas?"

"I would have said yes until the police received the information he stole."

"How did the police come to receive the data?" Rousseau directed at another seated at the table.

A thin, anemic man answered while nervously twiddling a pencil, "My contact at police headquarters said it was received from the Interpol office in Brisbane two days after the storm passed." Sweat peppered his gaunt face.

"This island you visited, Tomas, does it have computer access?"

"Nothing was seen to indicate such equipment," Tomas replied. "According to the natives there is a man living on the south side of the main island overlooking the lagoon. Police records indicate he arrived thirty-seven years ago. He had the necessary monies so they allowed him to stay. A year later, he purchased the southern end of the island for five-hundred thousand francs. He has had little contact with anyone since; even the natives know little of him. He lives as a hermit."

"So how does he eat? He must purchase food supplies," Rousseau continued to question.

"He buys everything through Caledonia Mercantile in Noumea. He radios in an order and when he intends to pick it up at Port Vila. They put purchases on the dock. He arrives during the night, loads up, and leaves. The merchant posts a bill to a bank in New Zealand and they pay it," Tomas answered.

"Where does the bank get this money?" Rousseau continued, frustration in his voice unmistakable.

A portly man mid-table answered, "Whenever the account falls below 20,000 francs the bank arranges a transfer from the United States in 10,000 franc increments. The funds come from an account listed to South Pacific Enterprises. Our associates in the United States say it is a paper front not unlike some we use, an entirely electronic operation."

"A very neat dead end!" the balding man spit out, slamming his hand on the table. "What is the nearest place he could have sent those records electronically?"

"Assuming Philippe survived and gave him the information, either Honiara in the Solomans or Port Vila. However, according to the Harbor Master at Port Vila the boat this man uses to pick up supplies is a battered, sailboat with a one-lung motor. It would take at least four days non-stop to make the trip. Even if he found the document the first day after the storm passed he could not have sailed there, considering the time it was received by the police," Tomas answered.

"The data was already unencrypted when received by the police," Henri said. He was the syndicate's pale but fit computer expert. "He would have had to know the coding or have highly sophisticated computers to do that. I think we are wasting our time with this hermit. Philippe must have handed it over to someone."

"Perhaps," Rousseau said as he slipped into deep thought. "Perhaps."

"Henri may be right. The only electronics observed on that island is a shortwave radio in the village. The over flights detected nothing to support any other form of communication," Tomas said.

"Do we know how Interpol received the information?"

"According to our contact it was received electronically from the address GuardianAngle at southerncross dot com," Henri replied, patting at beads of sweat on his upper lip. Everyone was sweating. They were frightened, but like Tomas, Henri was more confident. He made mental note to check the air conditioning. "It's part of an inter-island network based in Melbourne. Signals arrive via their satellite link. Just point a transmitter at the satellite on the right frequency and you can send or receive messages. The information could have been sent from anywhere; however, there are no records indicating any transmitters located in that part of the Pacific. The nearest are at Port Vila and San Cristobal in the Solomans, both over seven-hundred kilometers away."

"Four days journey in the hermit's boat," Tomas reminded them.

"How large a transmitter dish would be required, Cramer?"

"About three meters in diameter," Henri replied.

"It would possible to hide such a large piece of equipment?"

"No. It would be easily seen because of

transmission requirements and dynamics."

A young man seated next to Rousseau said. "I saw new technology on the Web only yesterday that uses a transmitter dish less than half a meter in diameter. Such equipment could easily be concealed in the jungle."

"Yes, but it is not available on the public market, yet," Henri answered.

"The timing of this was too perfect. As I intended to use the storm to dispose of Philippe, he used it to escape. If he were tipped off about my plans, then his departure was spur of the moment. No planning. On the other hand, if this were planned, the *Catherine* would have been found by now."

"If, as you say, this was planned, whoever helped Philippe might have intercepted him at sea, took him and the information, and then scuttled the boat," Tomas said.

"Perhaps a sea transfer might explain this. So far, it does not appear he put in at any port. If there was no transfer he would have been at sea when the typhoon overtook him. However, if he sailed directly from here to that island it would put him there just ahead of the storm."

"Actually, the storm surge would have overtaken him by that time," Tomas said.

"Hum-m-m. And the information was received almost immediately after the storm passed." Wheeling around quickly the crime boss said, "Cramer, track down how that information was relayed and from where. Tomas, I want you to go back to that island. Turn it upside down if necessary. If you find nothing, then work your way back. I must know if that brat is alive or dead. Use every available man. Bring others in if necessary."

Two days later Tomas stood on the bridge of one

of Rousseau's smaller yachts, a ninety footer, standing off the southeastern side of the main island studying it closely through powerful binoculars. A helicopter made another extensive fly-over with two, sharp-eyed observers, but all they reported was a massive pile of rock and a couple trails radiating from the peak toward the lagoon and one toward the village on the north end of the island. A place to harbor a boat larger than a canoe was non-existent except on the north end at the village. Much of the east side of the island was rock cliffs and inaccessible. The lagoon was impossible to enter because of the reef. The western side had stretches of beach, but coral deposits made it impossible to bring a boat the *Catherine*'s size within two hundred meters at best.

Tomas was a very careful man and had missed two important pieces of information. That bothered him. They said the hermit picked up supplies at Port Vila using an old, weather-beaten tub, however, none was seen during any of the fly-overs. It might have been destroyed by the typhoon. If not, the hermit may have left before the storm. If so, at best it might take weeks to find this man to question him.

The other thing that bothered Tomas, no habitation was observed where this man was supposed to live. A clue was provided from a casual remark by one of the observers. He'd seen some abandoned, long-range artillery batteries, apparently from World War II. So much junk abandoned to rust when the Japanese fled ahead of American troops. Doing a computer search, he made an interesting discovery. The mountain now owned by this hermit had once been a Japanese fortress during the war and honeycombed with tunnels. The hermit must be living in the mountain and those trails would lead him to the entrance.

Late that evening, the yacht captain carefully approached the smaller island along its south side and eased up to the reefs before dropping anchor fifty meters off shore. This was the closest possible anchorage. Tomas and his men would use a rubber launch to reach shore.

He chose this anchorage so the yacht would not be seen from the other island. Before dawn the following morning, Tomas lead five men ashore to a narrow beach quickly devoured by the jungle. While one stayed with the raft, he and the others worked west along the thin, rocky line of beach separating ocean and jungle.

Studying satellite photos, Tomas became fascinated by a white line arcing from island to island connecting their western ends. Closer investigation indicated that it lay shallow thereby affording passage by foot. An early morning crossing would not be detected.

Chapter 5

Hunters and Hunted

Philippe stepped from the cavern overlooking the north end of the island. He was five months old today. Much of his past remained scrambled smudges of incoherent scenes. The man he now called Tangata told him of seeing his boat go aground on the reef during the first moments of a typhoon, caught in the fist of the storm surge, and of pulling him from the pounding surf. Parts of that frightening memory returned, but not why. As Tangata asked, "What were a boy and dog doing alone on a great big ocean in a small boat just ahead of a category five typhoon?" And an expensive boat, too, at least that was Tangata's impression. When the helicopter flew over why was he so frightened? When a yacht circled the island, fear's talons gripped so hard to prevent him from breathing. Why? Why? Why? The answers were buried deep, refusing to budge from their secret hiding place.

When Johnny appeared, Philippe stopped giving any of those questions much thought. The boys became too occupied with fishing, diving the lagoon and reef, fishing some more, generally messing around, and lounging about talking. Johnny did most of the talking which invariably centered on girls.

Philippe taught his new island friend some Judo because he loved wrestling, but was not very good. Learning take-downs and pins helped. He would have taught him Kendo, but Johnny didn't have the required discipline. In turn, Johnny taught Philippe how to throw a spear, fish, dive deeper, and canoe open water. As they played together, Tangata return to work at the computer, confident the boys could be boys without outside interference.

When Philippe suggested visiting the village at the northern end of the island, Johnny nixed that idea outright without explanation. Philippe had the feeling the Islander wasn't particularly welcome. Tangata eluded to something about eligible girls and irate papas. From stories told during evenings on the beach that wouldn't be a surprise revelation.

Confining exploration to the north half, the two boys discovered all sorts of relics from the old war, but the water was the big draw, and Philippe felt drawn to the eastern barrier locals called *Kahuna's Teeth*, Kahuna being the Islanders' equivalent of King Triton, the sea god. From under water on the lagoon side, it was easy to see how the ragged remnants of the caldera and coral could be taken as teeth. In an arching line, the jagged rocks connected the two islands, pieces protruding cainine-like from calmer water. Those teeth had eaten Philippe's boat and it wasn't the only morsel they devoured. At a depth of twenty meters on the caldera side, they discovered the remains of an old sailing ship. Yes, the island was a marvelous place to explore with many things to divert him from remembering.

However, the time came Johnny felt it was probably okay to return home. With his departure, Philippe felt a sudden void as the previous life of solitude returned. Well, near solitude. There was, of course, Ellie. The Golden Lab never strayed far as they poked and prodded the volcano's wartime secrets.

One discovery made on his own was an overgrown trail leading to the inaccessible western shoreline. The previous occupants built a rope bridge across a narrow, but deep gorge. It had disintegrated from age, but using a ten meter piece of poly rope, he climbed a tree and out onto a thick branch to tie it off so to swing across. Ellie didn't swing well and didn't like letting go on alone, but her determination found a way across further upstream. Their discovery of the secret waterfall was worth the effort.

Philippe often wished to be as successful nudging out more memories no matter how dark they might be. Several days after that find, while stretched out on a flat rock listening to the sonorous sound of water dropping into the pool of his secret spot, he drifted into that twilight between sleep and wakefulness. The noise of the waterfall became the deep-throated roar of the waves crashing over Kahuna's Teeth. He already had a vague recollection of the storm and wreck, but this time it returned with all its hoary detail—raging, black waves higher than a four-story building with frothed crests resembling the mouth of a mad dog. Dog? Yes. Ellie is lashed to the wheel housing. Phillipe is overpowered by a hopeless realization they are about to die. The watery mouth opens to bear ugly, ragged teeth. In his mind, Philippe sees his hand reach out and cut Ellie's safety line. She immediately flips off the boat and disappears into the boiling water. His own ears cannot hear his shouts. High on the crest of a wave he sees the exposed reef, the ragged, knife-edged rocks in the trough below. The boat is hurling toward them. He fights desperately to cut his safety line. It severs as the bow slams onto the rocks. He's thrown against the stump remains of the mast. The boat shatters like a glass toy.

Philippe is in the water, some distance from the boat as it is masticated into small pieces. Now those same terrifying, watery mountains lift him higher and higher. He knows when the time comes it will drop him onto those rocks and certain death. Like the boat, he will be devoured, chewed into little pieces, and buried. The wave continues to carry him. Ellie is at his side paddling furiously, something in her teeth. A rope? His rope! She is trying to tow him to safety. He looks into the abyss of the trough. No teeth! Triton's wave has carried them beyond the reef.

Philippe awakened with a start. Ellie moved from a shady spot to lie next to him, placing her head on his chest as the nightmare fades. Scratching her ears, Philippe hugs the happy canine.

"Thank you, Ellie," he whispers as she replies with sloppy kisses.

Returning home, boy and dog barely entered the large, flat, open area Tangata referred to as a helicopter pad when a voice called out. "Hello." It was Johnny, coming up from the western beach.

"I thought you went home?'

"I did. Not good. Chief still angry. Had to duck spear."

"Holy cow! He tried to kill you? What did you do

to his daughter?"

The boy only shrugged. "Johnny needs do something to make Chief change mind. Johnny is good pearl diver. Always find best pearls, but Johnny needs something more. Needs to become great warrior."

"That may be difficult. There aren't any wars."

"I think about that while hiding, then paddle here. If Johnny kill creature on other island that would be important."

"Go over there? You're crazy. You'll get yourself killed."

"Molei worth it. You come with Johnny?"

"Hey, I'm not that crazy."

"That's okay. Johnny go alone. When come back we celebrate. If not, tell father I try bring him honor."

Hefting a spear, Johnny turned to retrace the path back to the underwater bridge. It was a slow walk as fear filled his breast. Arriving on the beach he knelt and began to chant, seeking help from his warrior ancestors. Finally, exhaling a deep breath, he stood. Just as his feet touched the water, Philippe came to his side, sword in hand.

"Don't say anything. I'm crazier than I thought," Philippe mumbled as the two began the passage.

"Is dog coming?" Johnny asked.

"No. I told her to stay. I don't want her to get hurt," Philippe replied as Ellie's whining lament carried out to them as they started the journey across the bridge. "So tell me why we are walking and not using your boat?"

"Johnny not watching where going when came to island. Was looking at island, thinking of creature, and Molei. Hit rock and put hole in boat."

"Well, I would appreciate you keeping your

mind focused on what we're doing now."

The sun began to set as they slogged ashore. The passage had not been easy, having to battle thigh-deep waves, sometimes having to swim. Upon reaching the far shore, the two dropped almost exhausted onto the beach.

"We can't stay here. It might see us," Johnny said through heavy breathing.

"If it hasn't already," Philippe replied glumly.

Gathering themselves, they ran into the dense jungle at which point Johnny said, "We stay here tonight. Look for creature in morning."

Philippe had charged off to his friend's aid without considering the time of day or bringing food. All he did was grab the sword and leave a cursory note that the two planned to camp out overnight.

An over-nighter away from the cave was not new. He and Johnny had done it several times. He began looking to gather material to make a bed, but instead, Johnny stashed the spear and started scaling a large tree.

"Follow Johnny," he said.

High up, he found a place where the branches intertwined wide enough to sit and settled in. Just below and to one side was another perch Philippe could occupy. Sitting with back to the main truck, they settled in. Johnny seemed comfortable, but Philippe only dozed sporadically for fear of falling. Climbing down that next morning, he was tired, stiff, sore, and hungry.

"We could have planned this little better," Philippe complained.

"If Johnny thought about this he would not come."

"Well, now what, Mana?" Philippe asked, referring to the well-known Polynesian wrestler from New Zealand, and trying to put his back into a more natural shape.

Johnny looked at him blankly.

"Obviously you haven't given any of this any thought."

"Maybe if we go to top of mountain," Johnny said, not sounding at all confident while searching the ground around the tree.

"What are you looking for?"

"Johnny left spear here. Can not find."

"That's a good omen. Let's go back."

"No. Don't need spear. Have good knife," he said and moved on, but what little confidence he might have conjured yesterday had withered appreciably.

The two traveled less than a hundred meters when they came upon a well-beaten trail. Each looked at the other.

"Not used by animals," Johnny said after inspecting it carefully. "Comes from beach where we crossed. We follow. Be careful."

"As if this were a Sunday stroll," Philippe answered sarcastically, clenching his jaw to keep teeth from chattering.

The trail meandered deeper into the dense jungle, skirting the western edge of the central mountain until coming to a small clearing. Off to the left was a cave.

"Do you think that's the creature's home?" Philippe asked as his voice quivered.

"I go look."

Philippe grabbed his arm. "Be careful."

"If creature get Johnny do not help. Run fast back to main island. Tell good story about Johnny."

The Islander crouched low, skimming the edge of the clearing until coming to the cave opening, quickly peeking inside before entering and disappearing. As the seconds seemed to drag into hours Philippe waited, watched, and listened. All he heard were the birds and the usual jungle noises. When Johnny reappeared it was at a full out sprint directly toward him. Dropping at Philippe's feet, Johnny breathed so hard to be unable to speak for a time.

Finally, he said between gasps, "Is place creature lives. Many heads. One very new."

"You mean there are others on the island?"

"Must be. I see other trail before go in cave. Climbs up mountain. We go up. See better."

The trail wiggled up the steep slope to the mountain's spine, but dense vegetation made it impossible to see very far so it was up another tree. What they saw chilled Philippe to the marrow—a large, white yacht anchored off shore about mid-island, the same one he'd seen weeks before circling the island when the helicopter flew over.

Seeing the great fear in his friend's eyes Johnny asked, "You know boat?"

"It belongs to my Uncle. He is trying to kill me," Philippe answered as more memories flooded his mind.

"Creature want kill us. Uncle want kill you. Not good idea we be here."

"I think I mentioned that . . . several times."

"Sh-h-h. What's that noise?"

From somewhere to the north they heard voices, speaking French.

"It's them!" Philippe said as panic began to overwhelm every centimeter of his body.

"Stay!" Johnny commanded as his friend began to shimmy down. "Hunters never look up. We safe here."

Philippe froze, hugging the trunk in a death grip

as the voices became louder. Then he saw them, five men, their leader a man in a white shirt. He knew that one. He was the only one who acted friendly toward him when he was at his uncle's place, but Tomas could be here for only one reason—to take him back or kill him. Philippe dare not move as they passed along the trail less than twenty meters away.

"Which way?" one asked as they came to a divide in the trail.

"Continue straight. That appears to take us to the beach on the other side. We should find the underwater connection to the other island from there."

"Well, I need to water a bush," the big man said almost defiantly as he stepped to the edge of the tiny clearing to relieve himself.

"Hurry it along, Frank. We must cross over before it gets too late," Tomas said.

The boys attached themselves more tightly to the high branches fearful any movement might draw attention, praying the hunters would move away soon. Finally, Tomas snapped the order heading them down the trail toward the beach. The boys audibly exhaled relief and were about to slip down when movement caught Johnny's eyes. It glided along the trail following the others, a formless clump of moving vegetation. Only after it had long disappeared did the boys venture out of their perch.

"Let's go back," Philippe pleaded.

"They go that way. We go other way to east end of island. We can swim back along reef."

Half running, half sliding, they plummeted down the trail toward the southern side of the island breaking out onto a small, rocky beach and headed east. About mid-island and fifty meters from shore, the yacht lay anchored. There was no way to hide as the jungle and basalt cliffs forced them to remain exposed on the shoreline. Crouching low and trying to keep to the shadows, they continued to slowly work their way east, but an occasional rocky finger protruding into the surf forced them to climb over until coming to where they had no other option but go around. Staying as low in the water as possible, and far enough away not to be dashed against the rocks by the waves, they carefully rounded the obstacle. That brought the boys to a raft lashed to a palm. A pair of shoeless legs were draped over the edge, the occupant apparently taking a nap. The boys had no recourse except sneak pass silently as possible. Just as Jimmy approached, he stopped short and stared into the craft.

Philippe looked, too.

The legs were attached to a headless body.

"This explains where creature found new head for collection," Johnny mused.

Philippe gagged before managing to say, "Let's get out of here."

They hadn't gone but a few meters when sand kicked up just ahead of them. Turning to look at the yacht, they could see a raft being lowered and several men on deck. Another spray of sand kicked up.

"They're shooting at us!" Philippe yelled the obvious while bolting into the jungle.

The shore rose less abruptly here, allowing them to duck into the vegetation as more bullets tore at their heels. If not for the gunfire they wouldn't have found the hidden path skirting the coast through the heavy undergrowth.

"They will follow. Come, we go this way," Johnny yelled, racing along the trail.

Johnny was right. When the second raft reached

shore and the three occupants discovered their compatriot, the chase was on. Passing another volcanic finger several hundred meters further, the boys once again had to return to the open beach. However, this projection was sufficient to shield their presence from the yacht's marksman allowing them to race up the beach, climbing over two more basalt fingers to reach the eastern end of the island.

Here the mountain appeared ripped apart leaving an estuary-like marsh connecting the north and south sides. On the east was a fragment of the mountain that dropped into the ocean. This may have been how the ocean gained access to the caldera. A trail rose above and skirted the marsh taking them to the north side. The boys just cleared the jungle and were about to plunge into the water when they heard a shout. Looking west, they saw the men from the yacht less than a hundred meters up the beach. A shot kicked up sand, intended to stop them. It only accelerated flight back into the jungle.

With complete abandon, Philippe plunged off the trail and lay flat in a thicket, Johnny right behind. Taking a deep breath and holding it, they watched as the men ran by. After waiting until certain they had gone some distance, the boys slipped back to the edge of the rocky reef. About to run into the water they heard more shouting. This time it was Tomas' group, closer than the others had been.

The boys could easily gain the water, dive out of range, and out swim their pursuers. The problem was the high, white tipped fin of a shark cruising just off shore. This was not the friendlier reef shark often encountered, but a canoe-sized man-eater waiting for dinner. Philippe began to wonder what happened to all those guardian angels supposedly hanging around to help people in dire need.

Turning back to the trial, they were about to take to the same hiding spot when they nearly ran head on into the returning ship's crew. This time there was no stopping, they tore into the heavy brush and up the steep incline with total abandon. Shots rang out, the bullets splintering vegetation just to Philippe's right. The last they heard was cursing, but no more shots.

Tomas lead his group in the chase while sending the others back to the lagoon beach to intercept the boys, certain they were attempting to get back to the main island. The boys realized this, too, and kept climbing until crossing a small trail that made progress much faster to the summit. Their only hope was that youth would prevail over the older men.

About mid-island, the exertion began taking its toll. Stopping briefly, Johnny scrambled up a tall tree to get a better view of their pursuers, and then sliding down just as quickly.

"They not far. Come, I have plan."

That was the first encouraging thing Johnny said since embarking on this disastrous adventure to get a girl's hand in marriage.

The boys set a rhythmic jog along the trail following the spine of the island to the western end where it intersected another trail, obviously more frequently used.

"I think this trail men followed first time we see them," Johnny said.

"They will expect us to take it to the beach," Philippe replied.

"So we go other way and wait until dark."

"But that will take us pass the creature's lair."

"I don't like but, yes. That's chance we must take. Maybe creature will hunt them, not us."

The boys carefully left indications in the soft ground that they headed north before jumping off the trail into the brush and doubling back to take the trail toward the south coast. It was a plan that seemed to work, but Tomas hadn't attained his position in the organization by doing the obvious. Being a cautious man he sent two men in that direct while leading the others toward the lagoon.

At the next intersection the boys headed toward the cave. It was not their intent to stop, but as they skirted the clearing the jungle directly ahead of them moved. Johnny stopped so abruptly Philippe ran into him. A couple meters in front stood a squat, sun-blackened figure covered with vegetation; a long, curved sword similar to Philippe's was pointed at Johnny's breast.

Automatically, Philippe pushed ahead, squared his body and held his weapon at the first on-guard position. The creature paused, an expression of surprised wonder etched on his gnarled features. Then, as if recognizing something, immediately dropped to his knees and bowed profusely while uttering entirely unintelligible words. At that moment a noise alerted them to the approaching pursuers. The apparition nimbly sprang to his feet and pointed vehemently toward the cave, again chattering something undecipherable.

"Come on," Philippe said understanding they were to hide in the cave.

"But we will be trapped."

"Come on," Philippe called back already near the entrance.

Philippe wasn't interested in going completely inside. There was no desire to see the collection Johnny mentioned earlier.

"If those men come in we can jump them before

their eyes adjust to the dark," Philippe said.

However, there would be no such intrusion. Two gun shots and a scream rent the jungle. When Johnny carefully crept to the opening and peeked out he saw two bodies sprawled at the edge of the tiny clearing. Their benefactor was no where in sight.

"Come on!" he said, bolting into an all-out sprint toward the lagoon.

Approaching the point where the white sand bridge crossed toward the main island, the boys had presence of mind to stop their head-long flight and melt into the jungle, climb a tall tree, and settle into a high crotch. Minutes later Tomas and his men came onto the beach to set an ambush. They watched the trail, but never thought to look up where they would have seen their quarry almost directly overhead.

As time lingered, the branch upon which Philippe perched began grinding into his thigh, but he dare not move. Being high up there was little shade and the sun bore down unmercifully. Adding to their discomfort, there was no breeze to cool them in the slightest. It felt like sitting in a sweat bath on splintered seats as sweat oozed from their bodies and run in rivulets. Below, the three men were no more comfortable.

"They should have been here by now," one of the men grumbled.

"If the boys turned back along the coast they would be seen from the yacht and they'd radio us," Tomas replied.

"They may have ducked into the jungle again to hide."

"So where's Paul and Grogan?" the hulking man replied. "I've got to pee."

Stepping off a ways, he faced into the jungle to

relieve himself. That's when Philippe thought to see the vegetation move. So did the huge man, but too late. He seemed transfixed a moment as the sound of his water splashed on the leaves, then to Philippe's horror his head fell off his shoulders and like a child's ball, rolled bumpily into the clearing. The body fell stiffly backward, red fluid shooting from where the head had been attached, spraying the clearing.

His compatriots first stared in disbelief before leaping into action, spraying the jungle with gunfire —Tomas from his pistol, the other from a semi-automatic rifle. The gesture was wasted. Their attacker had long since moved to the base of the tree where the boys perched.

The men alternately stared at the head of their associate, at each other, then intently at the jungle around them. As the minutes ticked, the tension grew, then there was movement again. Tomas must have seen it and fired repeatedly. His companion fell to the ground, Johnny's spear piercing his breast. Grabbing the rifle, Tomas walked to the edge of the jungle and moved in. He showed little fear. A few paces in brought him to the body of the creature.

Satisfied it was dead, he returned to the beach, looked up the long coastline, then toward the jungle trail apparently deciding which to take. The shortest route back to the yatch was back through the jungle. Within moments, he disappeared.

The boys painfully waited a while longer before descending, finding walking difficult after the arduous perch. With short, limping steps, they went to the body of the creature who had tried helping them.

"We should bury him," Philippe said.

"Yes, but let's tell Tangata first, then come back,"

Johnny replied.

Turning they came face to face with Tomas.

"I thought you might be close," Tomas said, speaking in French. It was a language Johnny knew as well. "Drop the sword, Philippe. Do you know that one?" he asked, pointing to the vegetation-covered body.

"No," Philippe answered. "I think it's the creature from stories about this place."

"Well, the stories are done. You'll come with me Philippe. Do not attempt to escape again. What I must do is for your own good. I will shoot if necessary."

"What of my friend?"

"I have no interest in him. He can start wading back to the big island."

"Go, Johnny. He will kill you if you do not. Please, go."

Johnny reluctantly entered upon the white shelf and started across the lagoon. When he had gone a hundred meters Tomas asked, "Tell me Philippe, where is the computer disk you stole?"

"I don't know what you are talking about."

"When you ran away, you stole a bag from your uncle's office. It contained money and a computer disk in a red plastic case."

"I do not remember that. I hit my head when the boat sank. There are many things I can't remember."

"Well, for your sake you had better remember. Your uncle has a sizable reward on your head and wants you dead because of that disk. I need to find what happened to it. There is more damaging information on it in a protected file. You unfortunately know the password. Besides wanting your papa's resort, that is why your uncle is so intent on finding and eliminating you. Let's go," Tomas said while motioning toward the jungle trail leading back to the yacht.

Following the death of Philippe's parents, the boy was sent to the older Bonnét. That's where he met Tomas, who seemed to reach out to the distraught child. The two took walks together and talked. Perhaps that familiarity caused Tomas to relax his guard for an instant as the boy stepped past, seeming resigned to the fate awaiting him. However, that split second was all Philippe needed to grab the pistol arm and easily flip the heavier man over his hip. In one continuous motion, Philippe tossed the dislodged pistol into the water, took up the sword, and pointed it Samurai fashion from the hip at the surprised man.

"It would appear the tables have turned Tomas," Philippe said as Ellie moved to the boy's side. Her sudden appearance was surprising. She had apparently disobeyed the command to remain behind, but now that she was here, Philippe felt more reassured and confident. "Do not consider anything foolish, Tomas. There has been more than enough death on this island today. Of all those who came ashore. You are the lucky survivor, unless you desire to be stupid."

Tomas looked up from where he now sat. An observant man, a trait had helped him succeed and survive. What he observed was a boy who knew how to handle that instrument of death, and he was in no position to challenge it.

"I told you the truth, Tomas. I do not remember the disk you speak of, nor have I seen it since awakening here."

Tomas stared into Philippe's eyes for a time before saying, "All right. Now what?"

"This is my home now. I want you to leave and

not come back. Ever."

Tomas' head bobbed agreement as he cautiously got to his feet. Johnny, having seen the change of events, returned in a great, splashing run. The two then escorted their prisoner back to the yacht. Tomas was secretly impressed how well they handled themselves for mere boys, better than many of his men. Any hope Philippe would lower his guard was out of the question. Then, there was Ellie, gentle, kind, lovable Ellie. Philippe was her boy and stood ready to protect him. Besides, Tomas had his fill of this place.

Just before stepping onto the beach where those waiting on the yacht could see them, Tomas stopped and turned to Philippe. "I believe you about the computer disk. It is obvious the contents reached the authorities too quickly. If you do not remember having it, then you obviously do not remember passing it off before sailing here. There is more on the disk, locked in protected files. You know the password. That is what your uncle fears most. I will honor your request, Philippe. Only I know you are alive here. I will tell your uncle you are dead, drowned in the storm, and your body is buried here. I do that . . . out of friendship. It would not do for you to appear on the beach where those on the yacht can see you."

"They already see us," Johnny said. "They shoot at us."

"From that distance you both look to be Islanders. That is what they shot at, two Island boys," Tomas said. "This paradise is now your prison. Your uncle has many eyes, greedy eyes. It would not go well for either of us if you are seen again."

Giving a two finger salute of farewell, Tomas turned and left as Philippe, Johnny, and Ellie remained hidden in the jungle. Only when the yacht turned away did they sigh collective relief.

"Do you think he will do as he say?" Johnny asked.

"He will," a voice said from behind, sending both boys spinning to a defensive stance. Ellie barked softly and leaped forward, tail whipping happily.

Philippe couldn't help himself. Upon seeing Tangata, the adrenaline dissipated causing knees to begin shaking. Dropping the sword, Philippe wrapped his arms around the man, savoring the feel of Tangata's strong, protective grasp. After a time, strength returned and they returned to where the creature lay.

Johnny bent over to look at something more closely the man wore. Pulling it from his neck he said, "This is necklace of someone from my village. There is story that on last raiding party they were attacked. Two died. One ran into jungle to avenge brother's death. They say he was crazy. Never seen again. They say he was killed by terrible creature who live on island."

"Tangata hunched over the corpse. "Maybe. This poor soul looks more Japanese than Islander. Well, whoever it was, his torment is over."

"Johnny will return this to chief," he announced, holding up a single, hook-shaped medallion on a leather thong.

"Then perhaps you will be able to stay?" the man suggested.

"Yes, and marry Molei and have many babies."

"I can't go back," Philippe said, sounding cast down, "to wherever I came from."

"I heard."

"I still don't remember anything about what Tomas was talking about," Philippe complained.

"I have the computer disk. It was in a waterproof bag along with a sizable sum of money. I found it washed ashore while you were recovering. That's why I burned any evidence of the boat."

"If my uncle finds out, he'll send more men," Philippe almost whined with fear.

"Unfortunately, yes."

Chapter 6

Escape

Walking a fine line became a way of life for Tomas since embarking on a career in crime, but this time that path become impossibly narrow and very, very slippery. The slightest mistake would not be forgiven. Having the ability to see the truth in a man's eyes, he knew Philippe had no recollection of the computer disk, nor knew of its present location. It was highly possible the boy had not taken the time to look in the bag taken from the safe. He made sure the disk was stashed beneath the bound stacks of cash. It obviously was not lost because some of the financial data surfaced. But how? Tomas could only hope Philippe would stay out of sight for a couple years at least. If not . . . life could become difficult for both of them.

Climbing aboard the yacht, the captain and two remaining soldiers greeted Rousseau's right hand man. "Get underway," he said brusquely before they could speak.

"Where are the others?" the younger of his men asked.

"Dead. Get under way." This was not the time to tell all, not just yet. Tomas the invincible had to think this out very carefully.

♦   ♦   ♦

Rousseau never saw his chief lieutenant looking so cast down as Tomas walked along the dock from where the yacht docked.

"Did you find the boy?" Rousseau asked anxiously.

"I believe so."

"And . . .?"

"He is dead."

"Too bad. I would have liked doing that myself. What about the computer disk? What of that? Did you recover it?"

"No."

"NO?"

"I do not believe he had it. The boy must have handed it off."

"Explain," Philippe's uncle growled.

"The stories of a creature inhabiting the smaller of the two islands were true. It is an island of death. I lost seven good men. Whatever it was rose from the jungle, an invisible beast killing with incredible speed."

"And . . ?"

"Philippe apparently was able to reach the island ahead of the storm, but judging from what little wreckage we found his boat was thrown upon the reef. I do not know if your nephew was killed outright or later by the creature."

"How do you know he is dead?"

"I discovered what appeared to be the boy's body just inside the jungle where the helicopter would not see it. I can only surmise it to have been his body. What remained was the same size and wore the same clothes I saw him wearing the day he ran away. The head was missing. No one on the larger island ever saw him. The hermit is just that, a man who desires to be left alone. Even the villagers shun him. And no one goes to the Island of Death."

"And how do you know he handed the computer disk off?"

"He could not have had it with him. The boy landed upon that island and died. There is no way for the information to have been transmitted from that area. The American living there lost his boat in the storm. It would have been impossible for anyone to have gotten to the nearest computer terminal capable of sending the data by the time it was actually sent."

"Do you believe he put in somewhere or met someone at sea?"

"I believe he was met. The last I saw the *Catherine*, she was about thirteen kilometers out, about where you said to dump the boy's body. At the time it was circling, therefore assumed my men were doing what they were told, kill him, and dump chum to attract sharks to dispose of the body. There were other boats, but not close. I was called to handle something else and did not see the boat again. Our people continue making inquiries among the islands, but did learn that a sailboat matching the Catherine's description, in particular the green and white sail, was seen off the north coast of Espiritu Santo twenty hours later heading in a northerly direction toward open seas. There simply would not have been sufficient time to make land, transfer the disk, and reach Vanuatu in that amount of time.

"I have studied the charts closely. The most likely place to head would be Port Via on Efate Island. Our competitors have a large cell there. They could have met the boy and taken the disk. Philippe is smart. He could not hide there, but going on to Espiritu Santo, it is sparsely populated and the east side of the island would have provided shelter from the storm. We have no interests there and he could hide for a long time. It would also put him in a position to contact any number of your brother's friends and find safety."

"Hum-m-m. You may be right, Tomas. I now recall my brother had some interests and business contacts on the island. It would make sense for him to go there. If the boy is dead, then the information may be safe. They will not know the code. Find who engineered this, and find that disk if is still exists."

"I have already ordered all our people to pursue that theory even before returning. I am not discounting other possibilities, and we will pursue those as well."

"Thank you, my friend. I know to count on you."

♦ ♦ ♦

Remaining just inside the jungle wall, Philippe watched his uncle's lieutenant climb aboard the yacht and set sail. Only then did he begin to relax and reflect upon what just transpired. Death once again reached out with its bony fingers, but Philippe somehow managed to slip through the grasp. He should have felt relief, but shuddered involuntarily as if that cold, deathly hand still lay upon his chest. A poor, deranged creature gave its life that he might live. The only consolation was that his uncle's chief henchman was gone, having failed an assignment for the first time, beaten by a fourteen year-old boy.

"They'll be back," the hermit said coldly as they stood side by side watching the retreating yacht.

"I must leave here."

"Yes."

"I didn't mean for this to happen," the boy spewed over teeth chattering like the staccato clatter of a machine gun.

The man wrapped a strong arm around quaking shoulders. "If that storm hadn't tossed you on the island you'd be shark droppings by now. Providence brought you here," Tangata replied. "Your uncle's tentacles are long and invasive in this part of the world. You'll have to go beyond that reach."

"You were very brave," Johnny said.

"I knew Tangata had come."

"How?"

"Ellie told me."

"The dog speaks?"

"Look at her, Johnny. Her coat is dry. That could only have happened if she came by boat, and the only person to come would have been Tangata. Tomas has an eye for detail, but thankfully, he didn't notice."

Climbing into Tangata's outrigger, Ellie took her place in the bow, and Tangata the stern to watch the boys dip paddles deep into the placid waters of the lagoon to skim the surface. As Philippe mulled over what transpired, Johnny expressed exuberance as a warrior's victory chant escaped smiling lips.

Early the following morning their native friend left once again. This time things would be different upon returning home. He performed a feat of bravery not accomplished since the old days prior to the Great War. At least the story to go along with the pendant would be sufficiently embellished to achieve that effect. The result, of course, would be the father of every eligible daughter fighting for a place in line to have him for a son-in-law. Johnny only desired one, and if the village chief still protested, Johnny was now endowed with some ability and confidence to stand up to him.

Remaining on the beach, Philippe and Tangata watched Johnny's canoe clear the western reef. As their friend became an indistinguishable dot on the gently rolling swells, Tangata picked up a cloth bundle he had brought and unwrapped two long, bamboo sticks.

"Shinai!" Philippe exclaimed with surprise, referring to the swords used in Kendo practice. "Where did you . . .?"

"I have also studied under Master Yamamoto. I guess you to be Shodan."

"Yes," Philippe answered in gathering awe.

"I am Shichidan," the man answered, referring to the 7th Degree black belt with its red and white stripes, and handing one of the sticks to Philippe. "It is time to further your education."

For the next hour, the two ranged over the expanse of beach as Ellie sat to one side, barking cheers. This was not traditional training as Philippe quickly learned. This was a real duel. Able to deliver a few blows, the boy found himself primarily in a defensive mode. Tangata was formidable and unrelenting. Unlike those teachers at the Budō camp, he did not hold back. At first Philippe received multiple, stinging blows until letting mind and body flow with the knowledge he possessed. When that happened, technique lurched to the forefront.

Seldom able to return the favors, at least Tangata's "sword" rarely made contact.

Both sweat profusely as the battle raged furiously, the clack of the Shinai like a drumbeat to which Ellie sang. Pushed to the limits of his training, Philippe began to smile as confidence increased. The man didn't smile. There was a particular seriousness in what they were doing. Suddenly, he stepped back, lowered the bamboo sword and bowed. It was over. A meter apart, the two knelt facing one another and bowed, placing hands on thighs preparatory to meditation, or so Philippe thought.

"The time has come young warrior for your greatest battle," Tangata said very softly, his voice sounding for the world like Master Yamamoto, serious, kind, gentle, agelessly wise.

Philippe closed his eyes and listened as the words flowed into his mind bringing to blossom stifled memories. They were words about his parents, the resort, his life in the before time. Memories as pictures sprang forth. Pictures of his mother, of his father, the special times they shared. Before this the things he'd been told were so many words, filling in gaps of memory, but not personal recollection, making them sound like another's life, not his. That life now returned to him. Philippe began to cry.

In the study, computer web sites provided visual confirmation. Staring at the pictures of his parents, tears again streaked his brown cheeks as those priceless, loving, memories tarnished by the return of knowledge why those beautiful people were forever gone. Philippe looked longingly at all that remained of his parents, pictures of their home, and memories, unable to take his eyes away lest they be gone forever. After a time, Tangata walked to a bookshelf along the far wall, removed several volumes to uncover a hole and reached in. An audible click sounded as that section slid inward to reveal a secret tunnel.

A series of naked bulbs strung on two bare wires tacked to the ceiling scarcely dissipated the blackness of the narrow shaft as the two plunged into the bowels of the mountain, Ellie at their heels, until a heavy steel, ships' hatch barred their way. As the man turned the center wheel, there came the soft whisper of grating metal. A push and the oval portal yielded, the pungent odor of diesel fuel immediately assailing their nostrils.

Stepping into a water-filled cavern, Philippe was amazement to see a sizable yacht resting silently in front of them. Except for a single floodlight centered on the boat, nothing else could be seen, although he had the impression something lay low in the water some distance beyond. Interestingly, there was no source of light to indicate how the boat got inside the mountain.

Ellie was okay with riding in a canoe, but showed fear at seeing the boat. Whimpering, she cowered behind Philippe's leg. Undoubtedly remembering what happened the last time she was aboard such a boat. Tangata spoke softly while stroking her golden-haired head, then lifted her aboard. Hopping on the sleek, white craft behind the dog, he flipped a couple switches to light the cabin and guided her below, and closed the hatch. Moving to the helm, he called out, "Release the bow lines, and get aboard." Flipping switches started the engine's deep-throated growl as if some prehistoric serpent had awakened.

Philippe barely made the deck as Tangata opened the throttle. The boat backed from the dock, turning until the bow pointed toward utter darkness. The whole boat vibrated as it leaped into the blackness with a thunderous roar. Somewhere in that void must be a wall at which the bow was directed. Philippe stared ahead then at the pilot bathed in green light from the control panel. The dock light rapidly diminished as disbelief and panic churned through his body.

A high-pitched scream filled the cavern with a cacophony that pierced the ears and gouge at the brain. Almost immediately, an ever-growing shaft of bright, tropical sunlight pierced the blackness as a section of wall ahead moved aside. With practiced dexterity, the boat passed through the opening, its cleaver-like bow effortlessly slicing the swells of open water as they left what had once been a secret, Japanese submarine base.

Philippe had seen many yachts come and go from his parent's island resort. Being a curious child, he'd visited most. This was a top-of-the-line, Hunter-49, somewhere around a half mil, considering the modifications he could see. The yacht lay some fifteen meters from bow to stern. A four plus meter beam provided stability. The mast and boom lay horizontal. That intrigued the boy until Tangata flipped a switch on the console raising it to its twenty-one meter height. Once in place, another set of motors hoisted the sails aloft. Obviously, the boat was designed to be operated by one person. When deployed, the iridescent blue sails flopped restlessly in the wind, eager, searching, until a slight turn of the helm brought them into position. With a thunderous crack, they snapped taunt and the boat lurched forward, vigorously slicing at the swells and sending a fine, cooling spray over the length of the boat. The dragon's growl fell silent.

Tangata's frequent spells of silence had been unnerving at first, but Philippe learned this only indicted he was in deep thought. That wasn't all bad. It gave him time to do what inquisitive boys like to do—explore.

Going below, he entered the heart of the boat. To his right the galley was not unlike a regular kitchen with a couple alterations, mainly lips on the flat surfaces to prevent things from sliding off, and secure door latches to keep the contents where they belonged. There were also stove, refrigerator, microwave, and ample preparation surfaces. It was pretty normal looking.

To the left was the navigation station, a small workspace with a wall-mounted computer displaying wind and boat speed, air and water temperature, a full battery of charts, and most importantly, a continuous, graphic weather update. Ahead was the spacious salon, modified to a smaller dining/lounging area so to have a work space, something like an office with desk, computer, a filing cabinet, reference books in a glass-enclosed shelf, and ship-to-shore wall phone. The head with shower for the two aft cabins was standard. A queen-sized bed filled one cabin while a twin filled the other. The man obviously slept in the smaller, compartment immediately behind the galley. Philippe was to use the larger cabin forward with its own head and shower.

Rummaging through the galley, he discovered the shelves, refrigerator, and freezer well stocked. After using the aft head, Philippe hungrily fixed sandwiches, grabbed a couple sodas, and went topside.

"Thanks," Tangata replied, accepting a china plate laden with slices of smoked ham and pepperjack cheese on rye, chips, and sliced kosher dill. "Take the helm. Maintain a heading of two-two-zero," he said rather brusquely, and taking the lunch, disappeared below.

Philippe took no offense to the rudeness as he sat at the second wheel. The Hunter was interesting because it provided two stations side by side on the stern. An opening between them exited onto a small platform and very large ocean.

Piloting sailboats was nothing new, especially after handling the *Catherine*. The sleek craft handled effortlessly. Tangata return an hour later to stretch out on a built-in bench alongside the companionway. Biting into his meal for the first time Philippe thought to detect the wispy hint of a smile.

"Good sandwich. You can handle the galley," he said while grinding a mouthful. "You're not a bad pilot, either."

Quickly finishing off the sandwich, Philippe's guardian went below again, lying down to sleep until nearly nightfall. When he reappeared, Philippe was sent below to prepare supper.

After eating and another turn at the wheel, the boy perched midships to gaze at the twinkling, celestial dance crossing the vaulted sky, wondering about the man with no name who expressed such disdain for humanity, yet showed him so much kindness. Was there some connection with this aberrant behavior and a toddler's portrait below? And, what of the boat's name—*Adrianne*? A boat's name usually held some significance to its owner, like Catherine did to Rousseau.

The sun set well above the watery horizon when Philippe was awakened by the whine of the sail motors and return of the boat's throaty, prehistoric growl. Ahead lay the lee harbor of an island not unlike the one they'd left, a narrow, sandy beach shadowed by sheer basalt cliffs cloaked in a multi-hued, green mantle. Within the harbor a grimy, tattered Junk rust at anchor. A man stood on the beach appearing as ragged, unkempt, and apocalyptic as the bromidic derelict.

This man's stance was not congenial with bare feet spread apart and dug into the sand, a fist firmly planted on each hip. He was a walking tattoo with geometric designs on his face, chest, shoulders, arms, and that part of his legs observable below the calf-length trousers. Philippe had seen many like him. Tattooing was a tradition among Islanders to make them appear ferocious. This guy didn't need any of them to achieve that effect. The only indication of friendliness was a big smile spreading a raven-black Fu Manchu mustache revealing dark-stained and missing teeth. In addition to the bluish-black artwork on his broad, weathered, oriental face was a light-colored scar down the left cheek, almost the same color as the large, gold earring dangling from that ear.

Philippe heard stories of such individuals—pirates—stories to frighten children much as Europeans told stories of the Boggy Man. No one need tell stories of this character. His appearance alone was enough to send chills pulsing through one's body. His only garment was a large, baggy trousers terminating at the knee and held in place by a piece of rope. A cowrie shell necklace with a bone hook hung from his neck while a wide leather belt angled across his chest from which hung a short, curved sword. A dirty, red piece of cloth covered his head, but did little to contain the shoulder-length locks of curly hair which appeared hacked to length by a dull machete. Philippe didn't have to look twice to notice the color of the man's boat and his skin where an identical reddish black.

"Look who come for visit," he greeted.

"How soon can we set out?" Tangata responded, stepping ashore.

"Close deal first. Ten thousand."

Tangata laughed. "You're a pirate, Rongo!"

"In old days, yes. Now respectable merchant."

"You're half right. One."

"I got better things to do for such tiny sum."

"You've been out of work for months."

"You think to know so much. Nine thousand."

"Competition scared off customers. One-fifty."

"Maybe not so scared as you think. Eight thousand. Last offer."

"Is that why people won't even ask you to deliver a grocery order?"

"Okay. Seven—American dollars."

The man reached into his front trouser pocket, withdrew a wad of clipped bills and peeled off a number of green notes.

"This some kind of joke, Jimmy? This only four thousand."

Philippe startled at the sudden revelation of a name. He had asked. When no answer came forth the boy surreptitiously poked around the man's study finding nothing to suggest a name—except! He now recalled a series of novels about a World War Two intelligence agent, "An authorized edition" penned by another writer to keep the popular series alive. He wondered at the time why the books had never been opened, as were others by the same author. Tangata was a writer! He had watched him at work from a distance. He didn't like anyone looking over his shoulder.

"Here's another thousand, for Rongo to keep

quiet. Take it or we leave," the man retorted brusquely.

Rongo shrugged with an obviously faked pout. "Who boy?"

"Your competitor's nephew. Philippe Bonnét."

"Red Face!" The pirate glared so hatefully Philippe could almost feel a knife twisting through his ribs.

"The kid's parents were killed in a plane crash so his uncle took him in. Ungrateful pup up and run off when the . . ." the man called Jimmy checked himself. "His uncle is trying to kill him."

"So-o-o! This is brat they turn islands upside down for. Offer bi-i-i-g reward. Ver-r-r-y big reward. Stole lots of money."

"Yes, I stole some money," Philippe confessed, "When I heard my uncle ordered me fed to the sharks I grabbed a bag of money from his safe and ran. He's pretty upset."

"No joke," the ruffian laughed. "He want bag back real bad and you dead for sure, kid. Must been lots of money. Maybe more than five thousand American dollars?"

"You looking to renegotiate, maybe?" Jimmy replied softly.

"No love boy's uncle. Even if I bring money and brat's head he still do not so nice things to me. I do this for free," Rongo laughed, handing the money back.

"Keep it. Think of it as a bonus."

"Okay," the pirate replied quickly shoving the wad of bills deep into the soiled jeans.

◆　　◆　　◆

"You look terrible, Tomas," Rousseau said. "Have

a drink." Tomas helped himself to a shot of whiskey as his boss continued speaking. "The police are trying to indict me for money laundering based on information they received off that CD. Those bloodsucking lawyers will finally earn their fee. I'll have a few political associates put pressure on the French and Australian prosecutors, too. It's also time to call in a few outstanding debts. That should make things go away.

"The cops obviously don't have the disk proper, just the financial record." Rousseau then called out to another man standing in the shadows. "Georgi, put the word out. The reward is double for that disk and whoever has it. And double it for the kid, too. I trust what you say Tomas, but that little bastard has more lives than a cat. I agree, he had help getting away, but someone filed papers blocking me from gaining control of my brother's resort, as if trying to protect his inheritance."

"Interesting," Tomas said, a bit shaken by the new development, careful not to show it. "I can understand that if the boy is alive, but if he's dead? That might be a smoke screen in an attempt to usurp your rights of inheritance. Who's handling the paper work?"

"Some ambulance chaser by the name of Tuskin."

"I assumed it was the boy's body from the clothes. It could be possible whoever planned this elaborate scheme to get the disk may have kept Philippe alive as well and put someone else on the *Catherine*."

"If so, he can't hide forever. If he does show up I want the kid alive. He will provide answers to many questions before he disappears . . . completely and forever, no trace whatsoever, and that goes for anyone who helps him. I want that disk."

"Yes, sir."

♦   ♦   ♦

Boarding the old, weather-blackened, and water-logged wreck took a great deal of faith and intestinal fortitude. It not only looked, but smelled as if resurrected from Davy Jones' Locker. Each footstep sounded with creaks and groans with visions of suddenly falling through to the next deck, if not out the bottom. One dare not touch anything. The wood was splintered, the metal rusted. A hand could end up looking like a reddish porcupine. A floating derelict until the engines roared to life and propelled it through the waves. Philippe was astonished. Whatever lay hidden below decks certainly wasn't a tired, one lung relic associated with dilapidated, inter-island rust buckets like this scrap yard fugitive.

"That's how the old pirate eludes competition . . . and the authorities," Tangata explained as the wind whistled through their hair.

"Can he be trusted?"

"Rongo's a scoundrel, but yes."

"So, you're name's Jimmy," Philippe said after a moment's silence.

The man said nothing.

"And you wrote those spy books."

The man still gave no conformation, but turned to the problem at hand. "Listen close. When we make port you need to . . ." He began outlining a plan.

Philippe and Ellie sat alone near the bow for most of the two-day trip, his stomach churning like a storm-tossed sea. His uncle's empire stretched throughout the South Pacific. He had "eyes" everywhere and that, as Tangata explained, was exactly what the plan depended upon.

Approaching Brisbane port the steady rumble of the powerful engines suddenly bowed to the labored chug of a one-lung, oil-spewing wreck as the boat took on its deceptive appearance. Shaken from trance-like thought, Philippe looked aft, startled by the sudden appearance of a sailor he'd not seen before standing at the pilot's wheel.

Cautiously walking back, it felt as if having been magically transported aboard an entirely different ship as it pitched, and rolled, and creaked, and groaned with every swell. The new pilot had black, wind-tossed hair hanging over sunken eyes reminiscent of an English Sheep Dog. A squared jaw and somewhat large chin sported a grizzled, black beard. Like the opened shirt, his body was oil-smudged and in need of a turn in the deep clean cycle. Philippe was about to question the new crewman until noticing something vaguely familiar.

"From now on, kid, don't show surprise when we meet," the man growled with a distinctively Australian accent.

"So where's the pirate?"

"Below and there he'll stay 'til this wreck sets sail again. He's not welcomed in this part of civilization. Soon as we dock, you be gone exactly like you were told. One step ahead, but only one. That's important for this to work."

As the rusty, creaking derelict bumped the dock in an older, seedy section of Brisbane harbor, Philippe jumped ashore as two of Rango's sons grabbed the hemp bow and stern lines and pulled several, quick figure eights securing it to the dock. He didn't look back, setting a brisk pace along the peer and inland acutely aware of questioning eyes following every move.

"Who was the bogan that came with you, Capt. Capon?" a port officer inquired while scanning the ship's forged documents and feeling as if he wanted to scratch himself. A stocky man in dark glasses stood off the boat skipper's shoulder.

"Reffo. Picked 'im up o'r Vanuatu. Says 'is boat swamped in the big blow. Passed o'r enough fer passage here. Din talk much," the man lied cordially. "Sure seemed to be in a bloody hurry. Soon's we docks he shoots through. Not so much as a g'dai.'"

The sunglassed man stepped away, immediately placing a call on his cell phone. Tangata smiled to himself.

Following directions to the letter, Philippe took a cab from the pier to the O'Sullivan Business Center in the middle of town and sat at the outdoor café. While sipping a latte, he noticed that the complex consisted of three high-rise towers. Two had a steady flow of people; the third was still under construction.

An hour passed before four men in shiny business suits and dark glasses exited a black limo and stood by the curb, looking around. Philippe instantly recognized them for what they were. As instructed, he walked briskly into the nearest tower. As he entered the elevator he saw them approach at a quick pace. Trapped in the lift, he watched them draw closer and closer. Philippe prayed for the door to shut. He wanted to jump to the control panel and push the close button, but was sandwiched to the rear. Finally! The doors moved. The lead man sprang for the closing door. His outstretched hand slapped the sealed door violently. He'd have made it if it weren't for some guy stepping into his path.

"There'll be another, mate," a brokerage-type

commented a bit sarcastically, brushing his jacket after being knocked down.

The man glanced at the bi-spectacled milquetoast while scanning the lobby. Frustrated, his natural reaction was to slug someone, but there were too many people not to mention a couple security cops.

"Chill," his accomplice whispered then began giving orders to his associates. "You two hang around here. Watch the lifts and stairs," he continued as a dozen more men joined them. "You two cover out front. The rest of you cover the back and delivery entrances. Lock the place down. I'll be in the security office. Now move it and don't let that kid get out or I'll personally handle demotions."

The next lift door opened and the milksop casually boarded, holding a briefcase with both hands in front with head slightly cocked to one side, peering over wire-rimmed glasses. Directing a congenial smile at the thug he'd collided with, the door closed and he was gone. For a brief instant, the thug thought the yuppie looked familiar.

"Police," the leader of the men trying to catch Philippe announced, flashing a fake badge at the security officer. "A wanted criminal got aboard lift six a couple minutes ago."

"That's an express to the fifteenth floor and up," one of the men stuttered.

"You see a kid about fourteen or fifteen get off on your monitors?"

"Not so far," another replied, then checking the console said, "That lift's coming down."

"Can you identify which floors it stopped on?"

"Yeah. Just a minute.

"Hurry it up. You other two start watching every floor from fifteen up."

"What's this kid done?"

"He may be carrying a bomb." That spurred the building security into action.

Philippe's elevator shot to the eighteenth floor, deposited all its occupants. Exiting, he waited out of camera view until another elevator appeared less than thirty seconds later. That carried him to the twentieth at the top. He was surprised how quickly it happened. Exiting, he hurried down the corridor to the third office door on the left and entered a semi-darkened reception room. As told, there would be no one at the front. Toward the back of the reception area were two doors. One bore a gold sign, "Mr. Tuskin." It stood ajar. Philippe gingerly pushed his way into the empty room.

"Go in, sit down, and wait," Tangata instructed. Philippe sat on the edge of a thickly cushioned chair next to the polished Teak desk looking for all the world like the deck of an aircraft carrier. It was totally void of anything except a lamp.

"I see you made it," a well-attired man with wire-rimmed glasses said as he strode into the office, plopping a briefcase on the desk, and pointed at the ceiling before placing one finger over his lips. Philippe thought to recognize the man, and then realized he was showing surprise. He instantly changed expressions. He also understood the gesture to mean their conversation was not private.

"I'm sorry to just barge in, but . . ."

"You did right, Mr. Bonnét," his disguised benefactor replied in the refined tongue of an English gentleman.

To the boy's astonishment his benefactor withdrew a CD from a briefcase and slipped it into Philippe's jacket pocket, motioning for him to be quiet.

"My name is James Tuskin," Tangata continued the ruse. "I have been informed that a computer disk in your possession would be invaluable to the authorities. Having been retained to represent your interests, I caution you that to withhold criminal evidence could put you in jeopardy of being considered an accomplice to your uncle's business enterprises."

"I didn't know I had it," Philippe said, answering with what they had rehearsed on the boat. "I knew there was money in my uncle's safe. I needed some to get away. I found a pouch in his safe and looked inside. I saw there was money, but didn't look any further. It must have been in the pouch. I just want to be rid of it."

"How did you escape the storm?"

"Two of my uncle's men took me out to sea with orders to kill me. I managed to toss them overboard, then radioed a boat I was told to contact. It met me, and a boy my age took over my uncle's boat. They took me to Lifou. The people who were helping me took the disk. They had this computer geek who opened some files on the disk and sent them to the police. They were all laughing about how they were getting even with my uncle. After they were done I then realized they had no need of me and I think they were planning to get rid of me. When they weren't watching, I grabbed the disk and ran. I still had the money and bought passage here. Papa said if I ever needed help to contact you."

"Yes. I handled some of your father's more personal matters. Acting on specific instructions from you father, I have filed papers with the court protecting your interests until you are either found to be alive or . . . dead. Specifically, your father wanted to block any attempts by your uncle to come into control of any part of certain properties. In fact, I was in the process of having you removed from his custody, but you took matters into your own hands and disappeared. Very well, then. Let's step into the next room."

Stretching forth a hand, he placed it upon Philippe's shoulder and winked. The boy was then escorted into a small, adjoining room where a casually dressed man milled about nervously. Tuskin closed the door behind them.

"Mr. Bonnét, this is Inspector Fenster from Interpol. This is the young man with the special information I told you about. We may speak freely in this room."

"Here," Philippe said, handing him the disk. "Guess I stole it from my uncle's safe when I ran off. I don't know what's on it, but it must be important. He's pretty upset."

"That would be a correct assumption," the young, blond-haired man replied in English. "There's a pretty sizable reward out for both you and this disk. We will, of course, provide whatever protection you need."

"That won't be necessary. Arraignments have been made in that regards," Tuskin replied.

"I guess you already have some of the financial data," Philippe said. "There may be other files on it. I think they're hidden and pass worded. I can't think of anything that might be helpful."

"We have people who specialize in recovering such data. I am certain they will be well amused cracking any codes, as we will be with the information on it. We are grateful, Mr. Bonnét," the officer responded slipping the diskette into his jacket pocket. "If this is what it is purported to be, your uncle will be much too busy worrying about his own affairs to be concerned with you."

Once the Inspector left Philippe said, "My uncle's men almost caught me on the lift."

"Yes, I know," Tangata replied casually. "I bumped into one on my way up. There are surveillance cameras in the corridors and voice recorders in offices, except for this room. It's been sanitized. Your uncle's friends are in security watching. Once we step into the corridor, they will know you're on this floor. It will take them four minutes to come up." Then glancing at his watch said, "Okay, follow me."

They exited the suite, locked the door, and moved briskly to the glass-walled entry of a vacant office at the end of the hallway. Using another key, Tangata opened the door, carefully locking it behind them before moving on to a private elevator at the rear.

"It will take them a few seconds to realize what's going on. There's a sensor in security alerting them to this lift's movement."

"They'll have men covering it. We'll be trapped."

"No," Tangata said coolly, reaching into the car.

Chapter 7

Bait and Switched

As the named implied, Rousseau was a ruddy-faced man, not large like the gang's behemoth soldiers, nattily dressed with a bright, red ascot, and always the center of abject attention like now as the words slithered from pursed lips, "Okay, explain how they could just disappear."

"I saw the kid and a guy on the camera come out of this office on the top floor leased to a J. Tuskin," the man who lead the chase reported. "They went straight into a vacant office down the hall. He had a key. Just as the boys arrived the private garage lift from that office was activated. I already had some guys down there. It was empty. There wasn't any way to get into that office. The glass entry could withstand a tank and it took seven minutes to get someone with a key.

Rousseau rolled his eyes, trying to remain calm as his blood began to steam. "Did anyone think of using that private lift to gain access to the office?"

"Yes, sir, but the door wouldn't open on that floor. It jammed. It took building security nearly an hour to get the guys out. Also, that guy at the elevator, the Yuppie Frank ran into causing him to miss catching the kid was the same one that sneaked him out of the place on us,"

"Who *is* this Tuskin guy?"

"Don't know. Security says the office is leased by South Pacific Enterprises."

"Now where have I heard that name before?" Rousseau said with a sarcastic tone. "Aren't they concerned that the office might be used for illicit activity, what with their paranoia about security?"

"What's illicit mean?"

Rousseau rolled his eyes and answered curtly, "Illegal."

"Oh, like us. Yeah, they asked once and were told by the Governor-General's office not to worry about it."

"Claude," Rousseau said, directing his words to a man standing off to one side, "Check with that girl you know in the Governor-General's office. See what's going on." Then back to the leader giving the report, "Go on."

"The office this Tuskin guy uses only has a couple desks and chairs. Nothing else in it. Not even a piece of paper. Until the kid appeared on camera, I didn't know what floor he was on. Afterward, I got them to roll back the video of the corridor, and got the sound bite from that office. I heard this Tuskin guy talk to the kid. He already knew about the CD and said Interpol was interested. When the kid decided to turn it over, they went into a soundproof room. The security guys at the complex are kinda upset about that. Anyway, I see some guy leave the office and get on the elevator. Five minutes later the kid and this Tuskin leave. Like I said, that's the first we knew what floor he was on."

"So how did they disappear?" Rousseau asked, his words as menacing as the Titanic's iceberg.

"The lift was a decoy," the man whined. "It stopped on a half dozen floors before going to the lower level garage. He had us running all over the place. They didn't take it at all. Went out onto the roof instead."

"Then what?"

The man nervously shrugged his shoulders. "The only way they could have got by us was to transfer to the tower under construction. The only way to do that would be using the crane. I questioned the operator. Said he placed a toolbox on that tower earlier in the morning. It would have been large enough to hold two people. About the time we were closing in he got a call to transfer it to the work site on the ground. He couldn't really see it from his position and was guided in by radio. After it was lowered, someone took over by remote and put it onto a flatbed truck with some other boxes. That's the only way out we didn't have covered."

"Where's that boat he came in on?" the crime lord snorted.

"Up and left about the same time we were chasing the kid. Only the kid and the captain got off and only the captain got back on board," another solider reported. "Didn't drop any cargo and didn't take on any stuff except food. There wasn't anything big enough for so much as a baby to hide in."

"I checked on that Tuskin, fella" another standing to the side reported. "He's some kind of lawyer."

"That's convenient," someone else snapped sarcastically.

"And he just happens to be the one filing all those court papers blocking me from taking over my brother's resort. Well, someone in the Governor-General's office must know him," Rousseau snarled as jaw muscles knotted and his complexion darkened.

"How come the boy is alive when Tomas said he was dead?" another questioned.

"Because there was a switch." Tomas answered as he stepped into the room. "Philippe had help from inside."

"Inside!" Rousseau yelled.

"Yeah," the man who had lead the chase said. "I heard the boy tell this Tuskin that he threw the guys who took him out overboard, then radioed somebody, and a boat came out to make a switch. Some other kid took your boat and whoever was helping him, took him to Lifou. Once there, they sent the info to the cops. Guess the kid figured they were going to get rid of him so he stole the disk back and made his way to Brisbane."

"I followed up on that," Tomas said. "It was the kid who cleaned the pool. I tracked him down after he quit. He was a plant to get friendly with your nephew. Apparently, he overheard your plans to kill Philippe and use the storm as a cover. He also overheard you talking about the computer disk being in the money pouch. His people saw a golden opportunity. By telling Philippe what you were going to do, it was a simple matter to encourage him to steal the money from your safe to buy passage to Europe. I don't think Philippe knew about the CD until later."

"Where is this informant now?"

"He was discretely removed."

"Ah-h, too bad. I especially enjoyed his company. Had a lot of promise, although the new boy is not bad."

"I am curious, Tomas, just how does a boy overpower two of your gorillas?" another at the table asked.

"He received a Black Belt from Master Yamamoto. His martial arts skills are better than we realized."

"What about the body you found on that island and said was Philippe?"

"I said it *could* be him. It was the same height and had the same clothes. The head was gone and mostly decayed. The boy who took over the *Catherine* was to sail to Briault on Vanuatu. Philippe was taken to Lifau to wait out the storm. Apparently the kid sailing the *Catherine* was blown off course and ended up on that cursed island."

"And who masterminded all this?!" Rousseau shouted.

"Red Pine of the Taiwan Triad."

The boss slammed a fist on the table preparatory to a Krakatoa-like eruption.

"Got a lead, boss," a diminutive weasel chirped with a high pitched voice as he barged into the meeting. "A bush jockey called. Just back from a charter. Ferried a Jewish kid and his father to Port Mosby to rejoin a tour group from Israel. Thought the kid looked familiar, but didn't put it together until taking another look at a picture of your nephew soon as he got back. Says the kid was wearing a disguise, but he's sure it was him."

"Israel!"

"Yeah. He saw them hook up with the group as it

boarded a plane."

"Israel! Damn!" Rousseau roared, slamming his opened hand on the table again. "Do we know anyone there?"

Tomas responded. "We could ask the Girabelli Family to get someone to the airport and pick the boy up."

"It shouldn't matter," the weasel continued, producing a computer diskette. "My contact at Interpol tipped me off there might be an exchange at the office complex. Got there just as the agent was leaving the building. Picked his pocket."

Philippe's uncle couldn't withhold astonishment as he took the disk from the soldier.

"You know something, boss," another said, "I went aboard that old derelict the kid came in on and nosed around. Port inspection. An absolute pigsty, but there was something in the galley that looked kinda odd. The makin's of a martini and a silver, metal shaker. Who'd figure some Chinaman be drinkin' martinis."

The boss' glower slowly dissolved as a smile turning the edges of his lips upward. It started as a chuckle akin to a hiccup, escalating into a rolling laugh.

"Well, whoever this Tuskin guy is, he's good. Real good. Played us like marionettes and to rub it in left a little message. Don't you get it? Shaken not stirred? And we bested him, anyway. "Tell Don Girabelli not to worry about the brat. Just send his head back in a box. I want to grind my cigar in it before feeding it to the sharks," he said, waving the disk and laughing.

◆　　◆　　◆

Marooned on a tiny island, Philippe watched the helicopter disappear into the scattered clouds. The transfer from off the business center roof had been nerve wrecking. A dark green, 4x4x6 foot steel box was setting on the back of the tower's roof. He got in as Tangata guided a construction crane's jib over. Apparently, the operator couldn't see from his position. When the cable was lowered, Tangata attached it, and using a two-way gave the signal, jumped in, and closed the hatch.

Inside was pitch black and hot as the container started to sway. Philippe began to feel sick, but the sensation was stymied when Tangata cracked a glow light. It's weird, green glow cast a surprisingly bright light inside the metal coffin. A few minutes later, the container jarred. He then heard voices outside and light scraping noises. Presently the box began moving, bumpy, not swaying.

"We're on a truck heading to a private airport," Tangata said, peeling rubbery additions off his face. "There's a change of clothes in that bag for you," motioning to a cloth shopping bag in the corner next to his left hand.

As their box bumped along, the fake barrister's face changed back into the one Philippe knew, then into that of a Jewish rabbi complete with a thick, bushy, white beard. Philippe changed into a white shirt, black trousers, and dress shoes. The addition of a curly wig complete with a long lock of hair dangling in front of each ear, and kippah finished off the transformation.

The change no sooner complete, the truck stopped. A tap on the outside signaled Tangata to open the door. Philippe was expecting overwhelmingly bright sunlight after adjusting to the near dark, but they were in a warehouse.

Leaping out, they made their way to a dark sedan parked nearby. The next stop was a charter air service a half mile away.

Less than fifteen minutes later the Hawker Beechcraft King Air turboprop leapt into the clear sky to wing its way north along the Australian coast, stopping at Cairns three hours later just long enough to refuel, empty bladders, and grab sodas and peanut rolls from an over-charging vending machine. From there the flight struck across the Coral Sea landing at Port Moresby, New Guinea seven hours after leaving Brisbane.

After passing customs, which Philippe thought was awfully fast, a shuttle took the Jewish father and son to the main terminal to become absorbed among a herd of kids his own age. If Philippe was thunderstruck at the ease in which every connection fell into place, and how Tangata easily transformed himself, what happened next only added to the wonder. Tangata was an American fluent in Islander French, British, and Aussy English. Now he spoke with the tour leader in Hebrew! The boy began to wonder how many languages this man spoke, and considering what had just happened, what were his connections?

Association with the tour group was short-lived, however. Passing through security, they began the final march along the concourse to board a commercial jet. On the way, Tangata pulled Philippe aside and directed him into a restroom.

"There's a tee-shirt, shorts and sneakers in your backpack. Trade out including that wig. It really isn't you," Tangata said as they ducked into separate stalls.

A few minutes later, they reunited appearing as themselves, the first time since leaving the pirate island. Exiting the restroom, Tangata stuffed the backpacks into a locker, discretely dropping the key as they passed a shoeshine stand. Doubling back toward the main terminal, they came to one of many locked access doors. Tangata swiped a credit card through the security reader and entered several numbers on the key pad. An audible click allowed them to open and pass through the door, down a flight of steep steps to an airport security pickup.

"Open this after you're airborne," Tangata said, handing the boy a small envelope. Whisked along the well-marked service road across the concrete tarmac, he came to a waiting dark blue, Bell 429 helicopter. Minutes later, he was in the air and over open water again heading east-southeast along the rugged Papua, New Guinea coastline. Philippe didn't especially mind that the security officer in the pickup, and now the chopper pilot didn't say anything. Digesting what was happening needed quiet, think time.

Once in the air, Philippe opened the envelop to find a map of an island indicating a trail along the beach to the opposite end with an 'X" just off-shore and a cryptic note, "Rango's son is there. Make yourself at home." An hour later Philippe stood alone on the sandy point of the teardrop-shaped island. Once the chopper left, he began walking along the sandy shore until coming to a point where the trees grew to the waterline. Passing through the thick vegetation, he reached the end of the island and lots of ocean. Anchored a football field's length from shore lie the *Adrianne*.

Stripping down to boxers, he carefully hung the civilized clothes on a small bush, intending to reclaim them later, not wanting to get them wet while swimming out to the boat. Lifting himself onto the rear diving platform, he looked around and called out. There was no answer until hearing a rapid clicking noise as Ellie shot up from below and raise up to plant both big paws on his shoulders, nearly throwing him backward into the water. Excited to see Philippe again, she slobbered kisses all over his face.

"Okay, okay. Nice to see you, too," he laughed and set her down gently. That's when he saw a black head coming up from below.

"Hi," he said with a slightly effeminate voice dipolar to his father and brothers raucous baritones.

"Hello Asuka," Philippe answered, using the name Rango used.

"I don't like that name."

"Oh."

"It is a girl's name. It means tomorrow smell pretty."

"I wouldn't like that either. Why would your father call you that?"

"My brothers started calling me that because I'm gay. My real name is Limu."

As Rango loaded everyone aboard his floating garbage scow, he wasn't too kind telling the boy to stay behind, treating him as an outcast of sorts. Now Philippe understood, but Tangata had need of him—to bring the *Adrianne* to this island.

Rango's youngest, Limu was three or four years older than Philippe. The pirate had seven sons, not one the same mother. The young man was much more slender than his brothers. They were by no means fat, but lacked muscle definition with smooth, rounded bellies. The young man was built much like Philippe except taller and less filled out. As his name implied, he looked like a seaweed next to them.

His skin was much lighter, too, like new copper

compared to his brothers' dark chocolate brown. Also, they all had black hair while his was brown with a hint of red. Straight, trimmed shorter in front so not to hang in his eyes, two, thin, tightly woven braids with interlaced green beads hung off the right side touching the shoulder. The remainder was long and tapered so to fall between the shoulder blades. A single, long, silver beaded earring hung from the left ear. That seemed to be a family trait as his father and brothers wore circular earrings on that one side as well.

Limu's face was shaped much like half a football, a narrow chin and wide at the cheeks. The dark brown eyes were not elliptical like most Asians, but more round, like Europeans, and unable to hide the sadness. Thin lips appeared to have not smiled in a long time. An intricately carved, bone fish hook hung close to the base of his throat on a leather thong while a beautiful crucifix on a silver chain hung over his heart. Like the rest of the family, all he wore was a knee-length pant. He was already starting to collect tattoos, having geometric bands on either bicep, one on the left calf, and a small dragon on his belly, its tail curling around the navel. He'd obviously been awaken from a nap.

Going below, Philippe tossed wet boxers into a laundry bag, quickly showered, toweled off, and don his favorite, blue lava-lava, tying a matching cloth about his head. Next was what any growing teenager would do—raid the galley. Limu had already prepared a sandwich and glass of milk before settling in at the bow to read, seeming to prefer being alone.

On deck, Philippe stretched out, back against the mast and ate, still trying to make sense of the flawless, whirlwind escape. As the last remaining adrenaline burned out, coupled with ship's gentle rocking, and full tummy, exhaustion caught up. There wasn't much to do until Tangata showed.

After a snooze, he moseyed below, sitting at the navigation desk to play with the maps and computerized calculator. If his guardian sailed from Port Moresby using Rango's boat, he might be a week arriving unless the pirate used the escape engine. Bored, Philippe switched to play a game. In the lower right corner a tiny envelope icon flashed. Hurriedly, he opened the e-Mail program. It was a message from Tangata.

> *Hope you are enjoying your holiday. Tying up a few loose ends. See you in four days if this rust bucket doesn't sink. T.*

Philippe spent the remainder of the day, napping, watching a video, and playing a computer game. Despite the Islander's unsociable attitude, Philippe did manage to start a conversation late that afternoon attempting to break through the young man's wall of withdrawal.

"That's a beautiful crucifix," Philippe said, sitting cross-legged in front of him.

"I made it."

The religious symbol was about two and a half centimeters wide, silver with an abalone inlay reflecting a rainbow of color depending on how the sun struck it. The boat's rocking provided ample movement. Slipping it over his head, Limiu handed it to Philippe for a closer inspection.

"This is beautiful. You are very lucky to have such talent."

"Brothers say it is work for girls."

"No offense, but they're crazy. A person who can do something like this must be sensitive to the things around them."

"Like women."

"You are hung up on that. One day I was in a real funk, beating myself up for something I had done a long time ago. Tangata said we are who we are. Let it go and get on with life."

"You don't care if I am queer?"

"Doesn't matter what I think. It's your life, not mine."

Feeling less threatened by what Philippe might think, Limu relaxed and became more sociable. After fixing and devouring a nice supper, Philippe opened a small drawer in the head where he left the shark's tooth necklace Johnny had given him. Slipping it over his head, the multi-colored, glass beads of the bracelet purchased in Australia seemed to sparkle in the mirror. It really looked worth more than the couple dollars paid.

At dusk, the two sat on the bow watching the sun disappear, allowing the steady emergence of stars until a blazing display filled the sky accented by an occasional meteor.

"Are you Catholic?" Limu asked.

"Yes."

"You do not wear a crucifix."

"It was lost when I was thrown overboard in a storm. I haven't had a chance to replaced it. Maybe someday."

"I hear anger in your voice."

Other than Tangata, Philippe hadn't spoken of the events of those last days on his papa's resort island and the encounter with Fr. Josteau, but here he was explaining it to a stranger. He felt a kinship with the young man with sad eyes.

"The priest was very hard on you," Limu said. "You have a right to be angry with the church."

"I don't know if I'm angry at the church or not. When my parents were alive, we attended church almost every week. Living on Tangata's island, there wasn't any way of going. It doesn't seem very important any more.

"Maybe you are angry at God for taking your parents away."

Philippe was silent for a time. He was angry at Fr. Josteau, but could he subconsciously be angry at God for taking away his parents?

"I do not think I am angry with God. I say the prayers my papa and mama taught me, and sometimes they seem to have been answered."

The two talked late into the night, until Philippe said, "I'm going to turn in."

"Do you want to share a bed?" Limu asked.

Philippe sat motionless, unsure what to say. He felt neither threatened nor offended. Finally, he said, "No." The rebuff wasn't hostile.

"Oh. I'm sorry. I thought . . .," Limu said, seeming confused, and pointing to the multicolored bracelet on Philippe wrist.

"Does this have some special meaning?" Philippe asked.

"It is the rainbow sign of queer people."

"Oh." He felt embarrassed. "It's something I bought from a guy while sitting at the coffee shop in Brisbane. He looked to need a dollar, and thought it was very pretty. Well, good night."

Until now, Philippe's mind had been in near over-load trying to keep ahead of his uncle's henchmen and death. For now, he could relax except for the nervous tickle creeping around in his stomach and up his back. A couple years ago when that feeling began, he had no idea what they meant. Whenever it came, running the beach, swimming, Budō, working in the resort restaurant helped to push it down and away. However, the unquenchable fire continued to smolder. When he and Jean-Peter saw the man and woman having intercourse in the bushes that feeling sprang up like a wind-fanned fire and his naïve brain began to understand. The fight to remain in control was difficult. When Limu invited him to share a bed, it emerged like a solar flare.

Finding relief as Jean-Peter did was out of the question. Fr. Josteau's acidic, sledgehammer condemnation was deeply etched into his mind. "When the procreative power bestowed by God is deliberately set in motion and consummated without achieving the natural divinely intended purpose as you did, that is a mortal sin."

That no one seemed to give heterosexual fornication a second thought was confusing. Many guests at the resort indulged in the privacy of their rooms. It was depicted in novels and in movies; there were houses to satiate one's carnal desires for a price. Society appeared to tolerate that. Even Fr. Josteau succumbed according to a news broadcast not long ago. Could there be degrees of mortal sin concerning the procreative power?

Limu's invitation did not seem any better alternative. While some railed at same gender sexual activity, Philippe was more tolerant. His parents taught him to understand that other's had weaknesses, but not acceptance of those things. Hate made an exception in his uncle's case. That Limu's manner was effeminate only made feelings of arousal stronger. That was a long, sleepless night, tossing and turning with the struggle, arising early committed to a solution.

Swimming back to the island, Limu and Elli trailed in a rubber dingy. As the two wondered off, he started with a tour of the island—a short tour. It wasn't quite 500 meters long by 350 at its widest at the south edge bumping against the ocean. The north quarter was mostly sand with a few small palms and bushes, the rest a dense jungle. A navigation chart aboard ship indicated this ink spot lay 800 meters from Mailu Island. Only 800 meters. Philippe debated making the easy swim to visit the fishing village facing the mainland eight kilometers further, but decided Tangata may not want anyone to know he was about. The *Adrianne* was positioned so as not readily seen.

Philippe set to working off the nervous agitation with stretching exercises before running the beach. The island's circumference was only a bit over one kilometer by his best estimate. The entire south end was a heavily forested, coral rock drop-off with no beach. That meant he had to start on the east corner, run around the pointed north end back to the west corner, and return. There was no way to cross the south end barefooted because of the sharp rocks. Five round trips was a respectable ten kilometers, and running in the surf provided resistance. He then cooled off with an easy swim along the east shoreline before returning for an hour of intense martial arts katas. Meanwhile, Limu remained at the southeast corner near the beached dingy, playing fetch with Ellie, reading, or sleeping.

Deciding to explore the reef, Philippe swam back to the boat and went below to retrieve a face mask, snorkel, and fins. There was also Scuba gear, but of interest was the small breathing apparatus no larger than the length of his hand. Tangata had demonstrated how it worked, taking oxygen from the water, and passing it to the diver, not unlike how the gills of a fish work. He decided to give it an extended try. Opening another compartment, he removed a large knife, strapped it around his waist, and took out a spear gun, thinking they might have fish for dinner, more than for defense. Back on deck, he fastened flippers to his feet, fitted goggles and snorkel, giving his lava-lava a toss before jumping feet first from the *Adrianne's* stern.

Water was a second home as he stretched out to glide over the surface, scoping out the coral below. He swam about the surface for a time before placing the breathing device in his mouth, activating it, and heading for the bottom to become just another fish exploring the fantasy world of pastel colors.

Coming upon a Wrasse cleaning station, he watched as larger fish settled in, opening their mouths to let the small, Bluestreak clean parasites from their mouth—the ocean's family dentistry. Other than that, there wasn't anything of particular interest. Nothing, that is, until a Blacktip shark swam into view like a silent minibus. Spear gun ready, Philippe held perfectly still as the gray torpedo-shaped creature glided gracefully over the coral. A juvenile no longer than the boy's height, he admired how effortlessly it moved, seeming indifferent until turning toward Philippe. He prepared to shoot, but the creature must have considered him too large and dangerous as it turned and raced off. This would not be their only encounter.

Surfacing at *Adrianne*'s stern, Limu was there to give a hand aboard.

"I saw a Blacktip break the surface so dog and I paddled out, but we didn't see any blood."

"He apparently thinks I'm too big and ran away,

but I didn't want to shoot dinner without being close to land or a boat."

"Good idea. What have you got?"

Philippe held up a thirty centimeter, yellow-eyed mullet. They would dine well.

As they were cleaning dinner dishes Limu said, "When Tangata come, I will leave.

"Leave?"

"Limu has decided to swim to next island and make his way to Port Moresby then to Cairns. I looked at the maps. My mother and a sister live there. I have not seen them for a long time. My mother says the people there are understanding of my kind."

"Have you ever talked to a priest?" Philippe asked, noting the crucifix on Limu's chest, wondering if he got the same railing lecture.

"No different from what was said to you. It is a crime against God to sleep with another man. I should go to confession to make my soul right again. I went every week and then slept with a man."

"Didn't the priest get upset that you confessed, and then turn around and did it again?"

"No. It was his bed I slept in."

That hit Philippe between the eyes.

"He said that it was perhaps better what we did. At least we would not create children, then go off and not raise them. I slept in his bed one, sometimes two times a week. Sometimes another would join us. He would hear my confession and say I was forgiven."

That's convenient, Philippe thought to himself.

"Did your father or brothers know this?"

"No. It was our secret. It was okay until the priest moved. Very sudden. But that was okay, too. I knew others who felt like me. That's when my brothers began to treat me badly. I don't understand. They lay with a woman and cause her to have a baby, go away, and leave her alone. Which is the bigger sin?"

"I am not sure one is bigger than the other. To break a law of God is not good. When a person confesses that he has done wrong, they promise not to do that again. To break the law again, a person is in much worse trouble because they broke the law and their promise."

The young man thought on that a while before replying, light heartedly. "Then Limu is in deep trouble. Probably will make one big bonfire in hell. Heat up the whole earth. Maybe come back as a big volcano." That was the first time the young man showed any joy. Philippe couldn't contain himself as Limu danced in little circles as if the deck was a bed of coals and yelled, "Whoop, whoop, whoop."

Philippe went to his cabin, returning to where his friend sat on the main deck staring out across the water. "Here," he said, handing him the colored bracelet, "To remember our friendship."

Limu looked up and smiled faintly. Taking the gift, he fastened it to his ankle and then removed a braided hemp anklet, and handed it to Philippe. "For you to remember me?" Philippe went to put it on, but had trouble tying a solid knot. "Let me tie it for you."

Scooting closer, Limu's long, slender fingers nimbly worked the cords, braiding a permanent knot so that it appeared to be one piece. Finished, he looked up into Philippe's eyes. They stared at one another for a time, and then Limu leaned forward and kissed Philippe on the cheek.

"You are a beautiful person, Philippe."

The shock was obvious on Philippe's face as he

stared open-mouth.

"I am sorry. I did not mean to embarrass you," Limu said and began to stand.

Philippe reached out and grabbed the young man's wrist to hold him from leaving.

"No. Don't go. I . . . I . . . No one ever showed me affection like that except my papa." A small tear began to trickle down his cheek, too small to be seen in the starlight, or he thought.

"I am sorry to have brought you sorrow," Limu said. He did notice.

"I wish my papa was here. I feel afraid, like the time I was little and a typhoon came. The lightning was so bright. It was like day. The rain and wind sound like some crazy monster trying to break into our home. Papa took me into his arms and held me tight, and the storm didn't seem so terrible."

Limu moved to Philippe's side and encircled an arm around a shivering shoulder. Philippe moved closer, envisioning the times his father or Tangata held him. The fear seemed to wither. The Islander thought of the times his mother held him this way, too and kissed his friend's head to make everything better.

Concentrating on the physical regimen of running and katas twice a day, and repeated long swims to explore the reef encircling the island, the remaining nights were no longer a sleepless problem. He was hard-pressed to remain awake after dinner, despite Limu wanting to talk. He listened the best he could until falling asleep.

He spent the morning of the fourth day ashore as usual jogging, and an hour of hard Kenjutsu katas in the soft sand and surf using a long tree branch for a sword before swimming back to the boat. Limu and Ellie lounged about the beach, he reading, she watching with crossed paws, eventually returning to the yacht in the raft. Philippe was smart enough to swim below the surface so as not to appear as a wounded meal. No other kinds of sharks appeared and there was plenty of food for the Blacktip to not bother bigger game, although it seemed to sense when Philippe was in the water and came around sometimes becoming a nuisance.

After grabbing a sandwich for lunch, Philippe stretched out atop the cabin to soak up the pleasant sunshine, and a comfortable snooze until awakened mid-afternoon by the deep-throated purr of an approaching engine. Raising up on one elbow, he was greeted by the vision of Rango's scrap yard coming in at flank speed. Looking through binoculars was not encouraging. The only one on deck was the pirate and a couple of sons.

"Uncle get disk," the pirate called out, looking downtrodden and giving the thumbs down sign as he pulled alongside. It was then Tangata stepped into view, seeming in good humor.

"Interpol had a leak," he said, jumping aboard. "We made copies of the disk before allowing the original to be picked out of Agent Fenster's pocket. The leak's been plugged. A couple others, too. Something folks thereabouts have been looking to do for some time. Your situation provided the perfect opportunity. The director of the Interpol office and Solicitor General send their deepest appreciation and best wishes."

"So that wasn't the original I gave the agent?"

"Oh, yes. A very special original. It has a little virus added, a present for your uncle's computers. Every time they log on to transfer data to their various accounts, we get all kinds of info, which is passed on to Interpol. They in turn will pass it to the appropriate local governments. Not exactly legal, but sometimes one has to knock down a wall to put out a fire.

"So, what about the data?"

"Both American and Australian cryptographers are playing with it."

"Tomas said I knew the password, but I have no idea what it could be."

"Not to worry. As Agent Fenster said, the computer people will be well amused for a time. I'm sorry to have taken so long getting here. Once you were safe, I had a couple things to tidy up before leaving Brisbane and join up with this pirate." Tangata had the satisfying look of a cat who just ate the canary and shifted the blame on Fido.

Chapter 8

The Odyssey

That evening the three men sat around a bonfire on Little Mailu's beach, eating fish Philippe speared a couple hours earlier. Rango's sons elected to remain aboard their Oriental yacht. With their appearance, Limu disappeared.

As the fire cracked and sparked, Philippe told how the Blacktip returned several times while he explored the reef, each time coming closer, but made no aggressive moves.

"Oh, you lucky, boy. Sound like girl shark looking for boyfriend," Rango teased, taking another big swallow from a bottle of wine. "Shark's eyes not always so good, though. Maybe boy shark looking for cuddle and can't tell difference." His laughter echoed loudly. "By way, where Asuka?"

"Limu left soon after you arrived," Philippe said, a

bit angry.

"Leave? Where he go?"

"I saw him swimming toward Mailu," Tangata said.

"He's gone to live with his mother and sister," Philippe said.

"Oh. He plan swim all way?" There was a flash of sadness in the old pirate's voice.

"Just to the fishing village on the big island then find a way to Port Moresby." Philippe didn't mention giving his friend money from a stash kept on the *Adrianne*, some of his uncle's money.

The sadness vanished as he returned to his usual, boisterous self. "Well, hope boy shark don't find him. They could play together for long time. Asuka be okay, but you be careful. Might eat more than small fish if find out you wrong kind."

The pirate was full of bad jokes, except some about Philippe's uncle and how he'd been outwitted were pretty good, or Philippe had drank enough wine to enjoy them. Tangata was laughing, too, and telling jokes about Rango's mis-adventures in earlier times. The pirate laughed louder than anyone. This was a side of the man with so many names and faces Philippe had not seen.

Halfway through a second bottle, Rango sat very straight, swaying slightly like a tall palm in a wind. Out of nowhere, he began a raucous sailor's song, a slurred, guttural sound approximating singing. Philippe spoke an Islander dialect, but only understood half the words spewed out. Obviously Rango used a more northern dialect. At another time Philippe might have been offended or embarrassed by the words, but right now was giddy enough to laugh and join in the chorus the third time through. Tangata rolled his eyes and laughed to himself. After all the boy had been through since the death of his parents, here was a moment's release. After cranking off a crude story about an escapade in Port Moresby, Rango took a big swallow from the bottle and laughed more loudly, drained the bottle, and gave it a toss. Without warning, his eyes rolled upward as he tumbled backward and passed out.

"Never could hold his wine," Tangata said, turning the pirate onto his side, partially to stop the volcanic, rumbling snores.

Philippe took another swallow from the brown bottle and announced, "I have to pee," and stumbled over to a small bush. Tangata picked up the boy's bottle and looked at it. It was almost empty. When he returned, Philippe flopped down on the sand.

"Well, it's about bedtime," Tangata said.

"Ah-h-h, not yet, Tangata. Please? I'm having too much fun," and drained the last of his bottle. "Is there any more?"

"Only what's in my bottle."

Philippe sat with his legs straight out. With that sad news he bowed his head and hiccuped. As his head came up, it and the rest of his body fell backward to join Rango leaving Tangata to tend the fire. Ellie got up, sniffed the boy, sneezed, and curled up next to Tangata seeming disgusted with her friend, but keeping an eye on him.

The next morning Philippe decided Tangata could either hold his liquor or didn't drink near as much as he let on. Certainly, Philippe couldn't. Raised on watered down wine, he hadn't graduated to stronger spirits until last night. He may have only consumed the equivalent of two or three glasses from the small bottle, but awaking that morning, felt sluggish and dull-minded, not to mention a headache, a dull pressure, nothing like the searing pain before. The swim back to the boat helped, as did several glasses of orange juice along with a bit of breakfast. By mid-morning Rango awoke and rowed his dingy to the yacht.

As the two captains conferred, Philippe lay in his bunk reading a book as that didn't seem to antagonize the hangover. Then Rango's voice boomed down the open hatch, "Good bye, boy. Don't let the sharks nibble that pretty body." His laughter continued until fading away as he rowed back to the Junk.

Going to the lavatory to wash, he saw it—Limu's silver crucifix with abalone inlay on a chain laying on the counter. He felt bad his friend had forgotten it, until realizing Limu never used the forward head. He left it behind deliberately with the rest of his past. Slipping it over his head, the crucifix joined the shark's tooth, two symbols of power. At noon the captains headed east on their separate boats.

Rango's Junk may have had a powerful engine, but under sail was hard-pressed to keep up with the *Adrianne,* forcing them to take in the headsail and jib to maintain eight knots at best. As the sun broke through the morning fog the second day out, they had traveled 350 nautical miles. Rango fired a shot from his pistol, waived, and turned south toward his hideout. It was 8 a.m. Philippe thought they would return to the volcano island, but grew suspicious by the course they were taking.

"Where are we headed?" Philippe asked.

"We'll put in at Honiara on Guadalcanal to take on supplies before going on."

"We're not returning home, are we?"

"No. You need to continue your education without having to look over your shoulder. How does the United States sound?"

"Okay," Philippe answered slowly, jolted at the prospect of venturing to a place he had only heard about, a horrible country everyone wanted to live in.

"We don't have to be in any big hurry, though.

Thought we'd kind of work our way through the islands before heading over to Hawaii then on to San Diego, California and up the coast to Portland, Oregon. It will probably take a couple months. We'll get you settled in time for school."

"School? In a real school?"

"Yes. Gonzaga College in Spokane, Washington has a good, Catholic prep school. I have some friends there willing to take you in."

"What about you?"

"Back to peace, and quiet, and no people," Tangata said, but the tone in his voice would convince no one that solitude was something he looked forward to. "However, your education isn't taking a hiatus until we get there. You'll find an envelope in the galley. Go enjoy."

Philippe found a large, cream-colored envelope on the galley work island. Stamped in upper left corner was, "American Embassy, Brisbane, Australia, Diplomatic Dependents Education Services."

"School work," he said to himself while eagerly opening it to spread the contents out. Above, he heard the whine of motors as Tangata unfurled the overlapping genoa and self-tending jib. With a freshening wind her speed kicked up to fifteen knots. Three hundred nautical miles later they put into port, in time for breakfast.

◆　　◆　　◆

Philippe enjoyed sitting at the kitchen table doing lessons as his mama prepared detailed assignments and menus for the staff. Other times it was at his own desk in his papa's office while Charles Bonnét managed business. Sitting in a classroom was an unknown, and he began looking toward the impending experience with some trepidation.

Seated cross-legged on a cushioned bench at the salon table, Philippe's pencil flailed at the first assignment on United States government as Ellie curled next to him and snored. Some lessons were via satellite Internet connection. Tangata resumed work on a novel. Piloting the boat was a shared chore. Galley duties were not. Philippe had learned to cook at the resort, enough to fix good meals. When anchored, the two did their work side by side, usually while seated at an outdoor café table, taking meals at restaurants.

Sailing directly to California from the Solomon Islands would have taken fifteen days, twenty tops. Instead, the odyssey became a slow meander, stopping at various islands to lounge on the beach, sit at outdoor cafés, hike, or otherwise act like tourists. They spent nearly three weeks hopping from one Hawaiian Island to another, but upon setting the *Andrianne*'s bow toward San Diego, she caught the wind and sliced through the ocean with the eagerness of a starved shark chasing a seal. Six days after leaving Honolulu Island, they arrived in San Diego, short of four months after leaving the volcanic island Philippe now considered home.

After several days touring the city and surrounding environs, they sailed north along the California coast. Docking at Alamitos Bay Marina in Long Beach, they spent a week visiting Disneyland and other wondrous LA tourist traps. He had never experienced such unbridled madness, bumping into people carrying on with childhood abandon, with the possible exception of some obviously frazzled, energy-depleted parents whose children continued on in hyper-dive.

Passing beneath the red Golden Gate Bridge for a couple days in San Francisco, Philippe thought of Limu, and how he'd find this city a place he could live without ridicule and scorn. Finally reaching the mouth of the Columbia River, they headed upstream to Portland where Tangata rented a car to check out the country as far as Seattle. All this Philippe absorbed like a sponge, keeping a journal as part of a school assignment, both written and photographic.

They spent a week with a friend of Tangata's in Sequim on the Washington peninsula. A widower whose children lived half a continent away, he was more than delighted having someone to boat with as that was often the most convenient way to get around the Venice of the American northwest. There seemed to be more about their relationship than just being mutual writers as they talked in whispers long after Philippe retired.

When Philippe remark about it, their host laughed and said, "We have collaborated on a thing or two."

"But that was a long time ago," Tangata put in.

"Too long. Too long."

As August began, the two drove over the Cascade Range to Spokane where Philippe met the Burkes who add him to their family.

Theirs was a grand, two-story house of stone and wood situated on a pine-studded hill overlooking a broad, green valley. It had a small, indoor swimming pool, and a barn full of horses. The family's two sons bracketed his age and attended the same prep school Philippe would. In addition were three girls, two older and one younger. He'd never experienced sisters and reveled in the attention as they fussed over the new arrival.

Life definitely changed. For one, he had to wear clothes and shoes, including for the first time, a coat, a heavy coat, against the cold and snow of east Washington weather. That inconvenience was mediated by the shoeless rule which allowed everyone to go barefoot in the house. He could have worn a lava-lava, but it tended to be cool in the house necessitating sweats. At least for now, the freedom of childhood days was gone.

Attending a physical school was a big challenge. Tangata accompanied Philippe a week before classes began to help with orientation. Seated in the principal's office, the boy's hands began to sweat. The Academic Vice President, Mr. Derek, sat to one side of the desk.

"We are very happy to have you come to our school, Philippe," Father MacArthur said from behind the desk. He was a slender man in his fifties with a Vandyke similar to Tangata's, but coal black. "Your guardian has explained your situation. All that anyone outside of this room will know is that you are an exchange student from France.

"I have looked over your transcripts. Quite impressive," Mr. Derek said. He was a friendly man in his mid-thirties, clean-shaven and athletic. A yellow dress shirt fit tight like a T-shirt. "You would normally be a sophomore because of your age, but these grades appear to give you junior standing. In order to offer you the best education to finish your last two years I would like to administer a couple test, if that will be alright with you?"

"That would be appropriate," Tangata answered. There was a different tone in his voice, one of a person in authority. "On another matter, the gentleman I mentioned will arrive in a few days and be in contact."

"I've informed our head of security to expect him. Mr. Murphy is excited to participate in the guest program, although I feel he should be included in this circle," Father MacArthur said, also sounding firm.

"I will leave the decision of including Mr. Murphy to the gentleman."

Philippe knew he was deliberately being left out of

something, and that didn't set well, but realized early on when something was important to know, Tangata would tell him, and not before.

The day Tangata and Ellie left was appropriately overcast and somber. As the car disappeared into the pine forest, the dog seated in the backseat like chauffeured royalty, Philippe experienced a great chasm open inside his chest. Everything in his world had been lost again. That feeling took time to cover over, but did not heal completely.

Any skepticism they may have had about Philippe's home schooling was shattered. His command of English was in some ways better than that of American-born students. The ensuing months of immersion helped tremendously to Americanize it. None of this distracted from continuing martial arts training. Even with the limited space aboard ship, he practiced, once losing to the boom.

Pulling him aboard using the trailing rope, Tangata said, "Well, if we ever need a sea anchor, you'll do just fine."

Katas were okay, but he wanted a live person with whom to spar. Fred Burke, his older "brother" and younger "brother" Kyle volunteered. They were game, but began to reconsider. Philippe's style was more aggressive. Fred proposed he come to Karate lessons with him, but doubted even his instructor was up to that level. The problem was resolved several days following Tangata's departure with a knocked on the Burke's door.

"Good afternoon," a man said in impeccable English.

Philippe was seated on the sofa reading a book, back to the door, facing the two-story windows facing the green valley. Upon hearing the voice, his heart jumped into quick time. He'd heard that voice somewhere before.

"I was asked to deliver this letter to you," the visitor said, handing over an envelope to Mr. Burke who turned it over and inspected a seal over the closing flap before opening it.

"Come in Mr. ah-h, I didn't get your name."

"Yamamoto. Michael Yamamoto."

Feeling paranoid, Philippe had slunk low to be out of sight, but hearing the name, he leapt to his feet, over the back of the sofa, and flew into the visitor's arms. Just as suddenly, he backed up, stiffened, to exchange formal bows.

"Mr. Burke, this is Mr. Yamamoto, the grandson of my martial arts master I told you about," Philippe explained, a quiver of excitement in his voice.

"Let's go to my office," Mr. Burke said.

After reading the letter carefully and adjusting his glasses, Philippe's host heaved a sigh.

"It seems your troubles continue. Your uncle has again doubled the reward on your head. You, my boy, are worth a million Euros to anyone ambitious or lucky enough to find you."

"But why? I thought once the police had the computer disk . . ."

"There has been a problem with that," Mr. Yamamoto began. "Our people have not been able to break the encryption."

"Our people?" Philippe asked.

"Yes, I am a member of . . . let's say, a counter terrorist organization. It seems that without the proper code any attempt to open the files destroys them. Fortunately, we have copies, but so far all our efforts have been unsuccessful."

"I'm sorry," Philippe replied softly.

"When your uncle raised the reward we began to ask why? What we have uncovered has caused him and his syndicate a great deal of problems. Such action must be for more than revenge. It was Tangata Aiwaiwee who proffered the suggestion."

"And that is . . .?"

"He knows you are alive, and you know the code."

"But I don't know any code! I didn't even know I had that infernal thing!" Then Tomas' last words before leaving the island of death came to mind. He did know the password, but what could it be?

"In any event, I have been sent here as your personal bodyguard," Michael said.

"My what?" Philippe said, then looked at Mr. Burke who handed him the letter.

Philippe read it over very carefully. Written in what he knew to be Tangata's hand, it explained everything as just heard. The piece not yet revealed was:

> *"Philippe, your uncle knows you are in America and has solicited help from organized crime families throughout the country. Master Michael will have your back, discretely of course. See you at Christmas time. Until then fly, but stay under the radar. T."*

Philippe slumped into a chair as if a great burden had just weighed down upon his shoulders.

"Not to worry, *wakai senshi*, young warrior. We have leaks, too. A word here, a whisper there, and they spend all their time searching the east coast. So long as you don't make the six o'clock news life will continue normally, if there is such a thing for teenagers." He laughed. "I hate to be a burden upon your family, Mr. Burke."

"That's why we have this big house. There's a room adjacent to Philippe."

"You will find sufficient funds deposited in your account to cover expenses, as usual. In the meantime, is there an area we could set aside for practice?"

"Yes. There is a large work area in the lower level next to the swimming pool. I'm only using a very small part of it."

"Thank you. Master Yamamoto asked me to deliver this," Michael said, handing Mr. Burke a small, padded envelope pulled from the inside, suit jacket pocket.

"What is it?" Mrs. Burke asked. She had brought a tray of tea.

"It's an *Ofuda* to replace your old one."

Just inside the main entrance to the Burke home were a framed photo of the Spokane LDS Temple which was central to their Mormon faith, and a copy of their faith's proclamation on the sanctity of family. There was also a small, elegantly, hand painted Shinto talisman, seven and a half centimeters wide by twenty-five long in a glassed, wood frame. Philippe read the Japanese inscription on the gift to himself as they all briefly looked at it.

"Elohim, New Zealand Shimada Shinto Shrine, protect this home from evil."

"We are most grateful Master Yamamoto remembers us in his prayers," Mrs. Burke said.

"He also sent this to you," Michael said, pulling another envelope from his pocket, leaving Philippe to wonder how many other things were stashed inside that coat. It seemed to be like Father Christmas' bag.

Opening the wrapper, he gazed at the small, rectangular cloth that came to a pointed end, decorated with delicate designs. The weight almost undetectable, he knew the cover protected a piece of rice paper. It was an *Omamori*, a personal amulet for protection. Issued by the same shrine, the paper contained a special prayer his martial arts master entertained on Philippe's behalf.

"Father thought, under the circumstances, you might need all the help you could get from the spirits, both as protection from evil, and for doing well in school."

"Thank you," Philippe said, staring longingly at the gift before slipping the leather thong over his head so that it would hang against his chest beneath the sweatshirt with the other talismans.

"Let me show you to your room and then we will see to the exercise area," Mr. Burke said.

Over the next two weeks, a part of the large, unused work area in the lower level was equiped with a woven rice mat floor properly cushioned to give it spring to absorb the shock when thrown. Outside, an archery range and fencing area were set up. Philippe helped Michael place a *Kamidana,* a miniature Shinto shrine, on the wall in one corner of the room near the door leading to the pool. Setting up a washbasin in the pool area made the water purification ritual convenient as it required clean, running water.

Although raised Catholic, Philippe had been feeling increasingly distanced from practice since his parent's death, thanks to Fr. Josteau unmerciful berating and subsequent behavior. Traveling to New Zealand during the cold part of the season, the boy quartered at Master Yamamoto's camp. It was there he became familiar with the religious rituals and began to participate in them as an extension of the training.

With Michael Yamamoto's arrival in Spokane, he began participating more. "It would not be heresy," Mr. Burke explained. "The shrine is as good a place as any to focus one's mind and soul upon God." Being more convenient, Philippe found it no different than kneeling in church or kneeling alongside one's bed. The shrine's presence was a physical reminder that praying was something he was taught to do every day.

Life continued for Philippe alias Philip Godeno', exchange student from St. Nazaire, France. Michael became an unobtrusive shadow, giving him the sense of what the American President's children must feel with their Secret Service. The Budō teacher was added to the school's security staff as a foreign visitor studying the American approach to school crime, as it was now becoming an issue in Australia. His presence was so discrete to be almost invisible. Still, Philippe felt the assignment must be difficult for him, although he never said anything.

There were challenges, of course, dating being one. Proving to be smart, witty, a great looker with a sexy accent, the young man became a hot item with the girls, but there would be no one-on-one adventures, not with Michael hovering nearby. Being around lots of young girls his age was a new experience, and Philippe became overwhelmed at first until his older, adopted brother, Fred, came to the rescue.

"Our church leaders ask us to not do any one-on-one dating until we are sixteen. I couldn't wait, but after a couple one on ones, I went back to group dating. It was just a lot more fun."

Actually, Philippe preferred that approach, too. He had enough stress adjusting to life in America and going to a real school. Another activity was the Boy Scouts. Neither Islander found comfort camping in the snow. The 'Polar Bear Swim' that April had to be the strangest and most physically cruel thing they ever imagined. Standing on a lake front, snow and ice edging the shore, Philippe watched as one boy after another ran into the water, ducked under the surface then sprinted for the heated latrine thirty meters inland.

Standing between his American brothers, bundled to the hilt and shivering, it came their turn. Taking a deep breath, off came sweat pants, parkas, and boots as the boys made an insane dash for the water in bathing suits, screaming. Minutes later, standing beneath a hot stream of water Philippe looked at the others, smiling until he thought his face would split. He loved it—every shivering, quaking, stinging moment—the games, the food, the camaraderie, and going home smelling of wood smoke.

Martial arts training resumed with daily workouts including both his new brothers and sisters, although they gladly sat on the sidelines and marveled when Shodan and Shichidan, went at each other. The teacher obviously held back during practice combat, but not much, pushing Philippe to his limits and stretch beyond.

Nor did Michael limit training one or two factions of the arts. Budō combines all the crafts of war, the physical along with spiritual and moral aspects. Lessons on combat tactics, *Bushido*, the code of honor, and spiritual development were necessary parts of the whole. Of course, Philippe loved Aikido and the physical contact, but there were other things to learn—*Kyudo*, archery, *Bo*, the staff, and Philippe's favorite, *Kendo*, the sword, the wooden kind that didn't necessarily kill, instead raised some nasty welts. The sixth day was given to serious combat using combinations.

Keeping a low profile was not especially easy as his popularity increased. With teachers, he was a delight in class, always alert, asking questions, and eager to participate in positive ways. With the guys, he was "cool," especially as the object of girls' percolating hormones, Philippe always introduce them to the boys who hung around like a spider around a sugar pot. A few girls tended to be shallow. Those he quickly learned to identify and steer a wide course around, but there was one he really, really came to like. Megan.

Between first and second period the first day,

Philippe finally relocated his locker as mayhem ruled the halls with students hustling to find their next class. Lost as an orphaned seal pup, salvation appeared when this girl hurriedly came to the locker next to his.

"Excuse me, please. Where do I find . . . room 126B?"

"That's in the languages section," she said. "That's where I'm going. Come on. We've got to hurry before the bell rings."

They were the last to enter just as the tardy bell sounded. The instructor, a tall, somewhat austere-looking woman in her forties, with an elongated face and hair tied into a large bun, glared at the arrivals who were looking for a place to sit.

"Juste à temps. Prenez l'un des sièges par la fenêtre," she said.

The girl stared at the teacher, not understanding what had been said.

"She said we just made it in time and to take one of those seats by the window," Philippe translated.

The instructor cocked her head back, mildly surprised. "That is correct, young man. You speak French?"

"Oui, je le suis. . . un étudiant d'échange à partir. . . Saint-Nazaire," he answered, saying that he was the exchange student from France.

The woman broke into a wide smile. "This might be a fun semester after all. Take one of those seats, please. We shall sort out a seating arrangement later. Alright, class, this is beginning French and I am Mrs. Waxman. Does anyone else here speak French? . . . Even a little ? Well, it seems it will be up to this young gentleman and I to help you."

Because Philippe already spoke French, and English with little accent, Mr. Derek assigned him to Mrs. Waxman's class as a teacher's aid, an elective. After class he didn't see the girl again until lunch. He was seated in a shady spot under a tree reading a book when she walked over.

"Hi. We didn't have time to be introduced. I'm Megan. Can I join you?" she asked.

Philippe jumped up. "Yes," and motioned for her to be seated. "My name is Philip Godeno'."

"Are you finding the rest of your classes okay?" she said.

"Sort of," he said, sitting cross-legged on the ground facing her.

From that moment Philippe felt attracted to the girl with the soft brown hair tied back in a pony tail that hung to the small of her back. As he learned later, it made no difference if worn back or flowing in loose curls around her head, the style complimented her slightly elongated face with broad cheek bones. However, what held him captive, were the eyes, large, dark, happy eyes, with a bluish-green tint. His whole body felt as if suddenly stuffed into a blender set on medium.

"Are you from Spokane?" he asked.

"No. Texas. My family came to Texas in the early 1800's from southern Spain."

That explained the girl's light, chocolate coloring and facial features suggesting Moorish ancestry. Having long, dark brown hair, large, expressive eyes, a slightly hawkish nose added power to the blender in his stomach. When her full, red lips parted into a big smile, the blender kicked into high.

Over the ensuing weeks they met for lunch where she practiced French. After school they met to do homework in the commons until Michael left work and drove her home. Of course, Mrs. Burke insisted she come for dinner one weekend. She just had to meet this girl Philippe never failed to mention, whether relative to the conversation or not. During swimming practice, Megan sat in the bleachers watching and doing homework. Friday nights, if he wasn't committed to a swim meet, they went to a dance and burgers at Dick's downtown, or Saturday events at Riverfront Park, which meant a couple trips on the carousel to catch the gold ring. There were also the assortment of school dances and activities. Of course, Michael was somewhere near, and one or two of the Burkes tagged along with their date. When it turned cold and snowy, it was either off to the Burke's mountain cabin near Mullen, Idaho east of Coeur d'Alene for snowshoeing and cross-country skiing, or snowboarding at Kellogg.

Michael seemed to struggle with boarding at first and the young men trying to help him laughed as he fell, traveling some distance on his backside. He was too athletic and determined to allow a piece of fiberglass be his master.

By noontime he whooshed passed calling out, "Last one to the bottom forfeits his French fries."

A highpoint in his life happened after a school dance. It was the fourth time they had gone out. He escorted Megan to her door. Reaching for the handle, she hesitated a moment before going inside.

"I had a super evening, Philip. Thank you," she said, then leaning forward, quickly kissing him on the lips before disappearing inside.

It was brief, but electric. Philippe stood on the porch in shock, tasting the fruity lipstick she'd left behind on his lips, until Michael's whistle shook him back to reality. Returning to the car, he got in and sat back, dazed.

"So, how was it?"

"What?" Philippe said back to Michael.

"That was your first kiss from a girl, wasn't it?"

"Yes. It was . . . nice."

"Nice? Just . . . nice?"

"It was wonderful. Ye-e-ah," he sighed, settling back in the seat and closing his eyes to silently relive the sweet moment over and over, licking his lips and tasting the fruity reminder.

The Jesuit-run school re-immersed Philippe in Catholicism, with regular prayers and religion classes. While prayer had not been a problem, Mass was. The school required attending Mass, despite feeling distant from the experience. Not long after the start of school, an early fiftyish priest taught a lesson on sexual promiscuity and the Church position. He didn't leave much off the table and every student felt uncomfortable, especially those who hadn't taken the admonition of celibacy seriously, but the lecture struck a raw nerve for Philippe. Something the young man did, a movement or facial expression, triggered warning bells to the priest.

"Mr. Godeno'," the priest said as the class began filing out of the room faster than usual. "What is your next class?"

"Study hall."

"Excellent. I have wanted to speak with you. I like to know my students better. Let's go to my office." It was not a request.

As they entered the room with a small, old wood desk, several over-filled bookshelves, equally used, he offered Philippe one of two chairs. He took the other so they faced one another with nothing between them.

"I sensed my lecture was difficult for everyone in the class. It appeared some wanted to jump out of the window, as others slid so far down in their desks I was afraid they would fall on the floor. That topic has interesting effects on students." He was smiling. Suddenly he turned serious. "I noticed you were especially uncomfortable."

Philippe squirmed in the chair, staring at his feet.

"How long has it been since you have taken of the Sacrament of Penance, Philip?"

The look in Philippe's eyes took the priest by surprise. So much pain . . . and hate? He waited for an answer.

"A while," Philippe finally managed to say. The priest didn't say anything, noticing the young man in front of him beginning to shiver as if chilled. "I guess I better do it." Subconsciously, he knew going to the area reserved for confessions would be sufficiently distant to take a detour.

"It does not have to be done in a confessional booth. We can do it here."

"Now?" Philippe's voice nearly squeaked, feeling panic rising. To go through what he'd endured before was not something to be revisited.

"Philip, whatever you did, are you truly sorry for having done it?"

"Yes." Haltingly, the details of what brought him to the last confession and results emerged. Anger rose in his voice when he got to the part about what happened after he confessed. The priest tried not to show or say anything against another priest.

"I am truly sorry a misunderstanding has caused you unnecessary torment. Sin is a very broad road with many lanes and it is quite easy to cross from one lane to another. If one signals, it is a deliberate act. If one does not signal, it is not necessarily deliberate, but a spur of the moment decision. Other times one may fall asleep at the wheel and drift over the line momentarily. I think what happened in your case, you were bumped over the line for an instant and came right back. You can't believe how many times I've counseled with a young man about self-stimulation. Entering puberty is not unlike having a bucket of Gatorade dumped on you. It comes all at once with little opportunity to get control right away. Masturbation is a miss-use of the procreative powers given by God."

Philippe groaned inwardly. *Here it comes again,* he thought.

"A one-time incident does not condemn one to eternal damnation. You recognized the misdeed, but emotionally unable to control what was happening in that one instance. You obviously were truly sorry for what you did and confessed to the proper authority. When you received absolution your soul became as clean as when you were baptized. You satisfied all that is required. There can be no further condemnation as long as you have refrained from further acts . . . . you have, I presume?"

"Yes. From that."

"Hm-m-m. Do I detect there might be more?"

Now Philippe was in a tight spot. Could this priest be trusted? He wished Tangata were here to ask. Maybe Michael. The priest just stared at him, waiting patiently. Philippe took a deep breathe.

"Yes, there is more, Father, but what I am about to tell you must be kept secret. Just between you and me."

"And God."

Philippe shuttered. He had been taught that God is everywhere. He knows all. The sudden realization God might have been sitting on the boat watching as he killed the assassins turned his stomach to the point of feeling ill. "God already knows," he sighed, feeling as if walking the last few steps to death.

"Philip, I am bound by sacred covenant, to never divulge what I hear during confession. I have been a priest for quite a few years, and some things I've heard were real ear scorchers. A couple should have been reported to the police, but they could not as they were committed to me within the sacrament of penance, thereby binding my tongue by the seal of confession."

Placing both hands on top of his head, Philippe pushed down as if trying to squeeze himself into an unrecognizable lump. It was then a reassuring warmth seemed to spread through his body. It was okay. He could tell. Slowly he began, releasing all the pent up pain and horror.

When finished, Fr. James sat back and exhaled. "That is . . . incredible." Gathering himself, he leaned forward, taking both of Philippe's hands into his. "What you did aboard the boat to escape was self-defense, Philip. There is no disagreement that it is lawful to repel violence, even to the taking the life of the assailant to protect one's self or another. Returning to dump the shark bait is a little iffy, but you may have acted more mercifully toward them than they would have toward you."

The blessing and extended absolution was followed by a lengthy prayer earnestly seeking God's protection for the young man. When finished, Fr. James said, "You mentioned having a problem attending Mass. To complete your penance, I want you to attend one of the weekly Masses held here at the school for the remainder of this semester, and continue your daily prayers. If you stay close to God, you will be kept safe."

♦   ♦   ♦

Tryouts for swimming and diving competition started with the winding down of football in mid-November. The young man's lean glide through the water, prompted Coach Joseph to ask, "Are you sure you're not a dolphin in disguise?"

Over the course of the next three months, the coach quietly looked on him as God-sent in that he not only put forth substantial personal effort, but encouraged and inspired others on the team. Swimming cut into social life, but he and Megan found plenty of mid-week, school activities to enjoy together. The biggest was the swimming banquet where he was center of attention, receiving several awards.

Philippe did have an adjustment problem no one knew about except Megan, to whom he explained one lunch period after she talked about a shopping trip with her mother and aunt to buy school clothes.

"Wearing clothes is still difficult for me," he tossed out.

"Oh, really?"

Revealing the truth of his past almost slipped out, until regrouping to cover. "I was raised as a nudist. We seldom wore clothing at home."

"I was wondering. Some girls have said some things. We're bad about gossiping. A couple of the guys on the swim team said something to them about your tan. They are a little envious, but wondered why you didn't have any tan lines."

"Well, now you know."

The adjustment went further than just having to bundle up against the cold weather. Dress slacks, polo-style shirts with a collar, socks, and shoes were the tip of the dress code iceberg. While he understood that students at the other high schools ridiculed the code, Philippe came to appreciate the professional feeling, such a seemingly simple thing, while those mocking Gonzaga looked like reject beach bums which effected their attitude, especially toward other people and education.

When Christmas arrived, so did Tangata who swept him up and loaded him onto a private jet, eventually ending up at Caliente Caribe in the Dominican Republic, a clothing-optional resort. They had barely set foot in the two-bedroom, ocean-level villa, than Philippe tossed his clothes and sprinted for the beach to join a volleyball game almost before the last sock hit the floor. Tangata watched, smiling that the young man was able to free himself so quickly of the depressing events of the last few years. Although Philippe hadn't said anything, Mr. Burke indicated something happened at school to change his attitude for the better. Tangata would look into what happened.

"I have unpacked for sir," a young Dominican valet said. "Does sir wish to select from the menu?"

"Yes," Tangata said, taking a food list and selecting the evening meal.

A staff member would prepare it in their private villa's kitchen. With all the travel, he wanted some quiet time to relax a bit himself. That first evening meal would be the only one the two would have alone together as Philippe invited a nearly unending string of new friends for lunch or dinner. Over the next two weeks Philippe romped and swam, rejuvenating his deep, amber tan while Tangata vegetated in the shade of a palm, reading a stack of books.

With the close of a successful swim season at Gonzaga, basketball fired up. Philippe didn't especially care to play the game, but enjoyed going because Megan worked in the concessions stand. When another student quit, he took the job.

It was a good year for the Bullpups, the last basketball game of the season being a championship game. The air filled with enthusiastic electricity. Gonzaga was a team to be reckoned with and the cross-town opponent of all nights did not play well. They lost —badly. As Philippe, Megan, Michael, and the Burke brothers walked to their car parked near the field house, they heard the high-pitch of girls screaming. In the dim light, it was obvious a gang had jumped some Gonzaga students.

Philippe reacted without thinking, something he was wont to do. Becoming involved in what would be a publicized situation was exactly what he was to avoid, but he neither could nor would stand aside and let six, football lineman-sized guys randomly abuse obviously younger and less endowed students. Without a word, he sprinted headlong into the melee.

Approaching the nearest he yelled, "Hey! Leave it go!"

One of the gang looking on turned to intercept Philippe and took a swing at him. Perhaps had the lighting been brighter the gathering spectators could have seen, but all they reported was seeing the strapping kid drop to his knees gasping for air. To Philippe it was a simple forearm block of the roundhouse swing followed by a straight knuckle shot to the solar plexus.

When the attacker dropped, two others jumped to his aide. Neither fared any better. The melee happened so quickly, by the time Michael and the Burkes became involved it was nearly over. Unfortunately, the younger Burke chose to challenge the only kid in the gang who obviously had studied more Karate. He was knocked to the ground. Michael was about to intervene when Philippe leaped forward. The kid grinned.

"Let's see what you know, Red Neck," he challenged and began a flurry of foot attacks.

Philippe defended. When the kid moved closer and began a barrage of hand attacks Philippe blocked them easily. Using his left foot, the kid's feet were swept out. He had barely hit the hard ground on his back than Philippe drove a fist into the rib cage. Bone cracked as the kid clutched his chest and groaned loudly while rolling into a ball and onto one side.

The attackers' defeat was astonishingly fast as bodies flew through the air, landing in sprawling heaps upon the frozen ground as if caught up in a tornado. When approaching sirens sounded, Philippe melt into the shadows just before the police arrived leaving the visiting school security member to explain, and the Burkes to become heroes. April had its better moments, though. The prom.

"I am under orders from your guardian to have you fitted for a tux," Mr. Burke announced one Saturday morning in February just before driving to a men's clothier downtown. He was very specific as he told the clerk, "An Eaton jacket with matching trousers, Sean John label, in black." The Eaton design is a waist-length coat with satin lapel. "A three-quarter pleated shirt, white, true French. He will also need a cummerbund with matching bow tie, apple satin color."

"And shoes?" the clerk asked, dollar signs spinning in his eye as on a slot machine.

"Black, patent leather. A Moreschi loafer will work nicely," Mr. Burke said. "We will also need a tux for this gentleman," he continued, referring to Michael.

"Single breasted, two button, black with Champaign vest and shar-pei tie. Same shirt and shoes. We have our own cuff links and buttons," Michael said.

"Those are special order items which will require a down payment."

Mr. Burke handed him a credit card. "By the first week in April, please." It was not a request.

After taking measurements and completing the order form, the three stepped back onto the sidewalk. It had snowed lightly overnight and there was a real bite to the northerly breeze.

"I believe a hot mug of chocolate with a dash of cinnamon is called for," Mr. Burke said.

"How much did all that set Tangata back?" Philippe asked.

"One never inquires the expense of a gift," Michael

admonished.

Seated in the coffee shop Philippe asked, "You said we have our own buttons and cufflinks?"

Once again, Michael reached into his Father Christmas-like jacket and withdrew a thin, long, narrow, black box. Philippe opened it and gasped. Inside were silver cufflinks with inlaid Abalone shell and matching buttons.

"Limu made these!"

"That is correct," Michael said with a big smile. "He made them especially for you."

"Then he made it to his mother?"

"Yes, thanks to the money you gave him, and then your uncle unwittingly set him up in the business of making extraordinary jewelry."

"My uncle did what?"

"Were you aware of what was in that bag you took from your uncle?" Mr. Burke said.

"I only looked to see there was money."

"Yes, there was money, two-hundred thousand dollars. There was also an envelope containing the account number and password for one of his secret bank accounts. When your guardian realized what was afoot, he made a discrete withdrawal on your behalf and set up your own secret account."

"I don't want anything that belonged to my uncle."

"James is well aware of that. The money is only used, as in Limu's case, to help others. Your personal needs come from the insurance monies your father set up and income from the resort, and other investments —all legal."

Recovering from the revelation, he asked, "There was another who helped me escape. His name is Napo."

"Ah, yes, the boy from Lau Island." Lines on Michael's forehead deepened.

"Is he alright? My uncle didn't . . ."

"Oh, he is alive and well. James moved to help him as well, but someone already intervened on the boy's behalf. He is living in England and attending school there."

Philippe couldn't see the order form clearly, but it certainly looked like a high triple digit figure. He was not used to spending money like that, but worth it when he and Megan entered the prom, arm in arm. Heads turned. There were a number of kids with rich parents, but none had a custom-made tux.

The second event making April an auspicious month was singing with the choral group. Singled out for a solo, he chose "Music of the Night" from *Phantom of the Opera*. The vocal instructor worked with him for months to develop his voice so that the song came out clear and strong. His tenor had begun to lower on its way to becoming more baritone. The audience was so impressed to give a standing ovation.

Backstage was nuts after the performance with adults and students scurrying about, putting away props and changing into school clothes. Philippe was being deliberately slow, enjoying the last moments of a beautiful evening. Megan had come to congratulate him with a full-blown kiss— she did that regularly, now— and left so he could change. He was just pulling the polo shirt over his head when he heard the door open.

"I'll be out in a minute, *ma douce*," he said, back to the door.

"I didn't realize you cared that much," a male voice said.

Philippe spun around and sprang into Tangata's arms.

"I hope you're not planning on kissing me like you did that girl."

He blushed. "No. It's so good to see you, again. You made the performance."

"Of course. Couldn't miss something like that. You were very good. Very good. Congratulations."

"Thank you. Will you stay long?"

"For the weekend, then I have some book promotion things, but I'll be back after finals. Thought we'd spend the summer together."

As promised, Tangata arrived the day of his last final. Following a family party, the two sat in the family room alone until quite late, Tangata in a lounger, the boy seated cross-legged on the love seat in front of him wearing a new lava-lava brought as a gift. There wasn't much to bring Philippe up to date about events in the islands. Not much changed except an occasional volcano, earthquake, or storm. The conversation mostly centered on every minute detail of Philip's experiences in America.

That next afternoon Philip, Michael and Tangata stepped out on the lawn where the two older men challenged the boy in every aspect of bujitsu. The Burke's watched the combat portion, often covering eyes and mouths as the fighting became intense. Many times, when it appeared Philippe would be killed, he rallied to return the favors. Suddenly, it was over. Tangata and Michael knelt side by side with Philippe facing them a meter in front.

After bowing Michael said, "I have been instructed by Master Yamamoto, Grand Master of the Seven Warriors. As you have been tested by two Shichidan, we are pleased to bestow upon you the rank of Nidan of the Seven Warriors."

Philippe was tired, but very proud as Michael handed him a rolled parchment bearing his name and the signature of the two 7th Degree Black Belts seated in front of him, and the signature of Grand Master Yamamoto. Gazing at the rice paper document, it dawned on him. It had been filled out before Michael left for America. He then surreptitiously glanced at the signatures hoping to have discovered Tangata's real name. No such luck. "James Elam." Philippe knew that to be the man's pen name. Irregardless, he now held the rank of 2nd Degree Black Belt. Bowing once more, the three stood and bowed again at which time Philippe embraced both teachers.

Saying goodbye to Michael and Megan was difficult, but Philippe's excitement keen as he and his guardian climbed into a spacious RV bus.

"Thought a road trip would be a nice way to spend the summer."

"Will it be safe?"

"It seems the photos received here in the States, oh, tut, tut, a terrible mixup. Some kid that died a few years back," Tangata said.

"Now, how do you suppose that could happen?" Philippe asked and laughed, but seriously wondered how the heck such things were managed.

"Just can't trust the mails these days. Doesn't seem to matter where in the world, things get mixed up."

Michael returned to New Zealand as the RV headed east to travel the historic American trails, briefly interrupted when Tangata was obliged to make some appearances promoting a recent book. Whenever that occurred he was not the man Philippe knew as his appearance changed so to be completely unrecognizable except for the eyes, the dark, studying eyes which seemed to laugh more now.

♦   ♦   ♦

Tangata would not respond as to why the need for disguises, and continued refusing to divulge his true name despite many covert attempts at uncovering the mystery. All Philippe and the world knew him by was,

James Elam. However, in time he didn't care, remembering what Shakespeare said, "What's in a name? That which we call a rose by any other word would smell as sweet." All he cared about was that he loved the sometimes irascible and mysterious hermit who pulled him from the clutches of a watery grave and nurtured his life back. Using seemingly unlimited resources, Tangata slapped the long-reaching hand of his uncle, helped restore his past, and protected his future.

That summer was one of joy and wonder as they poked touristy noses into every historical cranny from Maine to Florida before hoping over to the Dominican Republic to spend the last two weeks lounging on the beach. Well, Tangata lounged. Philippe was too busy socializing. Eventually the hiatus had to end, so it was back for a final year at Gonzaga. Philippe had thought Michael would return, but it was another member of the Seven Warriors School.

"Master Yamamoto came to study school security. How would it look if he came back?" Tangata explained. "Besides, you were getting used to his moves. I believe you know Master Yamata Orochi?"

Chapter 9

Betrayal

Oh, yes, Philippe knew the man standing in front of him in the Burke's front room. At five-six, the twenty-five year-old Japanese national was a strand of tempered steel wire, flexible, unbreakable, ready to coil, and smack an opponent upside the head. With a no-nonsense approach to Budō, he was unmercifully strict. Philippe had trained under him before and felt the guy got up in the morning with a lousy attitude and worked on making it worse throughout the day dragging everyone else down as well.

Philippe's bow was stiff, on the edge of offensive.

"The young Nidan is not pleased I have come to help him progress with his studies?" Orochi taunted.

"The last time you instructed me, as it may loosely be called, I ended up with a broken rib and an assortment of bruises."

"Your attention wandered."

"Your enthusiasm exceeded your judgment," Philippe countered, as Tangata stood back inwardly pleased with the young man's confidence.

"Your disrespect precedes your better judgment."

"You would not be here without knowing I have had to live my life under a cloud because of my uncle. I have been forced to defend myself when he sent men to murder me."

"And what did you do? Tickle them to death?" Orochi continued to taunt.

"When they came at me with their knives, I knocked them overboard, then dumped the bait bucket they were going to use it to attract sharks after killing me."

Orochi remained silent, but Philippe saw something flashed in his coal black eyes. Could it have been concern?

"Then you are a murder and used your training to accomplish that end," Orochi accused.

"The first tenant of Bushido is rectitude, unwavering conformity to the rules established by God or man. I have the right, no, I have the duty to defend myself and others from harm, even to harming the aggressor."

"But you disarmed them by throwing them into the water," Orochi continued.

"And what would they have done once back aboard the boat?" Philippe countered. "They were under orders from my uncle to kill me. Failure to do that would have meant their death by my uncle's orders. They were doomed the minute they took on the job. I hastened their death, and being eaten by a shark was more humane than what my uncle would have done."

A gleam in Orochi's eyes was almost undetectable behind the narrow slits serving as eyelids. "I have been looking forward to our training lessons and would like to start immediately."

Going to their respective rooms to change, Orochi was standing on one side of the center ring when Philippe appeared. Wearing only black cotton trousers, his brown skin seemed darker. Tangata stood at the edge of the circle ninety degrees to Orochi's right, facing the direction Philippe would enter onto the mat. He wore a black uniform with red and white piping on the left leg to match the belt. Philippe removed his jacket and handed it to Kyle before stepping onto the mat. The tatami felt cool beneath his bare feet. Executing the ritual bow, he walked to the center circle to face his new teacher. They bowed. This time Philippe was more respectful, not so much to the man he was about to engage in combat as to the tradition and history of Budō.

Tangata barely uttered, *"Hajime,"* or begin, than Orochi leaped forward with a great, guttural roar, launching a front foot snap aimed directly at Philippe's face. From all appearances, he was aiming to drive the young man's nose into his brain. Philippe's counter was pure instinct. Using a circular block of his left forearm, he deflected the attack so that it grazed his shoulder, forcing Orochi to turn sideways. Philippe's right foot shot out and caught the man's left thigh, continued a 360 degree pivot, finishing a roundhouse kick to the side of Orochi's head throwing him face first onto the mat. Philippe continued the attack, leaping on him and applying a choke hold, but Tangata intervened. The man was unconscious.

After a few minutes the Yondan regained his senses, but little else. Returning from the hospital,

Philippe still wondered what happened. He had just defeated a 4th Degree black belt with two moves.

The young man felt bad. X-rays showed a spiral crack in Orochi's femur just above the left knee. Added to this were a mild concussion, and broken nose. Philippe was shaken.

"You reacted exactly as you have been taught," Tangata tried to console him.

"But . . ."

"But, nothing. How many times did Master Yamamoto and Master Michael tell you to let your mind and body flow with what they know. The problem is how I am going to tell Master Yamamoto I'm sending his Yondan back when he gets out of the hospital and request another instructor. A Nidan defeating a Yondan that quickly, hm-m-m, he may send Master Sullivan."

"The gorilla?" Panic was justifiable. Tangata laughed.

Orochi stayed to put Philippe through arduous training exercises, unable to participate until the injuries healed. His superior attitude was more subdued as well. A student had never defeated him, either so quickly or soundly. Philippe understood the man had tremendous pride.

"It shall only be between the three of us," he reassured him.

"We shall have a rematch. Redemption," the man said. Philippe was sure there was a slight curl at the corners of his mouth.

♦　♦　♦

One of the first things Philippe did upon returning to Spokane, other than send his martial arts teacher to the hospital, was to call Megan. He had to leave a message. She didn't return the call so the next day he phoned her house. There was no answer. Her mother finally answered late in the afternoon.

"Megan isn't home. I'll tell her you called."

That netted nothing. The next Tuesday school began /and he didn't see her until lunch. She was sitting with a couple other girls some distance from where they sat last year.

"Hi," he said, approaching the small group.

"Hi," Megan said. She was acting distant and cool, as in Jack Frost cold.

"I called a couple times when I got back to town, but you were out."

"Yeah. I was busy. See you got your tan back. You go to that beach in the Caribbean and get naked?"

He recognized the stab as the other girls giggled. "Sure did. Was really nice. Not cold like here."

"You really go swimming without clothes?" another girl asked.

"Swim, play volleyball, Frisbee football, dance, sit around and talk. We even have dinner naked."

The girls were all turning red-faced and snickering.

"And what do you do after dark?" Megan came back.

"Well, after a long day, we finish off by sitting in a hot tub, talk, eat, the usual, and then go to bed . . . our own beds . . . alone. If you are thinking nudists jump in the sack with one another faster than clothed folks, you are totally mis-informed. We are people who aren't hung up about pretending to be Queen Victoria, all clothes and no morals." He was a little peeved at their childish behavior. "That's why we can come home and not make a quick trip to the confessional on the way."

"Hey, Megan."

"Hey, Justin," she said, sounding a lot friendlier.

"Queer boy bothering you girls?"

"I beg your pardon?" Philippe came back, watching as the senior put an arm around Megan's waist and pulled her close.

"Anybody that runs around with other guys naked ain't quite right."

"You are the epitome of ignorance," Philippe countered. He'd recently learned the word, epitome, and had been wanting to use it.

"You calling me stupid?" Justin said, releasing his hold on Megan.

"You ever watch the movie, Forest Gump? Well, stupid is as stupid says." With that, Philippe turned and started to walk away.

Sensing aggressive movement behind his back wasn't difficult. Awareness of one's surroundings was a major lesson in his training; besides, the collective gasp from the girls was like a quartet warming up. When the boy's hand grasped the back of his collar, Philippe launched a backward foot snap that caught the kid in the groin. Before he could gasp, Justin found himself in a hammerlock wondering which pain was worse, the one between his legs or in his shoulder.

"Hello, Philip," Fr. James said as he stepped up. He had been moving closer to the group, seeing an altercation brewing. "Nice demo, but I don't think Justin can use that in wrestling, can you Justin?"

"No, Father," he said, forcing the words passed the pain.

"Philip, I've wanted to talk to you about your summer," Fr. James said, taking him gently by the arm and starting to walk away. "Oh, Justin, just a thought, but you shouldn't try to get wrestling pointers from someone who is a Black Belt in martial arts. Totally different. Wrestling is a sport. The stuff Philip knows hurts people . . . bad."

That was the end of Philippe's relationship with Megan, learning a lesson about fickle, teenage relationships. While he didn't date anyone steady, he wasn't without female companionship, often having two or three girls hang out with him during lunch or seek his help with their French.

The school year activities quickly filled with involvement in choir, the school musical, and swimming. He gave a try at diving, but didn't quite have the desire others had, but desire was not a problem in the lanes as he did very well with the breast and backstrokes, and looked like a torpedo in the freestyle. When the musical closed its last night he searched the crowd for Tangata, but didn't see him until after changing into street clothes. He was waiting outside the dressing room door.

"Got something to discuss with you," he said, leading Philippe out to his rental car, but said nothing more until arriving at Starbucks. Seated in a very private corner with peppermint-spiked hot chocolates, Tangata pulled out some documents from his inside coat pocket and laid them in front of the young man. "Guardianship papers," he announced.

"You say what?"

"You are still under the age of eighteen. Signing these papers will completely stop your uncle and make life a bit easier for us."

Philippe nearly knocked the table over as he leapt up to hug the man who had become a father-figure. He couldn't sign the documents quickly enough.

"Does this mean I can call you papa?"

"Yeah, I guess. If you want."

"Then papa, will tell me what my name will be?"

"You needn't change your name."

"I know using my birth name would still be dangerous. Godeno' is okay, but it's better suited to someone else. So, I could use your last name . . ." He held both palms up seeking an answer to the question.

"Elam."

"But that's your pen name."

"It works."

Philippe showed real disappointment. "A papa should be honest."

"It's not a name you would want to be associated with. If you think Bonnét is dangerous . . . well, just consider Elam is pretty safe, and it's the name I'm known by at the IRS." Picking up the chocolate mug he said, "A toast. To Philip Elam. I'd christen you with a bottle, but with your hard head probably wouldn't break it, and that's bad luck."

To keep things simple, no one was made aware of the name change, so that on Friday, the 31st of May, about to be seventeen year-old Philip Godeno' walked across the stage to receive his high school diploma. It should have been a great feeling, however, he had mixed emotions. Tangata hadn't showed up, delayed by work Mr. Burke said. Walking across the stage with diploma in hand he waived to the raucous cheers of his American family, but there was a hollow feeling in his heart. After waiving, he turned to leave the platform and made eye contact with Tangata's smiling face at the bottom of the steps. There was no holding back emotion as he literally leaped into the man's arms. Michael stood to one side and received a hug as well.

The Burkes threw a grand party that went late into the evening with gallons of punch, a pickup load of snacks, a live band provided by Localboy Promotions, and many of his school friends. Megan was there, too. She'd broken up with the jock, but their relationship remained polite. Philippe had specific plans for his future and a girlfriend bent on marriage wasn't a part of that. For old time's sake, he introduced her to a friend.

The following day Philippe stood on the tatame mat wearing his white, cotton jacket, pants, and 2nd Degree Black Belt, facing Orochi for the first time since he was put in the hospital. For whatever reason, the Japanese martialist did not mend quickly, suffering several setbacks, something about the spiral fracture and calcium deficiency inhibiting healing. He was declared fully recovered only a week before the test, but they did not spar.

"I need to get back into shape," he said, working katas to the point of almost wearing a hole in the mat. Likewise, the punching bags took a beating as well.

Philippe's education continued throughout the year, as well, working through katas and against Fred and Kyle who had progressed greatly with individual instruction from Philippe. Sometimes he felt a little like spying as he watch Orochi workout, studying how he moved, and picking up on the small ways he telegraphed attacks.

Standing on opposite sides of the circle, Tangata on the edge between them, they stared at one another, then Orochi said, "Nidan, do not expect to be so lucky this time. I am your shark."

Philippe had been very nervous about the test. Not that he wasn't prepared for promotion to Sandan. The last time the two met, something snapped inside his head. He saw the heel of the man's foot coming straight at him in a way that could, no, would have killed him. That memory plagued him repeatedly as he continued training. Why?

"Gentlemen?" Tangata said, indicating both to kneel where they were. "Philip, you have the right to know. Orochi came here to kill you."

Orochi looked at Tangata, the brown pigment in his face fading as if being flushed down a toilet. Philippe's heart slammed a beat as if shifting into high gear without using the clutch as anger began to rise, feeling the heat on his cheeks.

"Oh, yes, Orochi, we've known all about the plan. The communiques you have had with New Caledonia? You were actually talking to Master Michael. We infiltrate as well."

"He could have killed me any time over the last nine months and you let me alone with him?"

"Orochi has a fetish, Philip. He likes to kill with his feet. The injury you inflicted during your first meeting was substantial enough for us to stretch out his recovery, making him think he wasn't healing, until nearing this moment. What better way to complete the job, and make it look like an unfortunate accident during Sandan promotion? You see, we like to play our little games, too."

"So, you think he can beat me?" Orochi said. His arrogance was sickening.

"Yes." Then to Philippe he said, "Because Orochi intends to kill you, you have the right to respond according to the first tenant of Bushidō."

Despite receiving absolution for what he did, the memory of that day in the straits off New Caledonia still chilled the young man's bones. Now, he was about to face the same threat.

"Philip, there is something you need to know. If Orochi does kill you, then he must face me, which will be more preferable than facing Michael. If he fails to kill you, he will be hunted down by your uncle's people and his death will not be pleasant."

"Then what you are saying, any way you look at it, Orochi is a dead man," Philip said.

"Yes," Michael said. "But there is something else you need to understand. He has taken the oath of an assassin. Failure means disgracing his ancestors."

That just upped the stakes. Orochi was not going to see the next sunrise, however he would not bring disgrace upon his family, although being a hired assassin didn't seem to be a very honorable occupation to Philippe's notion. That both Tangata and Michael felt he could defend himself bolstered confidence, but could he kill again, despite it being in self-defense? There was one catch. To enter into this combat, he had to have only one objective—in this case, not just to win, but to survive. His uncle had his father and mother killed, and Philippe wanted to see that man pay for the crime, so survive he must— whatever the eternal consequences.

Philip stood slowly, hands at his sides, and took a deep breathe. Orochi stood, with only one objective —to die with his view of honor.

Bringing his hand down between them as if breaking a board, Tangata began the test. "Hajime."

Orochi didn't come straight on this time, but started with a slow circle left. Philippe stood his ground, watching his enemy's eyes as he had been taught. They always betrayed the attacker. Orochi watched the young man's feet. Philippe sometimes had the bad habit of crossing them as he moved sideways or in a small circle.

Mentally he said, "Thank you for reminding me, Orochi."

Philippe let Orochi make the first attack, a low

squat with a roundhouse sweep to strike at the ankles to knock him off balance. Again, the man telegraphed the move with his eyes so that as he swept, Philippe was already airborne. The only thing that saved Orochi was reflexively turning his head and falling back as the ball of Philippe's foot grazed his cheek. From that moment the battle became a flurry of feet and fists flying like a whirling dervish in a tornado, but as much as he tried, Orochi was unable to land a solid strike. Neither could Philippe, but the blows that made contact, stung. Then the Asian began to tire. Having been kept from practice by the phony diagnosis, his stamina had weakened, while his opponent had gotten stronger from swimming, running, and rigorous practice. He was going to loose. A 4th Degree Black Belt was going to lose again to a 2nd Degree child.

Realizing there was no way to win this way, Orochi mentally changed tactics and began to maneuver into position. Philippe instantly became suspicious, until Orochi's eyes betrayed him once more. When the assassin dove off the mat to grab a sword, a real one from the rack, he turned to find Philippe holding one with the highly polished wood and Abalone handle found at the island. The young man forgot it had been next to the shrine as Michael tossed it into his hand. Orochi also forgot that Kendo was the young man's favorite part of training.

The ring of steel and grunts ricocheted off the concrete walls. Whirl, kick, strike, the battle continued to rage on and off the mat in the large room. Philippe defended everything the assassin tried. As Orochi's energy grew weaker, reflexes slower, sweat covering him from head to foot, Philippe went on the attack. Orochi faultered for a split second. Philippe executed an unfamiliar move, one seldom taught, but Master Yamamoto insisted he learn. The flat of the ocean-born sword slammed across Orochi's arm. As the sword dropped from the broken wrist, Philippe did a 360 degree spin to add momentum, bringing the blade flat against the lower back knocking him breathless to the ground. Orochi struggled to his knees as the tip of Philippe sword touched his breast.

"It is done, young warrior." Uncle Rousseau's assassin admitted defeat. Then without warning, he grabbed Philippe's blade in both hands and drove it into his heart.

Philippe jerked the sword free as the man slowly rolled backward, eyes wide with wonder and surprise, toppling sideways. Tangata stepped up and touched Orochi's carotid artery.

"He's explaining to his ancestors why he failed," Tangata said.

"Before making a journey to the land of fire," Michael added.

Philippe stood back, air coming in great gulps as he stared at the body, repeating, "I didn't do it. I didn't kill him."

Tangata put an arm around Philippe's shoulders, taking the sword and passing it off to Michael who restored it to its usual resting place after cleansing it with running water. As the two left the combat zone, Philippe looked over his shoulder to see Michael grab one of Orochi's ankles and drag the body toward the door.

"What will happen to Orochi's body?"

"It will be disposed of," Tangata said.

"Disposed of? Just like that? No funeral? Nothing? Just disposed of like so much garbage?"

"Yes. We cannot allow the authorities to find it and start asking questions. You needn't worry. You did nothing wrong."

"I know that. He killed himself. I wanted to, but . . . How will he be disposed of?"

"You needn't concern yourself about that."

"Yes, I do."

"Well, some will be added to the river, some will be buried here and there in the countryside."

"Some? Like in pieces?"

"Yes. Very small, unidentifiable pieces."

"But . . ."

"This is a very different game we play, Philippe. It's for "keeps."

The hot shower was so long Tangata thought the young man was trying to drown himself. He stayed close, handing him an over-sized towel when finally exiting. Retiring to Philippe's room, Tangata sat in a wingback chair used for reading while the young man sat on the edge of the bed.

"Uncle knows I'm here, then."

"All he knows is that you are in America. He still thinks you're on the east coast. Orochi was a member of the Yellow Dragon gang affiliated with your uncle's syndicate. When Michael came to America for an extended visit, they were pretty sure it was because of you. So, when Michael returned, Orochi wormed his way into becoming the next visitor. We were suspicious, but when he tried to kill you at that first practice, that pretty well cinched it."

"He could have . . ."

"Not really. You may hold the rank of 2nd Degree, but your skills are far more advanced, Philip. The only thing holding you back is age, not ability.

"He sent reports back to your uncle. We intercepted them and forwarded them on to Michael who then sent bogus messages to your uncle."

"But he could have killed me at any time."

"Under guise of being your uncle, we encouraged him to take his time and do it his way. As I said, knowing Orochi's fetish for killing with his feet, we capitalized on the injury you gave him, faked the medical exams and X-rays, kept him in a cast and therapy, and off the mat with you. Until now."

Two days later Michael reappeared and a promotion ceremony performed. Philippe Bonnét, now Philip Elam, was granted the privilege of wearing the 3rd Degree Black Belt. He was Sandan.

"Your next promotion will be more difficult," Michael said after handing him a new belt and certificate.

"Who do I have to kill for that?" Philippe asked, sarcasm edging the words.

"Hopefully, no one, but you will have to face both men seated in front of you. Not to worry. You have two years to prepare."

As the summer passed, Tangata and Philippe traveled the western states, a much relaxed vacation as the memory of the battle faded somewhat, at least enough that Philippe could sleep nights without seeing Orochi's face as he slid off the sword in death. However, there was one question that plagued him, but reluctant to ask, until sitting by a small campfire on a rock outcrop overlooking a broad valley cast in the growing shadows of night, a blanket of stars firing up overhead.

"When will my uncle know he has failed to kill me again?"

"He already knows."

"He'll double the effort to find me."

"I think not for a while. He was sentenced to prison a couple days ago. He has too much on his plate right now, besides which, he's frightened . . . of you."

"Me?"

"Yes. After the gift you sent him, he has become a very frightened, little man."

"What gift?"

"Orochi's head."

"What!"

"When he thought you had gone to Israel, he gave orders to have assassins there send him your head. Instead he got Orochi's with a short note attached. You are a man of few words . . . sometimes. It said, "Dear Uncle, this is for you. Place it on the shelf in your office where you planned to put mine, but leave space next to it for yours. See you soon. Your loving nephew, Philippe."

"The hunter becoming the hunted? That's ironic."

"Something like that. He doubled security around him. Didn't matter. He kept finding little things now and then with a cryptic note of greetings from you. Even the first day in prison. Hope you don't mind."

Eventually, the fairy tale days of summer drew to a close as the well-traveled RV passed a monument of Abraham Lincoln on Interstate 80 west of Cheyenne, Wyoming and rolled down Telegraph Canyon into Laramie, and the beginning of another chapter in his life.

Chapter 10

A Bad Decision

"Of all places, why Wyoming?" Philippe asked, looking out at a nearly treeless prairie sandwiched between two mountain ranges and dotted with a hodgepodge of houses.

"A good education comes from the least expected places," Tangata said.

Fall was just getting underway when Philippe arrived in the hardy community of Laramie. The sky was clear, the sun shone brightly, the temperature mild and pleasant as conversation around about focused on the only two passions of importance, football and hunting, not necessarily in that order. In addition, the wind was a light breeze at nearly forty-eight kilometers per hour.

With registration taken care of, all they had to do was move in. As a Resident Assistant for McIntyre

Hall, an engineering junior, opened the door, Tangata stuck his head inside and said, "Ah, remodeled claustrophobia. Looks a little like a jail cell without bars."

The size of a bedroom, the twelve by fourteen space was stuffed with two single beds, two wardrobes, and TV stand. A shared desk, actually a counter across one end had two desk chairs tucked underneath. There were already a duffel bag and a couple black, plastic garbage bags on the back bed.

After a damage check, the RA reminded them of the Western barbecue later that afternoon before hustling off to snag another freshman.

Soon as the young man left, Tangata took a look inside a micro-fridge on the counter-desk.

"Hm-m-m. A six pack of beer. Looks like you have a roomie planning to party while at school. Obviously has a taste for horse urin."

Philippe glanced over his shoulder and wrinkled his nose. "Maybe I can educated him about a good New Zealand stout."

Tangata needn't admonish Philippe about carrying alcohol consumption too far. There was no glamor in something that had been a part of growing up. "Good luck finding something like that in this town. Toss your stuff on the bed and let's go shopping," Tangata said.

They passed a WalMart coming into town and it didn't take long to fill a shopping cart with housekeeping items like bedding, a desk lamp, and school supplies. Back at the room to put those items and his personal effects away, they met Philippe's roommate, a lanky, fresh-face kid with cowboy boots and accompanying drawl. Respectful, he came off as a nice kid.

As they headed for the campus bookstore, Tangata's cell rang. Looking at it he read aloud, "William Sublette Longley, nickname Will, eighteen last May, Pinedale, Wyoming, high school steer roping finalist, GPA 3.57, prefers four-legged girls over the two-legged variety. Owns a bay, purebred Quarter Horse mare, and a new Ford 250 pickup, a graduation present from his granddad, Frank. Has a two-horse trailer bought with money earned stacking hay bales. His granddad still likes a tight stack that can only be achieved by hand. Clean driving record. Well, almost. One speeding ticket at age fifteen. Nothing since. Guess his granddad's admonitions behind the barn are still effective. Ag business major . . . Good Christian family. I'll drop a hint to his granddad about the beer."

Philippe rolled his eyes, having given up wondering about his guardian's connections.

"Prices haven't change," Tangata grumbled as they loaded down with the required texts. The checkout tally exceeded five-hundred dollars, and most of those were used editions. The new ones were the budget killers. "I honestly don't know how kids can afford to attend school with these prices." It was the first time Philippe had ever heard him complain about expenses.

"Is this costing too much?" Philippe asked.

"Not for us. I'm just thinking of the average kid whose parents want something better for them," as he laid down six one-hundred dollar bills from a wad secured by a silver money clip.

With the last text neatly stowed on Philippe's end of the desk, the roommate walked in. Tangata silently shook his head. Another long drink of water, the kid didn't look a day over fourteen. He noticed that becoming an interesting perception as he aged —people, especially people this age appeared a lot younger.

Unexpectedly, Tangata slipped into a slight western drawl which seemed to fit comfortably.

"Since ya got lost the first day at Gonzaga, how do ya feel about findin' your way around all these buildings?" Philippe's mild panic looked was enough answer. "Thought so. Let's mossey 'round campus. Ya wanna tag along, Will, or ya plannin' to hang out with Miss Peggy some more?"

Longley looked startled. They hadn't exchanged names and certainly nothing was mentioned about his mare. Still apprehensive about living in the big city, he hesitated, but Tangata put an arm around the kid's shoulders and all but hustled him out the door. "Ah-h-h, yeah, sure. She's fine," he said.

"So how's your granddad?" Tangata asked as they walked the residence hall toward the elevators.

"You know him?"

"Stacked bales for him a couple summers. Was all of twelve. Your granddad had a way even then of settin' a guy on the right path. Your dad was jist a knee-bouncer them days. Sorry about the accident. We still keep in touch."

Class schedules in-hand, Tangata conducted a tour taking them to the center of Prexy's pasture, a large, open grassy area encircled by stone and brick buildings. "It's pretty easy gettin' around, actually," Tangata said, and pointed out the buildings they needed to remember. "Oh, by the way, if Miss Peggy gets a hankerin' for grass, you can't ride a bike on the pasture, but she can graze here. Just love those old laws." That he had been here before was pretty obvious, but wouldn't elaborate. "Okay, I smell barbecue. Let's go chow down." The drawl definitely wasn't a put on.

Philippe decided to pursue a degree in Political Science with an eye on International Politics and Law. As usual, his guardian was correct. The University of Wyoming's Political Science Department was unusually good. The only negative was the declining thermometer.

By October 14th the temperature had stiffened all animate objects to the consistency of Jell-O jigglers. Philippe was cold, colder than most. Accustomed to the perpetual warmth of the Pacific, his blood was still "thin" despite two years in Washington. Bundling against the deepening chill that Friday evening, he attended a pep rally on the eve of a big conference football match with an arch rival from Utah.

The following morning many students, like his roommate, were already in the mountains for opening day of Elk season, while the rest headed for the football stadium. Philippe still struggled to understand American football, but just being caught up in the excitement was enough as he prepared for the game by encasing himself in layers of warm clothes—thermal underwear, wool trousers, insulated cotton shirt, insulated ski pants, down-insulated coat, insulated boots, knit cap, and down gloves. With the hood of a brown and gold Cowboys sweatshirt pulled over his head and latched down, he waddled through the lobby and stepped through the glass door displaying a hand printed sign reading, "Welcome to Wyoming," and stepped into a half meter of snow that fell over night. Yes, welcome to Wyoming.

For the Islander in Spokane, snow was a novelty, and enjoyed the soft, powdery stuff piled vertical on anything horizontal. This was surreal as the wind ripped at the senses and drove the white stuff horizontal along with anything else not anchored down. Even more surreal was sitting in the stands sipping hot chocolate as the grounds crew repeatedly shoveled snow off the yard markers so the players could plow on.

At least occasionally glimpsing movement on the field, he guessed the game was still being played. And did the blizzard diminish enthusiasm? He and several thousand people screamed hysterically as the final seconds ticked off the clock and their brown and gold gladiators kicked a desperation field goal for the win. Did it go through the posts for the win? Could anyone see it? From the invisible south goal came the resounding cannon. Boom. Yes! And as the sign facing the opposition read, "Welcome to 7,400 feet above sea level," and to Wyoming in October.

Polar differences made adjusting to the climate a challenge as Philippe switched from ocean to snow sports, favoring cross-country skiing and snowshoeing—solitary, reflective activities. Studying in the dorm was as nuts as the weather with the racket from students experiencing their first tastes of freedom from the oppression of parental snoopervision. Philippe found the necessary quiet in a cubby at the back of the lower level of the library. That's where he met Sandy.

"Hi," the young woman said as she walked by carrying several books from the stacks.

"Hello." He recognized the redheaded girl from the Intro to Political Science class. She sat in the back. She was in his American History class, too.

She set the books down on the cubby desk on the other side of his. "You look frustrated."

How could she tell? Was it the fact that he had just snapped a pencil in half? "Yes."

"Surely it can't be that bad already. It's only the first week."

He liked her smile. "I'm really lousy at taking notes, and the History teacher talks fast."

"She really does. Someone needs to mention it to her. I never learned to take notes in high school and that became a real problem when I started college last year, and then a friend suggested I use a tape recorder. I record the lecture while taking notes, then play it back later to add anything I missed. That helped a lot. Most of the instructors will let you do that. You just need to ask permission and sit somewhere near the front of class."

"Thanks."

"Hey, would you like to look at my notes for now?"

Philippe and Sandy began their own study group. A big help was that they had a lot of interests in common, not to mention she came from Coeur d'Alene just across the state line from Spokane. They spent spare time together at the library, student center, an occasional movie, huddled under a blanket at football games, and weekend trips to restaurants. Neither were enamored with dorm food, but then who was, as they found the off-campus places crowded with fellow students.

With only a three day break, there wasn't enough time to drive north to spend Thanksgiving with her aunt and uncle in Idaho with whom she lived, or he with the Burkes. Instead, the two joined a couple of her friends in an off-campus apartment to celebrate with dinner that Philippe took a major hand in preparing, and watching football on the TV. Christmas was different. Finishing final exams December 13th, they didn't need to return to school until a week after the New Year. The Burke family was excited having him back.

A week's worth of gear and food securely strapped to the top, the Burke army along with Philippe and Sandy packed into the van and headed east to a cabin outside of Wallace, Idaho for cross-country skiing.

Upon arriving in America, Philippe found snow a mystical wonder he had only read about. With youthful enthusiasm, he jumped headlong into snow sports. The appeal of cross-country skiing was the incredible silence broken only by the muffled crunch and scrape of snow beneath the skis. Coming upon wildlife such as the doe and yearling crossing a clearing one sunny afternoon was just some of the added perks.

The bright sun riding across a pale blue sky cast a radiating warmth, but as it made a final dive for the horizon, the temperature plummeted. Returning after a day in the mountains, unloading the equipment from the Ranger Rover, and storing it in the shed was accomplished quickly. Entering the cabin, Philippe was instantly bathed in warmth from the wood stove as the smell of beef stew bubbling on top invaded his nose causing his stomach to growl from hunger.

There were two bedrooms downstairs along with a small kitchen and large living room. Mr. and Mrs. Burke used one while the girls shared the other. The boys slept in the open loft. Heavy, down coats hung next to the side door, and boots parked on towels to absorb any melt. Sounding like a herd of Elk, the boys headed up the steep steps to change into lighter weight clothes.

"I'm putting dinner on the table," Mrs. Burke called after them. They wouldn't need a reminder except to wash their hands.

Philippe peeled off the layers, finally removing the special wicking, long underwear which invoked snickers from the guys.

"What?" he snapped.

"Mr. Elam sure knows how to buy boxers," Kyle said. Philippe was wearing Porkie Pig.

"Yeah. Great, aren't they. He got them for my birthday."

His adopted brothers had seen Tangata's interesting selections lots of times and didn't miss a chance to tease him about the cartoon character boxers. They also were a source of endless giggles the first time he undressed in the locker room preparatory to gym class at Gonzaga. As it happened, it was wrestling day and there were no snide comments after dumping and pinning the state champ three times. Philippe became a fashion trend-setter as animated boxers began appearing above sagging belt lines—off-campus. The Burke brothers were no exception.

Since Mrs. Burke and the girls made the meal, it was up to the men to clear and wash. Philippe lead the KP detail before joining her in the living room as a movie began on the player.

"How are you doing?" Sandy asked as he sat on the floor next to her.

"This has been a terrific day," he replied, exhaling a satisfied sigh.

"Did I notice you limping when we got out of the car? Did you get a blister?"

"Feels like I might have. It'll be okay."

Sandy scooted down his outstretched legs, sat cross-legged, and took one foot in her lap to pull the wool sock off.

"Sure do."

"Here's the first aid kit," Mr. Burke said, handing her a small, black leather-bound kit as he joined them, sitting on the sofa with his wife.

The blister, about the size of a nickel, had sprouted on the left heel. Using a sterilized needle, Sandy opened the bubble to drain the fluid, then applied an antiseptic and blister plaster. Checking the other foot, she was satisfied there was no trouble there.

"Before we go out tomorrow let's put a moleskin pad on it. If you start feeling a hot spot on your foot, let's take care of it before it gets like this." Then she began a deep massage of each foot and up the calf.

"You're good at that."

"I wanted to be a sports therapist when I left high school. Went to school for two years and interned in the college sports department for a year, then something else came up. I got interested in International politics."

"Hey, when you get done with him, how about

me," Fred asked.

"Do you got a blister, too?" his mom asked.

"No, but my feet feel awfully tired."

"That line is lame," his dad said from behind a newspaper.

A long day skiing, a hearty meal, and sitting near a warm fire finished off the day. By the time the movie was over Philippe and Sandy were the only ones left to enjoy the dying embers in the fireplace. He watched as she got up to retrieved a small box from the mantle and sat in front of his crossed legs.

"It's a little early, but I have something for you," she said, taking out a one centimeter wide, metallic-like band, and fastening it around his left ankle next to the one Limu gave him. "Just something to remember me by."

"I don't think I'll forget our friendship," he said. Reaching into his pocket, he pulled out a small box and removed a silver charm bracelet, and put it on her wrist.

Scooting up to his side, she kissed him on the cheek, and then rest her head on his shoulder as they watched the crackling fire. Neither spoke. Just being together seemed enough.

The following morning, he sat upright in the sleeping bag and stretched. Fred and Kyle were rattling around the kitchen below. Suddenly the thud and clack of toenails on the steps echoed off the wood panels. Blinking several times to clear his eyes, he saw Ellie bounding headlong in his direction. Knocked back she pinned him to the floor and happily slobbered dog kisses over every part of his face. Scratching her ears did little to calm the excited canine. Averting his face from another round of slobbers, he happened to glance toward the large, picture window at the back of the loft that framed the trees beyond, their dusting of newly fallen snow glistening like tiny diamonds. He squinted into the glare. Someone sat in the lounger in front of the window, backlit to appear as a silhouette.

"School teach you to snore like that?" a familiar voice said as the figure stood.

Leaping up, Philippe flew into Tangata's arms.

"You know, every time I show up you greet me without clothes. What will people think?"

"That's their problem."

♦　　♦　　♦

As the spring semester closed out in May, the white blanket of snow pulled back. There was a whole month before the start of summer classes, but the problem was where to live as the dorms shut down. He had to move. It was Sandy who came to the rescue and introduced him to a grad student-friend from the PoliSci department, Clarence Rowenstein. Clarence had a house a block off campus and three of the five guys renting rooms were leaving for summer jobs. Philippe moved in.

Clarence's live-in girlfriend provided meals for a little extra money. With Sandy joining a couple girlfriends on a summer junket to Europe, he had time to make several discoveries, the first being the incredible beauty and solitude of the Laramie Range mountains sixteen kilometers east of town. Mounting a Suzuki Marauder, he found a perfectly secluded spot to mediate. For the first time since leaving the islands he was able to toss clothes aside, settle on a blanket, and read the latest Elam novel. When summer school started, the first four days of the week quickly filled from sunrise to late night. With much of the curriculum covered in weeks instead of months there was substantial homework. That meant the only time for trips to the mountains were on Friday, Saturday, and Sunday.

That became a welcomed and needed seclusion because of an English class which prompted the second discovery. Early Friday morning at the end of the first week of summer school, he gathered equipment and food for camping out and headed to the secret spot. Sitting on a blanket, legs stretched out, leaning back on his hands, Philippe watched pillow-like clouds drift slowly overhead. Suddenly words began to enter his mind. Grabbing pencil and notebook he scribbled furiously.

Sequestered amid the rocks and Ponderosa trees north of Vedauvoo, another memory slowly slid back into its rightful place; the memory of sitting on a rock projecting into the sea bathed by a warm sun as puffy clouds lazed through the blue sky. Philippe's mother sat there with him reciting poetry, poetry she composed, poetry that encapsulated the panoramic grandeur and beauty of their emerald world floating upon the everlasting waters reflecting the blue sky. What he scribbled on that and following days were not things about the islands, but of where he sat at that moment. He discovered an ability to create poetic descriptions of the things he saw.

Another memory returned a couple weeks later on another beautiful, Columbine afternoon. Stretched out on the blanket, hands clasped behind his head, eyes closed, he visualized his father seated at a piano, fingers gliding over the white and black keys. He played for guests, happy, lively, melodious music, music he had composed. Philippe heard a melody swim lightly just above him. Reaching out into that ethereal world he gently brought the tune into his head, giving it voice with his lips, first humming, then vocalizing the melody.

The previous spring semester included a music appreciation class. As most of the students let it pass unnoticed, Philippe silently wondered, "How did the Masters do it? Mozart, Beethoven, Bach, Williams, Bacharach, the others? Having need of no more than quill and paper, they compose music that would endure to the end of time—perhaps beyond." Somewhere deep in his memory vault a door open to reveal a vision of his father sitting at a piano, playing something previously unheard. How?

Now sequestered among the sacred rocks as some of his most precious memories returned to stay, the adolescent becoming a man understood. That music was always there, floating about, like an apple on a branch swaying gently in a breeze, waiting for someone to reach out with their mind and pluck it. Those were the precious, eternal gifts a father and mother gave their son—poetry and music. Viewed at first as only sublime hobbies to soothe his soul, they would not always be so encumbered.

Summer classes were a compacted whirlwind leaving one nearly breathless by the time weekendd arrived. By July he turned the blue Marauder west into the Snowy Range, favoring the back roads above Centennial. Leaving each Friday after class to return Sunday evening, the time was spent riding, exploring, reflecting, and writing. He couldn't write down the music flowing through his head like the many streams tumbling from winter's snow-pack, but he could sing, sing into the tape recorder. One of the remaining house-mates majored in music. Having the necessary equipment and software, the new friend employed a digital keyboard and computer to put the melodies on paper, fleshing them out with harmonized orchestration.

A couple weeks before fall term, Clarence and his girlfriend made good on plans for a road trip to Yellowstone National Park. Insisting Philippe come along, the trio rattled across Wyoming in their psychedelic, '65 VW love bus. The adventure was wild, wacky, wonderful, and awe-inspiring. However, before heading into geyser land, they stopped in Cody, Buffalo Bill's door to Yellowstone. A nightly rodeo was playing and Philippe's first year roommate was in it.

@ Living in the American west, rodeos seemed to be the number three activity behind hunting and football. This was his first experience. Will Longley and Miss. Peggy were fifth out of the gate in the roping event. He didn't have any idea how well his college roommate did, but Clarence indicated it was a good time. Then came bulldogging. Philippe watched closely, figuring if not so intimidated by horses, that was something he'd like to try. Again, Will and Miss Peggy did well, placing second this time. When it came to bull riding, Philippe was shocked when Clarence cheered for the bull.

"Anyone nuts enough to get on one of those things deserves to get throwd," he said, a great booming laugh escaping the thickly bearded face.

They stayed another day in Cody, taking in all

the wild west environs, arriving late that evening at the Madison Junction campground inside the park. It was cold, but this was still Wyoming as Philippe snuggled down into the cocoon-like bag inside a small dome tent. That morning, breath condensing in vaporous clouds, Philippe stuck his head out of the tent flap. He needed to pee. Less than five meters away a buffalo casually grazed among the tents. The size! The hair! From such a lowly angle, it looked like a trunkless Mastodon.

The creature's eyes stared at the tiny thing on the ground. They were soft, brown eyes. There was no fear, neither within Philippe nor the great beast, as they understood each yearn for that which had passed, never to return, the days of freedom, the total, unequivocal, freedom of youth. In the quiet, hazy moments of that morning Philippe composed some of his best poetry and plucked an ethereal apple as the beast lay upon the ground, chewing its cud, listening, both oblivious to camera flashes.

Fortunately, Philippe was attempting one of those scraggly, chin beards adolescents grow as they enter manhood. That, and the Sherpa cap helped hide his face so that when pictures appeared in newspapers across the country and on YouTube, no one would recognize the person communing with the buffalo. The captions read, "City boy and Wyoming buffalo smoke peace pipe." Of course, that referred to the clouds of steam each exhaled and caught on film.

Upon his return to Laramie, Sandy was waiting. They spent the entire night on Rowenstein's front room floor talking about their adventures. The following day he moved back into McIntyre Hall, sharing a room with Will Longley again, a gimpy

Will. A dark blue cast, from toes to knee, held things together to help mend a broken ankle from a bad dismount.

"So, how many points did the calf get?" Philippe couldn't resist, become the young man's pack mule as he hobbled around campus on crutches. He also had the pleasure of exercising Miss Peggy, an addictive experience once overcoming the initial fear.

One of the holes in Philippe's memory was his actual birthday. Tangata easily discovered it in church records, but the boy chose to celebrate that event on the date he washed ashore – August 8. Interestingly, that would have been about the time Philippe's mother conceived.

The day of Philippe's eighteenth birthday, he finally slid out of bed. It was late, nearly noon. Normally an early riser to take advantage of every second of daylight, he had been up until nearly four, trying to recreate the words on a computer screen as they poured from his mind until succumbing to exhaustion. Stepping from the shower and into the hall, he held an undersized towel with one hand while fluffing wet hair with the other. Happening to look up, he spotted Tangata leaning against his bedroom door. Towel dropping to the floor, he flung into the man's arms. Once again, Tangata appeared into his life like a mystical apparition, just as he had when the boy opened his eyes the first time upon the volcanic island.

"Happy birthday," Tangata said once they separated, and handed Philippe a small, white box.

Philippe gingerly fiddled with the gold bow until it yielded. Removing the lid, he gasped.

"You remember that?"

"Yes," Philippe replied, swiping at a flood of tears. "It was my mother's locket. But how . . .?

"You might want this, too." Tangata withdrew another small box from his jacket pocket.

"Father's watch!"

"One of them. He had several. A friend saved their things before, well, before they would have been lost."

"Thank you, Tangata. Thank you." Philippe threw arms around his guardian. "This is the best birthday ever."

"Well, at least one of the most appropriate I suppose."

"Huh?"

"Celebrating your birthday in your birthday suit?"

Philippe looked down and laughed as a guy and girl stepped out of a bathroom together, each wrapped in bath towels.

"Hello, Will. Still an unofficial co-ed floor, I see," Tangata quipped.

"Hi," he said, his smooth cheeks turning red as if a favorite aunt had just pinched them.

"Technically it's not. Girls are on even numbered floors and boys on odd. They are not supposed to get off the elevator on the wrong floor after hours," Philippe answered, grabbing up the towel and heading toward his room with it draped over one shoulder while admiring the treasures.

"Let me guess. Stairwell."

"Yup. Gets so busy at times they need traffic lights." Tangata notice the young man was picking up a Wyoming accent.

Will and the girl sat stiffly on the edge of Tom's unmade bed as Philippe dressed.

"So, you have a girlfriend yet?"

"Not really. I've got a girl who is a friend, but we don't shower together."

It was a really good teasing dig Will usually responded to by throwing a boot at his roomie, and would have if not for Tangata standing there.

While dressing and quickly brushing long hair into a damp ponytail, Tangata glanced at some of the writing on the desk. "Pretty good, stuff" he said. "See you have gone western," he remarked as Philippe pulled on a pair of cowboy boots.

"A birthday present from Will. Whadeya think, pahdner?"

Tangata laughed. "All you need is a ten gallon."

Philippe pulled one from the wardrobe and put it on.

"Well, I'll be darn, if'n the city slicker hain't turned cowpoke. Ya still serenadin' bufferlo?"

"Nope," he said softly, and putting a hand to the side of his mouth as if trying to keep Will from hearing, said, "but Miss Peggy sure likes it."

"Let's have lunch," Tangata said, scooping up the writing folder and following Philippe out. Before closing the door, he turned to Will and said, "As I recall, last time you tried riding a bronc, you broke your leg." Tossing him a small, foil package, his parting shot was, "Best cinch up before climbing aboard."

"You plannin' to tell his granddad about that?" Philippe asked as they waited for the elevator.

"Naw. Frank raised him pretty good. He's an adult now, old enough to make his own choices and live with the consequences. So, how are you coping with something like that?" Tangata asked as the elevator headed down.

"I get a lot of studying done in the fishbowl. That's the study lounge at the end of the hall, or at the library. That doesn't happen much, like his drinkin' beer. I jist can't stand the manure-kickin' music."

"Yeah, and your eyes look it."

Patronizing a bar off-campus, Tangata's nose filled with the smell of frying hamburgers and onions.

"This takes me back to when my dad and I frequented a similar place on Saturdays for lunch, a couple beers, and a game of pool. These are just as greasy and delicious as I remember."

"Might as well be drinking horse urine, what with the kind of imports they got in this country. Did find a decent micro-brew here," Philippe said as Tangata racked up the balls for a game of pool.

"You break. Not bad," Tangata said, taking a swallow.

Lingering over drinks at a back corner table, they exchanged stories of what had transpired during their separation. As usual, Tangata said little about his work, preferring to read more of Philippe's writing.

"This is good. Quite good in fact, but that's my

opinion. I tend to be biased toward certain individuals. May I show these to a friend?"

"Sure, if you think . . ."

"I think. Now, let's crank up that motorcycle of yours and show me around."

Over the next four days, the two became inseparable again. With his best friend on a rented bike, Philippe piloted through the Laramie and Snowy Ranges. Occasionally stopping to sit beneath towering, old growth Spruce or Lodgepole, they just talked as if back home on the beach of the volcanic lagoon. Then all to soon, Tangata was gone and another season of school and snow began.

Taking an overload of eighteen credit hours, Philippe was far too busy to be homesick. Even Thanksgiving time was filled to overflowing as he and Sandy joined Clarence and several other students for the traditional stuffing. It wasn't until the Christmas holidays that he began feeling those pangs, anxious for Tangata's return. True to form, he appeared in the dorm after the last final as suddenly as usual.

"How about a break from all this snow?" Within the hour, the two were driving toward Denver and a plane headed for the Bahamas.

The sun may shine on Laramie 320 days a year, but there is precious little time to use it for tanning. Summer trips to the mountains helped, but being so close to the sun, if not careful, a body tends to burn before toasting. Another problem was that while Wyoming was beautiful in all aspects, Philippe was perpetually cold, even in the summer when camping in the high country—and every part of Wyoming is high country. Days were great, but at night one either hunkered deep inside a sleeping bag or bundled in layers of clothing, lots and lots of layers so that a person looked like a space cadet from across the tracks.

As Tangata held down the porch of their rented cottage on the lee coast of Eleuthera Island, Philippe swam, jogged, played volleyball with others, or stretched out on the beautiful pink beach. For a brief time he was able to relive his former life and feel the marrow in his bones begin to thaw as the once deep, brown tan was renewed.

Not having to look over his shoulder or at every adult male with suspicion, the displaced Islander settled into the routine of three yearly visits from his guardian—summer vacation, birthday, and Christmas. With a seemingly endless procession of classes in between, he completed a bachelor's degree in three years. Crossing the stage and shaking hands with all those important people was great however, none measured to the one waiting at the bottom of the steps.

The two toured the western states that summer before settling Philippe into an apartment preparatory to beginning a Master's program at the University of Utah in Salt Lake City. He actually felt sad leaving Wyoming with its memories. When Tangata left, homesickness began to sneak up to became a problem. When his guardian couldn't make it for his birthday or Christmas, then an e-mail came that he couldn't come that spring as planned, homesickness became almost unbearable. The world had become a troubled place and Philippe understood that had something to do with Tangata's absence, but it didn't help mollify the feeling.

Finishing all necessary course work by spring

left only the thesis to complete. That's when Philippe finally convinced himself, "After all this time it should be safe to return. Besides, I'll pass through Australia too quickly for anyone to notice." Without further thought, he headed home—home to the mountain garnished with an emerald cloak, its feet in the warm waters of the Coral Sea.

◆　　◆　　◆

With increasing excitement, Philippe stepped off the Quantus flight in Brisbane. Some six years had passed since leaving his volcano island and he looked nothing like the orphaned boy thrown upon that lonely rock. Topping out at one-hundred-seventy-eight centimeters or five foot ten inches by American measure, he was no longer a long drink of water, as Tangata sometimes referred to him, with the long, narrow face. Wide cheeks narrowed to a firm, slightly cleft chin. The deep, golden bronze color of his smooth skin almost gave him to look like a Native American. He'd given up trying to grow a beard having inherited his father's hairless genes. The fine, chestnut hair tied into a ponytail extended just below wide, muscular shoulders with a swath overshadowing mischievous, sea green eyes. A Nehru shirt stretched tight across a broad, deep chest with a small, gold, five-franc coin on a chain gleaming on the white material, the first profit his father made from their resort and his mother's favorite locket. Unseen was the crucifix next to the skin he hoped to return to its owner someday. He felt comfortable Uncle Rousseau's syndicate would not recognize him, having changed a great deal since leaving what seemed eons ago. That's why he told no one of the impromptu trip, even Tangata. It was to be a surprise.

That proved a mistake. Walking by several limo drivers holding signs of who they were to chauffeur, it was his luck that one of them had worked for his uncle on New Caledonia at the time he escaped. As eyes briefly met, the driver's curiosity peaked as the young man walked alone through the terminal. Philippe wasn't completely naive nor unaware of his surroundings and knew instantly he was in trouble.

Chapter 11

The Hidie

Traveling light, the backpack contained one change of clothes, toiletries, a book, notebook, and tape recorder. His front pocket held an American passport and wallet with cash, driver's license, and credit cards all bearing the identity, Philip Elam. The man to whom he owed his life was good at providing such things. Traveling light facilitated passing through customs with relative ease, as was ducking out the main doors, flagging a taxi, and disappearing into the menagerie of traffic. Whoever tried following would be quickly lost in the crowds by the unexpected speed of his departure.

However, Philippe's caution was to the point of near paranoia. Giving a familiar address, the business complex where he disappeared years ago, he left the taxi. There, he took an escalator to the third floor retail center, crossed over the footbridge to the next tower, down, and onto the street on the other side where he hired another taxi. Anyone following would be sufficiently duped and lost. Wrong. Passing through a less favorable part of the city on the way to charter boat services, he noticed a dark blue sedan not far behind. How'd they do it?

Traffic suddenly became congested and slowed. He could walk faster. "Looks to be a bloody bingle ahead," the cabbie called back, referring to a car accident.

The paranoia cloud opened to begin a downpour. Why was Philippe skeptical of that explanation? The driver had been on the two-way radio, but it sounded like the usual exchange with a company dispatcher, but then he only caught snatches of the conversation. The sedan moved within a half block. All the occupants of that car had to do were jump out and catch him. He tossed the driver a bill large, enough for the fare and tip, popped the door, and bailed.

Ducking into an alley the cab had stopped next to, Philippe turned on the speed. Long legs well-conditioned to running and an extra burst of adrenalin-fortified speed left any pursuers far behind, but a foot race couldn't continue forever. Bursting onto the next street, he looked in both directions. Another dark-colored car came to a squealing stop, ejecting three men. Spotting a vacant building to his left, Philippe ducked inside as four oriental men puffed their way onto the street, two from the alley, and two at the corner, joining the others.

When Tangata helped him elude pursuers before, he learned the secret was to keep moving, so continued through scattered debris inside the derelict, apparently an abandoned hotel. Heading up some stairs, he was cautious to make no noise. At the top floor stairwell he found the roof access door. Back in sunlight, he nimbly crossed one attached building after another until finding an open door near the end facing the previous street. Glancing over the parapet, he spotted the cab parked at the curb and the sedan abandoned to interfere with traffic. There was no accident ahead. Slipping through the door, Philippe entered a dark staircase, latched the door closed, and quietly worked himself toward the street level.

This was some kind of apartment building judging by the number of doors off a long hallway, but there didn't seem to be anyone around. Making his way to the first level, he crept to the front, cut glass door, parting the lace curtain just enough to look outside. Several loads of suited men were exiting an array of cars and fanning out. Turning back into the house, he saw double doors leading into another room. From behind came the soft sound of romantic music and the voices of several men and women. Unobtrusively peeking through the side crack of the door he gasped silently and stepped back. Of all places, he landed in a bordello.

As one of the call girls began to lead a customer to private quarters, Philippe quickly removed his tennis shoes in preparation to heading quietly back upstairs. Just as he slipped the second one off he thought to detect movement at the end of the hallway, but it was dark. Staring for a moment, he didn't see anything, chalking it up to imagination. Shoes in hand, he ascended the wood stairs three at a time. Randomly picking a room near the middle left side, he pressed an ear to the door, and listened intently. From below a man and woman argued.

"Look upstairs," the man ordered with a thunderous tone.

"How dare you barge in here and push us around," a husky, woman's voice responded loudly.

"Shut up and get out of the way."

"Della, call the jacks."

"You call no one, dog."

The exchange of foul epithets continued as heavy footsteps climbed the stairs. Philippe tried the door latch. It yielded. Taking a quick peek, he slipped in, closing the door quietly behind him.

The average hotel-size room contained a bed, sofa, and makeup table. More importantly, it appeared vacant as he scanned around. Pressing an ear to the wood door, he listened as other doors were opened, usually accompanied by a woman's startled scream. Stepping to the window, a quick look outside was not encouraging. More men took positions along the street sealing off the entire block.

"Well, Uncle's men are still thorough," he chided himself.

"You'll find the scenery inside much more appealing," a sweet voice said.

Philippe spun around to confront a girl about his age attired in a thin, lavender nightshirt. Stepping from the bathroom, she glanced out the window.

"They looking for you?"

"Yes."

"So many. What did you do?"

"It was a while ago."

"I recognize a couple of them. They frequent this place though I haven't entertained them personally."

"They're my Uncle's men."

"Your Uncle?"

"It's a long story. I better leave. If they find me here it wouldn't go well for you."

"I don't like them, and it sounds like they're out in the hallway. You better hide. Come here," she said walking to a curtain and pushing it aside. A closet.

"That's the first place they'd look."

"Yes, but not here," she said, pulling a cardboard box aside opening a hidden panel in the sidewall next to the floor. "This place used to be raided a lot in the old days. Has all sorts of hiding places."

Philippe dropped to his knees and crawled inside as the girl closed the door and slid the box back into place just as the hall door was forced. She let out a slight scream.

Reaching into his backpack Philippe quietly removed the tape recorder. Opening the battery compartment, he removed the power cells and pressed another latch. A small derringer slid into the palm of his hand. Made of fiberglass-reinforced polyurethane, it had no metal parts. Firing a modified .22 cal. bullet, it was lethal, a gift from his benefactor during a mysterious side trip last summer. A number of lessons with a nine-millimeter, Ruger P95 while on the island, and practice in the mountains surrounding Laramie helped Philippe become a good marksman. He only used this pistol on inanimate stationary and moving targets, but he wasn't about to fall into his Uncle's hands. That was certain death.

"Out of the way," a man's voice growled.

A small ventilation grill next to the floor beneath the dressing table afforded a view of the room. He heard the closet curtain pushed brusquely aside and clothes moved around, then saw a man's black leather shoes stomp past the grill. He looked under the bed and into the bathroom. Apparently satisfied, he left, but not without touching the girl's breast and making a crude remark.

The hunter was gone, but the girl didn't come to get him, instead sat at the vanity to apply makeup. "Don't move," she whispered. Suddenly the door sprang open again. The girl turned abruptly and threw something at the intruder who slammed the door closed, laughing boisterously. They were good. If she had come to Philippe that sudden reappearance would have been deadly.

Standing, the girl walked toward the closet as if to get something and whispered, "Stay where you are. It will be a while." She continued out of sight and into the bathroom.

After a time the search noises diminished followed by a light rap on the door. "Christie," a feminine voice called out as it opened.

"What's going on Chelsea?" the girl answered, her bare legs and bottom of a towel coming into view from the bathroom.

"They're looking for a boy," the new arrival said.

"A boy! Here? Don't they know to pick them up on the street, not in a place like this?"

"Oh, you're being silly, Christie."

"What'd he do?"

"I don't know, but they want him awfully bad. They're gone, but the street's full of the hoons."

A chime sounded.

"Customer," Chelsea announced and hurried out.

When the door closed, Christie walked to the closet to slip on a tight, low-cut dress and high heel spikes.

"I'm sorry, but you better stay where you're at for a while," she whispered and left.

After a time, the girl returned accompanied by a man. Once inside she began to disrobe him as they embraced. Once naked, they crawled into bed and began their sexual play. An hour later, he dressed and left. She got up, slipped on a near transparent, lavender gown, and combed her hair. It wasn't long before the bell sounded again. This time Christie slipped on a red dress and left.

Five times the routine played out as she addressed the needs and desires of men of various ages. Philippe dozed between customers, otherwise stared in disbelief at the activity on the bed in front of his portal. Only once before had he seen such things, and then only briefly—on the beach where he had been a child. Now Philippe found himself on the front row of a full-length, live porno show. After the last man left, the girl showered, but this time dressed in a flannel night gown.

"That was the last one," she whispered, opening the closet curtain, moving the box, and sliding the secret panel open.

Philippe crawled out. After twenty hours on an airplane and nearly eight crammed in the hiding hole, every muscle was horribly stiff.

"I'm sorry you had to be in there so long, but they're not giving up. That last was one of the mongrels, though he was naughty in bed."

Philippe's stomach growled.

"When did you eat last?"

"On the plane," he cast a quick glance at his watch. "Fourteen hours ago."

"Oh, you poor dear. We're locked for the night, or rather the day. It's morning. If you'd like to take a shower, I'll slip down and get some brekkle from the kitch."

"Will it be safe?"

"Oh, yes. They're tearing the other buildings apart. If they come back I'll ring the bell twice. That's the warning code. You can hide."

The door latch clicked as she left. Another safety precaution. Anyone forcing their way into the room would make a lot of noise and probably break a shoulder. It was a stout door. Downstairs, the girl made a couple of sandwich plates and started to leave when a heavyset woman in her late fifties entered the kitchen.

"You worked up an appetite tonight," the husky-throated woman remarked.

"Yes."

"Enough for two."

The girl flushed.

"I wondered where our special guest went. Saw him shoot up just before those mongrels pushed in. Stash him in the hidie?"

"Yes," the girl replied weakly.

"It's alright, dear. He looked to be a growing bogan. Let's take up a spot more. I'll help. Besides, I want to meet this bloke who's so bloody important."

Philippe just stepped from the shower when he heard the door latch snap open. Flipping off the light, he hastily wrapped a towel around his waist, and palmed the pistol out of sight behind his thigh.

The door closed and re-locked.

"It's me," the girl's voice called out softly. "I've got some food."

Philippe peeked around the door frame. He was surprised to see an older woman at the girl's side. Both had their hands full of food.

"Well, I see you've taken off more than your shoes," the older woman said with a canvassing smile.

Philippe stood silently.

"I own this place. I'm Evelien, but everyone calls me Eve. I saw you earlier when you didn't wait on the formalities and shoot up on your own . . . just before those hoons barged in. So, what's your name?"

"Philip. Philip Elam."

"Elam?" She ruminated over the name while setting the food on the vanity. "You look familiar."

"I don't believe we've ever met. I'm from America."

"I never forget a face. We've met, I'm sure . . . You look a lot like . . . Holy dooly, yes! Charles. Charles Bonnét." Philippe went totally pale. How could a prostitute know his father so well? "But, no. Charles is dead, God rest his soul, and you're too young."

"He was my father."

"Of course! Little Philippe!" With a squeal, Eve threw her arms around him in a crushing hug. "Oh, my dear boy, I am so sorry," she moaned in his ear before holding him at arm's length by the biceps. "Your mother was a dear, dear friend. We grew up and went to school together. I was her bride's maid on their wedding day. She was so pretty, so very,

very pretty. I visited their island paradise many times. They had wonderful parties. The last time I saw you . . . you look so like your father, but there's a lot of your mother there, too."

Philippe thought age had offered change, but hadn't considered how much he might resemble his father. One seldom stands before a mirror to compare. His father was a well-known businessman in this part of the world. No wonder recognition was so quick. Sliding the pistol's safety on, Philippe laid it on the table.

"Here, sit down and eat. My, but you are so like your father," the older woman continued to croon, her painted, brown eyes watering.

"I'm sorry, madam. I don't remember you."

"Probably not. You were just a kidiwink, and so full of energy, constantly shooting here and there, always the delight of your dear momma, and papa, and the guests. I'm sure the parties were a bore."

"Momma and papa loved them. Wait a minute. I remember an elegant lady in bright dresses who came often. I called her Aunty. She was always so kind. She always brought me presents. Once she came in a particularly striking blue dress. Gave me a lava-lava of the same material. I love blue. Wore it for years even after it became so worn it looked like waxed paper. I was wearing it the day my parents . . ."

"I still have that dress, yes, though it doesn't fit quite as well any more. Age has a tendency to change one's figure here and there." She laughed, a laugh that hadn't changed, and he loved hearing.

Unbridled, Philippe threw his arms around the woman and hugged her close as he had whenever she came to the island resort. She still wore the same perfume. Some time passed as they clung to one another until slowly, reluctantly separating.

"Well, that explains why they want you so badly. You really have caused a lot of trouble for your uncle. He just got out of jail . . . on a technicality," she said sourly. "He wants your papa's, well, it's yours . . . he wants your property real bad. It's worth millions."

"Yes, and the only way for him to gain control is for me to be dead. He keeps trying to have me killed. I'm not done with him, either. The day will come when he will be broken, completely broken, and no technicality will come to his aid," Philippe spat bitterly.

"To accomplish your end and not his you'll have to stay here a while longer. They don't give up easily. They know you're in one of the buildings on this block. You're safest right here. If they show up, I'll ring the bell twice. In the meantime, I can't think of a better person to tend to your needs than Christie."

Aunty Eve took Philippe by both hands and kissed his cheek, as she had so many years ago, then spinning her ample figure about with unexpected grace, left, latching the door behind her. After finishing his meal, Philippe looked around the room.

"If you have a blanket, I'll lay on the sofa."

"You'll do no such thing," Christie replied. She had stripped the bed and spread fresh linen while he ate. "You will sleep right here."

"But . . . where will you . . .?"

"Next to you, of course."

He stood stiffly.

"How old are you?" Christie asked while fluffing

a pillow.

"Twenty-two."

"You've never been naked in the presence of a woman before?"

Philippe gulped, "Well, yes. My parents owned a nudist resort, but never like this."

"You're a virgin?"

Philippe stammered, feeling the heat rise to his face before admitting, "Yes, but . . ."

"If it's not your wish, don't worry. I'm tuckered as you must be. We'll put a sheet between us," she said, a sincerity in her soft, brown eyes.

They lay upon the bed, he beneath the sheet, and she on top, the comforter over both. Philippe had no idea how he would be able to sleep, but it was late afternoon when movement brought him awake.

"Hello," the girl said softly, looking at him through the vanity mirror while combing her hair.

"Hi," Philippe replied sleepily.

"Eve brought up food." She pointed to a tray near the window.

Philippe stood, took up a piece of toast, and peeked around the edge of the blackout shade. There were men still roaming the street.

"Darling grundies," she teased.

"A joke. I seldom wore clothes growing up except a lava-lava. During formal parties or going off island, I had to wear clothes. I never wore underwear after leaving diapers. When I went to America that changed. My guardian buys these as a joke."

"And you wear them?"

"I love him as if he were my father. It may sound

strange, but like this necklace and watch remind me of my parents, these silly things remind me of him."

"It may be a few days before you can safely leave."

"If at all," Philippe said dismally. "They're like vultures waiting for something to die. I was foolish for coming."

"Well, I for one am not sorry you came."

The little bell sounded. Philippe flashed a panicked look at the girl.

"That's only one. It means a customer has arrived, asking for me. Take the tray," she said while opening the hidden door. "If you need to use the dunny, shoot down the ladder and slip the panel. It's across the hall."

Philippe slipped in. The girl pushed a pillow and blanket in and closed up. The size of a closet, he sat while eating as Christie entertained a customer. So the night proceeded, a seemingly endless procession of lusting men. There was a lull around midnight so the two could share a meal, then her work resumed until early morning when he came come out, showered, and slept, a bit more restlessly this time.

Fewer of his uncle's men prowled the street, but like a cat with a cornered mouse, some still lurked about, patiently watching. Eve said there was a plan in the works to be in place by the next day. Philippe wasn't sure he could take another night. After the first, he didn't watch, but it was hard as the sounds crept through the vent, circled his head, and burrowed through burning ears into his mind.

"This is my night off," Christie said.

"That's good. I don't know if I could take another night in there."

"We could sleep beneath the same cover." Philippe did not reply. "You can have private time, if you like."

"No," he almost snapped, then calmed. "I don't do that." The subconscious connection between having masturbated and the death of his parents stilled stung. Intellectually, Philippe understood that was bogus, but the priest so burned the prohibitions against such acts into his young mind it was impossible to overcome.

Christie looked at him with longing, truly wanting to help.

"Oh," she suddenly said. "Are you gay?"

"Huh?" Philippe replied, shaken by the question, then understood how she might come by that impression from his responses. *No. Men don't hold any sensual appeal,* he thought, then to tried to explain. "I was accustomed to living among people who were naked. My parents owned a nudist resort. Very first class. I understand it still is. I own it, but have no interest in its operation. My guardian arranged for others to do that. Guests do not wear clothes unless they desire to. Growing up, I seldom did.

"Papa was very strict. If guests wanted to have sex it must be in their cabins, never in public. Such things are a very private matter. Occasionally a guest, a male guest, would become aroused. At such times they were expected to cover themselves until gaining control. Actually, that happened infrequently.

"Growing up, it was natural to see a naked body and not be aroused. That is not to say I do not have natural urges. Seeing and listening to your employment has been very difficult, but I guess somewhere in my past the seeds of celibacy must have been sown. It is a feeling very difficult to overcome."

"Do you think you will ever marry?"

"I think so. I hope it will happen, then perhaps I shall feel free," Philippe said, pausing a moment before continuing with a slight smile, "and make up for lost time." They both giggled.

With the shades drawn, the room was dark as nighttime, permitting sleep, but it did not come to Philippe as he tossed and turned repeatedly. With death lingering on the street below waiting for its victim to appear, being physically excited by the environment, and knowing a woman laid a sheet's breadth away, sleep was impossible.

Christie left the bed. He was sorry for having disturbed her rest. Cracking one eye open, he watched her go into the lavatory. There was a strange hissing noise, almost undetectable. A few minutes later, the girl returned. He determined not to move so much. The bed bounced as she settled back in, then a hand crossed over his shoulder, resting on his chest as she snuggled close, beneath the sheet, her bare skin soft and warm against his. He didn't move as her fingers played with his right nipple, surprised at how hard it had become. When the hand slid down to gently scratch the belly, she draped a leg over his.

Yes. No. The argument roared in his head, louder and louder. When her hand slid beneath the elastic band of the boxers, *Yes!* screamed so loudly Philippe was sure it could be heard down on the street.

Philippe opened his eyes, staring at the ceiling, blinking several times. Turning his head to the right he gazed into Christie's face.

"Rest well?" she asked as the hands of the clock approached six p.m. and her fingers played over his chest.

"Yes," he answered.

"Upset?"

He looked at her worried expression, smiled. "No." This would require a trip to the confessional, but he would shop around for someone understanding, like Father James, and for some reason, he didn't expect much reaction to something like this. From what the priest indicated, this was a sin he heard a lot.

"Alright you two, naughty time's over," Eve said, bounding into the room and opening the curtains to flood the room with light. "It's all set. You leave in a hour. Go shower."

"Thank you, Aunty Eve," Philippe said, sliding his feet to the floor to sit on the edge of the bed a moment before walking to the bath.

Eve sighed, picking up cartoon boxers from the floor and laying them on the bed. "My, my, my. Little Philippe's all grown up."

"He certainly has," Christie said with a dreamy sigh.

Chapter 12

Under Cover

As dusk settled about the neighborhood, Philippe and Aunty Eve stood out of sight just inside the ornate front door waiting the commencement of another rescue. Philippe felt bad always having to impose upon others to bail him out of trouble. Christie stood on the bottom of the staircase. Tension was heavy. Their visitor now wore a dark, dress topcoat over his travel clothes, a fedora pulled low over the eyes. The backpack was fitted to the stomach to give the appearance of a paunch.

A black limo pulled to the curb. Nothing out of the ordinary. A tall man with a paunch wearing a dark, dress topcoat and fedora pulled over the eyes exited, walked up the steps to the door, and stepped in. As the door was about to close what sounded like someone banging on a trashcan filled the quiet street. Bang! Bang! Bang! That could have been gunshots. The stakeout across the street turned to look toward the sound. There was shouting. More gun fire-like noise. The man in the dark, dress topcoat and fedora hurriedly stepped from the door and entered the limo, which sped away.

Philippe looked back through the smoked glass window of the limo at the departing brothel, then ahead. "Where are we going?" he asked the driver.

"Home, sir," the driver answered with a crisp, Aussy accent, but from the timbre it wasn't an Anglo voice.

The limo glided rapidly through traffic. Obeying all the rules, the car eventually pulled onto the compound of a business center. Stopping at a small security hut, the driver rolled down his window. The stop was surprisingly brief as the heavy, steel gate began opening before the guard had time to review the credentials. The car moved ahead around a series of concrete barriers before heading into an underground garage and down two levels. Once parked, the driver exited, and opened Philippe's door.

"If sir will follow me please," a thickset, Black man said and escorted him to an elevator. Once inside the small compartment the chauffeur, an Aborigine, reached around the corner, pressed a button and stepped back as the steel doors closed, not once displaying emotion, neither smile nor frown, nothing in the dark brown eyes to indicate anger, happiness, or even boredom.

Alone, Philippe's feet pressed into the carpeted floor as the lift rose quickly. An annoying bell announced each level until the door opened on the eleventh floor.

"Hello, Philippe," Tangata said. "Once again it seems your fat is pulled from the fire."

"Sorry," Philippe replied, throwing his arms around him. "I just got so homesick. I'm sorry."

"I know. It worked out. Amazing how lucky you

are. Should take you to the gaming tables. Come with me. Really is amazing. The only place you could have escaped that manhunt was that particular brothel run by an old family friend. Yes, my young friend, we do need to visit a casino."

The two walked down a long, starkly sterile, fluorescent-washed corridor passing a number of pale blue doors with various names until arriving at one reading, "Mr. Tuskin." When the door closed behind them, Tangata did something totally uncharacteristic—initiate a hug.

"It's really good to see you again, despite everything. School goes well?"

"After all these years I know you needn't ask, but yes, it goes well."

"A's and what was that B+?"

"Tough grader. That was the highest grade in the class."

"I understand. Some people can be arrogantly unrealistic. Not to worry. Her department head had a heart-to-heart about things. First time she had an entire class pass. Well, it is the holidays. Need to do some shopping, eh?"

"That may be difficult. I obviously can't show my face in this part of the world. I thought I could, but didn't realize how much I look like my father."

"Then we shall change the face. Remove that ridiculous coat and hat. They really aren't you. The shirt, too, and sit on that chair," Tangata said, the usual brusqueness returning.

Philippe obeyed, marveling at the strangeness of the office. Its only furnishing was what appeared to be a barber's chair with headrest in which he sat. A folding chair off to one side became Tangata's seat. A large mirror and counter littered with various containers, large, small, square, round, and oval dominated one wall. A light rap on the door admitted a stout, middle-aged woman wearing a black apron over a tan shirt and trousers.

"This is Lorette. Best cosmetologist in Australia, other than me," Tangata said with a wink.

"G'Day mate . . . Holy dooley!"

"What's wrong?" Philippe said.

"Ripper! Nice cheek bones, good, strong chin," she said gripping Philippe's jaw and turning his head from side to side. "Bonzer skin. Oh, thanks heaps, Mr. T. You'll get a pash for this. A real canvas to work with for a change. And this hair . . ." Having untied the ponytail, she ran her fingers through it several times. "You should take better care of it. This style is too feral. Shame to cut it, but it'll sprout out if you insist."

Philippe wondered if she thought her own pile of frizzy, auburn hair was so great. If so, he was in trouble.

That was the last Lorette spoke as she began to hum a jaunty tune. Tying an over-sized napkin around his neck, she set to work. An hour later, the chair was brought upright. Philippe stared into the mirror, but the person staring back was someone totally different. The cheeks were softer, the chin cleft gone, the nose wider. He also sported glasses. His ginger-blond hair was now a short, dark pile flowing from a left part, dipping to just above the right eye. Philippe rather liked that, except it would take more care than the previous wash, comb back, tie off, and run style. Contacts had changed his eye color as well.

"Well, that should do very nicely, don't you agree Mr. Adams," Tangata said, christening Philippe with another new identity.

While Tangata snapped several photos, Lorette

beamed at her latest masterpiece and left, looking back one last time, obviously satisfied with her handiwork. A half hour later Tangata answered another rap at the door and received a large, vanilla envelope, opened it, and began handing over its contents—a passport with a picture of Philippe's new face and an ID, Jeremy Lawton Adams, age 21, 5'-10", 185 pounds, brown hair, brown eyes, born Reno, Nevada. All the current physical details matched. Then a wallet. Same information on a Wyoming driver's license.

"There's corresponding data on file in the States to match. According to your driving record, you should slow down a bit," Tangata said.

Philippe looked at the credit card bearing his picture.

"Never leave home without it. Actually works. Credit history, not bad, small bank account. All the necessities of a college kid. Oh, and this."

"An airline ticket?"

"Used. Arrived this afternoon. How else did you get here?"

Philippe opened the photo compartment of the wallet. There were pictures of parents, a brother, two sisters, family dog—a Golden Retriever that looked suspiciously like Ellie, and a girlfriend, Mickey.

"Cute girl. Who is she?"

"So, you've taken up noticing girls now?"

Philippe's face reddened.

"Well, shouldn't be any surprise since you took up residency in a cathouse of all places. Longest any man's stayed there in its 110 year history. I have a hotel room. Very accommodating staff, but not like you're used to. We'll do some holiday shopping tomorrow."

Back in the underground garage, the same Aborigine driver stood leaning against a car as they stepped off the elevator. He said nothing while opening the door of a silver Porsche. Actually, this was the first Philippe had been up close to one of Australia's natives. He'd seen pictures in history texts. The gentleman looked like some Islanders, yet different. An oval face with very wide cheekbones, the black face enveloped by a thick, short, neatly trimmed beard, and very curly, dark brown, very dark brown hair beneath a navy blue driver's cap. Both beard and hair showed signs of salting giving him an aura of distinction.

Philippe recalled how in one history lesson he learned that the Aborigine migrated from Africa 55,000 years ago and never moved out of the stone age until the arrival of the Europeans. They were better equipped to survive the outback than white prejudice. Yes, he was black as coal, had an extremely thick, wide-flaring nose and generous mouth with thick lips, still . . .

Philippe hesitated getting into the car, obviously staring at the man.

"Many of my people are no longer pure," he said with a gravely, bass voice that rumbled like distant thunder.

"I'm sorry, I didn't mean . . ." Philippe stammered.

"No problem, sir."

"Don't worry," Tangata said as they sat in the back seat. "Joshua has an uncanny knack of reading people's minds, so stop fretting."

"Like you?"

"It's a trick one learns. It's in the eyes. He can see that your curiosity is virtuous. About the only part that's left."

"Hey! I didn't go there on purpose, and I didn't initiate sex with Christie, and how the heck do you find out all this stuff about me?"

There was only the vaguest hint of a smile on Tangata's lips as a low, rumbling chuckle drifted from the front seat of the car.

"We have as many eyes and ears as your uncle."

"Oh, geez! You weren't watching?"

He neither denied nor confirmed the accusation.

"Your guardian understands dream time," Joshua tossed over his shoulder, suddenly becoming talkative. "Besides, what happened was necessary to prevent you from exploding like a skyrocket and alerting those on the ground of your presence."

"He knows, too?! Holy cow! How many others?"

"Well, let's see . . ." Tangata began silently counting on his fingers, tapping three.

"That's all? I can live with that I guess."

"All the girls in the naughty house want young sir to return," Joshua cast back.

"And girls accuse men of telling."

"Well, from the way it's passed around, you were pretty spectacular for a virgin," Tangata added.

Philippe slumped so low in the seat to nearly slide onto the floorboards, wishing the driver and his guardian would be less inscrutable and more silent.

When told they were heading to a hotel what came to mind was one of those nice, quietly comfortable places like a Marriott. What he got was the Reef Hotel in all of its palatial splendor, quite the change from a dorm room in the University of Wyoming towers and efficiency apartment in Utah. Something like going from a broom closet to the American White House. On top of that was the greeting upon exited the car.

"Good evening, Mr. Adams. Right this way, Mr. Adams. Did you have a pleasant day, Mr. Adams? Yadda-yadda-yadda, Mr. Adams." All five stars worth in perfect British English for someone Philippe thought was supposed to be low-key.

"This is my nephew, Jeremy Adams. Just arrived from America for the holidays," Tangata introduced the boy to the Concierge, "He's one of the most important and knowledgeable persons to know in these settings," he told Philippe as they walked through the lobby.

The suite was a two bedroom house with a big screen, 3-D TV in the living area, a kitchen, and fully stocked wet bar. Beds were king size clouds to be stretched out upon and absorbed into, although just before nodding off Philippe wished he weren't quite so alone and considered giving the Concierge a call before falling asleep.

Following the initial reception at the airport and ordeal of the past several days he never thought to casually stroll about anywhere in this part of the world. Attired in a polo shirt, slacks, and tennis shoes, uncle and nephew started the day with breakfast in the swank hotel's dining room. The U of W didn't provide breakfast steaks except to the football team, and those dudes never heard of Eggs Benedict. Philippe stuffed himself with both.

Waddling out to the entrance, Joshua opened the rear car door to chauffeur them again. Today the man was very business-like in a dark gray suit, and thankfully silent.

Their first stop was Lord & Lord, Ltd. Philippe knew this was not going to be like shopping Target as they passed through a thick, smoked glass door beneath a carved, dark oak portal. A nattily dressed man in his late thirties met them before covering four meters.

"G'day, Mr. Adams," he said, giving Philippe a close inspection. "And what may we provide for you today, sir?"

"My nephew just arrived from America and is in need of something to replace his lost luggage."

"Yes, I can see a need." Philippe wasn't sure how to interpret that crack, except by the tone which sounded pretty snooty.

Since forced to wear stuff other than a lava-lava, clothing tended to casual. College and hanging out with Clarence Rowenstein's hippie crowd probably instilled a bit more casual than the norm. He was partial to stone washed, straight leg jeans, tight T-shirts, and bare feet.

As the clerk totaled the bill, he changed into a pale yellow, pinpoint twill shirt with royal blue ascot that almost appeared to be black, black slacks, tweed sports jacket, and dark brown, suede shoes. Being wrapped were medium gray trousers, polo shirts, leather sandals, and a medium gray Ralph Lauren tux with dark gray cummerbund, a chino shirt, and patent leather shoes. He'd outdistanced the first tux by high school graduation.

He was okay with all this stuff, not really knowing what Tangata had in mind, but when his guardian yelled across the sales floor, drawing everyone's attention, "Hey, Jeremy, this is definitely you," almost sent him out the front door. He was holding up a pair of black, silk boxers with the exaggerated, toothy grin of a horse holding up the Richard Nixon victory sign. Philippe shook his head and the salesclerk wrinkled his nose, but they found their way onto the sales receipt. "A reminder of dear, old Wyomin'."

The next stop was to purchase garment bags

for all this stuff, followed by lunch at Half Moon Bay Marina overlooking the Coral Sea. Looking around, he understood why Tangata wanted him to wear the "casual" attire. Philippe wouldn't have been surprised to see the Prince of Wales taking lunch at the next table.

"G'day, Mr. Adams. Your usual table is ready," the Maître d' said, personally escorting them to a very private section of the establishment.

"What would you like, Jeremy?"

"A Carl's Jr., but they probably don't have anything like that here."

"Well, you might be surprised."

"Actually, what I've missed the most has been *real* fish and chips."

And that's exactly what Philippe got, not the American version of fried white-something and manufactured French fries all previously frozen at least a month or so before. This was snapper from the morning catch, fresh potato chips, served with kiwi, and a tankard of James Boags beer from Tasmania.

As they left to do more shopping, Philippe looked out at the boats at dock and said, "Isn't that the *Adrianne* over there?"

"Yes. Fifty-five dollars a day. Not bad for first rate service. The most expensive is not always the best value."

"And how do you classify the places we've, or rather you've been unloading tons of your money?"

"Best value. And it's not my money."

"Don't tell me you put this on an expense voucher?"

"No. You ponied up for your own clothes . . . and thank you for that delightful lunch."

Once living in the States, Philippe had need of

money for the first time. There was access to a bank account in his name with a comfortable balance. Remembering his father's lessons, he tended to the side of frugal. He guessed there were insurance monies, and the resort still made money, but never went beyond asking how much.

That evening, the two left the suite in formal attire and headed straight for the Reef's casino. Tangata obviously had tired of speculating about Philippe's luck.

"We'll start with the machines," he announced, pointing for the young man to take a seat. Then standing at his shoulder Tangata began giving instructions on how to play Blackjack.

Philippe didn't fare too well at first as he struggled to grasp the rudiments of the game, but after an hour, he had nearly broken even, but more importantly thought to have a working handle on the game. That meant graduation—to the tables. Tangata picked one with no customers.

"The kid's just learning," he announced to the dealer, who called the pit boss over and explained the situation.

"How about a few practice hands?" the thin, Chinese man asked.

Philippe felt sweat begin to bead his forehead as he played the chips with shaky fingers. The nervousness began to dissipate after five or six hands at which time the game began for real.

"How much do I have to play with?"

"Oh, let's start modestly. Say . . . fifteen thousand, Australian.

Philippe choked. The pit boss made a phone call. Tangata wasn't kidding.

"Verified. Fifteen thousand," the man said as the dealer started stacking chips in front of him.

"Remember, never drink anything stronger than soda while playing, despite what the cute sales girls offer," Tangata said and left.

Although moderately successful at first, he began to lose when he choked and didn't play smart; however, confidence and understanding began building. Several more people joined the table, but were not nearly as lucky. A crowd began forming as they do to watch a big winner.

"You are a very good player," a man said as he took the empty seat at the opposite end of the table from where Philippe played. Glancing up, Philippe nearly leapt up and ran. It was Tomas. He froze and stared.

"Is something wrong?" Tomas asked.

"Huh, oh, no. You just remind me of someone . . . ah, a teacher back home. He died," Philippe quickly covered, wondering, "Does he recognize me?"

"Well, I assure you I am not a ghost."

If his uncle's right hand accomplice did recognize him, he wasn't saying or doing anything, but then Tomas was a very cool person.

"Well, Tomas, long time no see."

Tomas turned to greet the person addressing him and paled slightly. Philippe had never seen him so unsettled. Recovering somewhat, he answered, "Yes, it's been a while." He almost stuttered.

"Having any luck?"

"I just arrived. Saw this young man doing well and thought to give the table a try. And you?"

"Roulette," Tangata said, shuffling a stack of high-end chips in his hand. "You've picked a good table. My nephew is one of the luckiest people I've ever met, other than the two of us, perhaps."

"Your nephew?"

"Yes. Jeremey, this is Tomas Bonnell, a . . .

business acquaintance. My nephew, Jeremey Adams."

"Howdy," Philippe said, hesitantly reaching out to shake Tomas' hand.

"American?" Tomas said.

"Yep."

"His grandpa owns a cattle spread in Wyoming, but the boy's not interested in staying down on the ranch. Wants to travel, see the world a bit, so I invited him to come over."

"I'm sure you will enjoy Australia and this part of the world . . ., Mr. Adams."

Tomas appeared to have no idea who he was talking to. Miss Lorette's work was truly amazing.

"Thanks. I'm hungry . . ., Uncle. How are the steaks here?"

"Not bad, but I want to introduce you to one of the most mouth-watering lamb dishes you'll ever experience," Tangata said coming up behind him. Looking at the stack of chips in front of the young man he said, "Obviously, you're buying." then whispering, "Leave a nice tip."

The pit boss issued a receipt for Philippe's winnings after both he and the dealer received a hundred dollars each. Tangata was right. He was living a charmed life.

"It has been a pleasure meeting you, Mr. Adams," Tomas said.

"Likewise. Good luck with the table," Philippe said as they left.

"Would the gentlemen desire wine with dinner?" the sommelier asked after the Maître d' personally escorted them to a table along the far wall.

Before Tangata could even respond Philippe said, "I saw some people having sea bass."

"Yes. A superb dish prepared with braised

endive and balsamic vinegar."

"I haven't had bass since I was little. That requires Côtes du Roussillon. Do you have that?"

"Excellent choice, Monsieur. We have several vintages. May I suggest 2004?"

"1997?"

The gentleman's left eyebrow almost shot into his thick hairline as a great smile broke across his face. "As a matter of fact, we do," he said, and a few minutes later returned with Philippe's order. With the cork's pop, a memory flowed back from the nether depths of his mind.

"I remember," Philippe said as his eyes glistened. "Papa instructed me very carefully in wines. At evening meals, I was the wine waiter. I know what you're thinking. Yes, we dressed for that. More than just a bow tie. Evening dining was a formal time."

Tangata laughed. It was loud and sincere. "You're catching on, and with that expertise order on."

A tomato bisque was set before them just as Tomas strolled up to their table.

"Excuse the interruption, but I was wondering if Mr. Adams was planning on returning to the tables this evening?"

Philippe looked at Tangata, a touch of panic in his eyes.

"Yes," Tangata said. "Why?"

"It was very interesting, but after your nephew left, the golden glow disappeared as well."

Philippe looked at him curiously.

"That means the table went cold," Tangata said to Philippe. "We'll be back after dinner, say, an hour, or so?"

Tomas smiled. "Thank you. Enjoy your meal."

"You know Tomas?" Philippe whispered after the man left to take a table further across the room.

"We've met. Your uncle was importing a shipload of drugs into the region seven years ago. Tomas was head of security when the ship . . . let's just say, it developed a hole and sank. I gave him a lift to shore."

"With the *Adrianne*?"

"Ah-h, no. Another boat. Something that sits low in the water. Very low. Now, what do you suggest for an appetizer?"

After dinner the two exited onto a long veranda where Tongata pulled a cigar from his inside, jacket pocket and lit up.

"I didn't know you smoked?"

"After a wonderful meal like that, there is nothing like a good cigar, don't you agree Tomas?" They encountered him again standing at the banister looking out over the city.

"Definitely," he said, turning to greet them.

Philippe had yet to take up that "pleasure." Another memory escaped captivity. His papa enjoyed a cigar with a glass of wine after dinner. Whatever these two smoked was mildly aromatic with hints of cedar and various spices, much like what his papa smoked, not like the obnoxiously pungent aroma of burning rubber and gym socks his uncle incinerated.

"Would you care to join us?" Tomas said, offering him a slender, nearly black stick.

"No, thanks, Mr. Bonnell. I only chew, and then only where I can spit without carrying a bottle."

Tomas wrinkled his nose. Tongata's tummy bounced slightly with a chuckle.

"Did your papa enjoy a good cigar after dinner?" he asked.

"No, but grandpa sure does. Heads off down by the corrals. Says the cows complain a lot less than grandma." In truth, his mama enjoyed the aroma as they sat quietly on the veranda overlooking the ocean, holding hands and talking quietly. They enjoyed one another's company.

Tangata was secretly impressed with the young man's poise and attention to Tomas' fishing expedition, picking up on the tenses used in seemingly unobtrusive questions. There was no way for him to know this was the boy Rousseau sought, or was there? Tomas seemed to study Philippe with a microscopic eye for detail, as was his forte. Tangata chalked up Tomas' curiosity as to who would hang out with a man that nearly killed him, and then turned around to rescue him from a most unpleasant end.

The three hung out for several hours in the casino, actually Tomas stayed close to Philippe as the young man continued his winning ways at the Black Jack table. The two did very well as Philippe overcame initial apprehension.

Back in their suite, Philippe loosened his tie, and flopped onto the sofa, obviously exhausted. Tangata handed him a one-third shot glass from a tall, slender bottle from behind the bar with a Bushmill Malt 21 label. This was the young man's first taste of real whiskey. It had the faint scent of spice and orange as the amber liquid slid smoothly down his throat leaving a sweet, dry taste with a faintly liquorice aftertaste. As it settled into his stomach, a warm sensation swelled up to soothe his exhausted body.

"You did well with Tomas," Tangata said, downing a similar quantity and pouring another and reading the label. "One of the finest true Irish whiskeys. They distilled this one about the time you were born."

Philippe slipped the remaining liquor to enjoy the flavors. "I was tied in a knot the whole night, watching how he phrased questions. I don't think I slipped up."

"He's very good at walking a fine line and phrasing questions to extract what he wants to know. I couldn't have handled him better," Tangata replied, pouring Philippe another drink. "Do you know that the word whiskey is Gaelic for "water of life?"

"I sneaked some, once. A friend and me. I thought I'd never be able to breathe again. It didn't taste anything like this."

"If it's one thing the Irish know, it's whiskey."

Not long after siphoning the last drop from the glass, the tension totally dissolved. He vaguely remember going to bed, but a light rap on his door the next morning brought him awake to burrowed out from beneath beneath a pile of cloud-like bedding. Wandering out in his boxers, Philippe was greeted by Lorette.

"Time for our daily date," she said, eying him as if he were a blank canvas and envisioning the possibilities. "Go bath up, then you can down some brekkle while I refresh a few things." As the bathroom door closed, she called out, "Would you like a tat? I do a very nice job with new paints that last for weeks, even with repeated sprinkles."

Mid-morning of the fifth day, the two boldly walked past two men loitering about on the Half Moon pier. No doubt, they were syndicate. Philippe thought to have seen one of them before. They stared at him for a moment before turning away unconcerned.

Sporting a blue headband, sleeveless tank top, shorts, and flip-flops, he hoped they got a good look at the tattoo of two dolphins swimming around the yin-yang symbol on his left bicep. Lorette said he had perfect skin texture and coloring for the paint to work. He was honestly considering making it permanent. Boarding the yacht, he fired up the engines, eased it toward the breakwater, and set a course for home as Tongata lounged atop the cabin and watched.

"I wonder why those guys were on the peer? Do you think Tomas recognized me and they were supposed to nab me?" he said.

"He wouldn't send only two men. Not for you. It'd be an entire army. You've got quite a reputation, and you're with me," Tangata said, getting up, removing a pistol from the small of his back, and putting it in a water-proof compartment next to the starboard wheel.

Chapter 13

The Navigator

Once into open water, Philippe piloted the yacht as his guardian stretched out on the recessed bench next to the hatch leading below. They talked, or rather Philippe talked about the experiences and feelings while meditating in the mountains above Laramie. The comments were in response to questions, Tangata's way to probe deeper into the young man's inner psyche, and help bring it into focus. Philippe came to understand that those things which at the time seemed insignificant and meaningless often held supernal implications. Then the conversation took a sudden switch.

"So, how do you feel about your experience at Evelien's?" Tangata asked.

Philippe knew exactly what Tangata was getting at, and it wasn't about being chased and hiding from his uncle's goons. "I wondered when you'd come around to that."

Tangata didn't respond. Whenever he asked a question, it was for a reason and he didn't expend further effort to explain. There's the question, now answer it.

Philippe looked sideways at lots of water, looked upward at a Frigate bird circling overhead, then at the man. Letting out a deep breath he asked, "Do we have to?"

"No."

"But you think it's important."

"Maybe."

Philippe hated when Tangata took a blasé approach. There must be something important or he wouldn't broach the subject. "Where should I start?" he asked.

"Wherever."

"The girl, Christie, hid me in a secret place behind the wall, a space between closets facing each adjacent room. It had an air vent to each room along the floor. I think it was more for seeing what was going on than for air circulation. If something went south in one room, a person could hide there or exit into the next room. There was also a ladder leading up and down. I don't know where it went going up, probably the roof. Going down came out on the ground floor. I used it a couple times to visit the lavatory.

"That's where she put me when my uncle's goons first searched the house—the hidie, not the labatory. The guy looked in the closet, under the bed, in the lavatory, and walked within a meter and didn't realize I was there. Christie was smart. She told me to stay put, which proved right. He made a surprise return expecting if she had me hidden I'd come out."

"Were you scared?"

Philippe paused to think a moment. "No. No, I

wasn't. Tense, but I felt in control. I had the pistol you gave me."

"Were you prepared to use it?"

"Yes."

"On him or yourself."

Philippe startled at the question. He'd not thought about that. "Suicide is a sin against God."

"So, you'd shoot your way out if necessary?"

"Yes."

"With how many shots?"

"Two."

"Then what?"

"I have my hands, and feet, and anything I can grab." Philippe paused. "Yeah, and his gun, and anyone else's gun. I will not return to my uncle alive and he'll be missing a few of his hoods in the process."

"Their type are easily replaced. So you would go out like a blazing meteor?"

"I'd survive, somehow."

"With that mindset . . . and your luck . . ., no doubt."

Philippe then saw what Tangata was aiming at. Survival is a mental attitude, and there are options available. Maybe not many, but some, and it was good to consider them.

"So, Luther missed you," Tangata said.

"Luther? You know him?" Philippe was stunned a moment that Tangata knew so much detail. "Okay, enough. You drive me crazy sometimes. No, a lot of times. You know stuff like you were there. How?"

"Evelien told me."

Philippe suddenly felt very stupid, missing the obvious.

"I know Luther because our paths crossed a time or two, although he doesn't realize it. He's one of Tomas' men."

"Well then, you know everything so why ask?"

Tangata tilted his head down as if looking over a pair of glasses and stared back expecting him to continue without answering.

"Alright," Philippe said with a sigh. "Anyway, Christie felt I should stay put, and she went to work as if nothing was out of the ordinary until morning. Her last customer was one of goons hovering around outside. Probably another way to check out the place."

"Yes. At least you got some rest in that hiding place."

"Not likely!"

"You watched?"

"Yes, I watched. It was bloody hard not to," Philippe countered, feeling frustrated and embarrassed. "I'd never seen stuff like that. Well, once, but only briefly." Philippe suddenly went silent.

"And?" Tangata continued to prod.

"And that lead to doing that which is prohibited by God. For a long time I thought that was why my parents died. God was punishing me."

"So you've said," Tangata responded flatly.

"So Father Josteu said."

"Ah-h, a man of intellectual tact, spouting conjured gibberish to control the masses."

"You don't like God, do you?" Philippe now prodded.

"God and I have an understanding of one another that transcends priestly intrigues."

Philippe paused to consider. His parents had been Catholic, more than the twice-a-year, in name only sort. They attended Mass regularly, planning business trips to include Sundays near a chapel. When they couldn't, time was set aside early Sunday morning to pray. Family meals never began without prayer, and every night when he went to bed, either his mama, or papa, or both knelt with him by the bed for prayer.

"Is not religion given to us by God to provide structure and guidance so that we may be like him?" Philippe challenged.

"Perhaps. For the weak or lazy, structure and direction are necessary. But what good is that structure when it destroys?"

"Religion is to build and strengthen a person. How can it destroy?" Philippe asked.

Tangata replied by arching an eyebrow, asking the silent question, "How?"

Philippe thought back. He and his friend happened across two guests engaged in intercourse. His friend was aroused. Philippe, too. They retreated to their favorite, secret place by the rock protruding into the sea. Philippe's friend masturbated. He'd protested, but the argument and urges were too powerful to overcome.

All his short life, Philippe heard about the sin of self-stimulation. It bothered him. He confessed to Father Josteu and the priest railed on him. That confessional flooded back as if taking place at that very moment as the priest's words screamed in his mind.

"What you have done is a grave misuse of the procreative powers God has bestowed upon men and women. When it is deliberately set in motion and consummated without achieving the natural, divinely intended purpose that is a serious sin. That shows genuine lack of love for God. You have revolted against God and turned your heart away from Him, and shown contempt for everything He and your parents taught you.

"You have committed a mortal sin with full knowledge that such acts are prohibited by God for a reason and you did it deliberately. You have been

baptized which makes it all the more grave. You have removed yourself from the State of Grace which denies you the reward of Heaven. Should you die with this mortal sin on your soul you shall go to Hell."

"He said that?" Tangata asked softly. "And you were what, thirteen? It would have been kinder to shoot you in the head."

"I was working on absolution," Philippe said, tears flowing freely down his cheeks. "I confessed my sin to Father Josteu and God. He insisted I spend a month with him doing penance, but God apparently was not satisfied. After the funeral, Father Josteu said I was being punished. That He took away my parents. That God allowed two people to die just to punish me for my transgression. It made no sense."

Tangata could see the anger, consternation, and confusion in the boy's eyes. "So, you and God are on the outs?"

"The god Father Josteu spoke of seemed heartless and cruel. When I was at Gonzaga and in the Burke home, that was not the same god. That god was understanding and loving. I eventually spoke to a priest at Gonzaga about it.

A picture of that meeting came clearly in his mind. Leaning forward in his chair, the priest looked straight into the boy's watery eyes and said, "Philippe, when you confessed your sin, God forgave you right then. That you have done penance and refrained from further acts has only added to your stature in His eyes. Your parents did not die because of what you did, and Father Josteu was mistaken. I regret saying that about a fellow priest, but the Holy Father has made God's feelings on this very clear. Your parents died because of your uncle's greed. For him there will be no easy road to forgiveness."

"In that I totally agree. Issue closed," Tangata said. "But, returning to my original question . . ."

"How can religion destroy? When manipulated and distorted, and used for man's gain, not God's." Philippe answered.

Tangata's head nodded slightly in agreement before continuing to prod, "So, after that thorough explanation of what constitutes sin and its consequences you eventually ran off and spent a couple nights in a whorehouse to be educated in the finer points of fornication, and then hopped in bed with a prostitute."

Philippe cringed at Tangata's coarse description. "It wasn't exactly my idea. I have this adversity to being killed. I worried about that and told Christie so. There wasn't anywhere else for me to hide. She put a sheet between us, but that didn't matter. That first night I was so exhausted I fell asleep. Not what a *normal* guy would do, huh?" Philippe said, making quote marks with his fingers in the air around normal.

"In that instance, exhaustion was quite normal. What about the second night?"

"I didn't watch. I turned my back to the air vent and tried to sleep."

"And?"

"Do you know how much noise people make when they are having sex?"

"Another sleepless night, eh?"

"Christie is a very pretty girl and very smart. She recognized I was worked up and offered to help, but that would violate God's laws. The priest at Gonzaga instructed me about having sex outside the marital covenant. Yes, Christie and I lay in the same bed, but we again had a sheet between us . . ., but I couldn't sleep and tossed. It interfered with her rest. I felt so very sorry about that and determined to force myself to lay quiet. She went to the lavatory. When she returned she slipped beneath the sheet, moved close, and put a hand on my chest."

"Ah-h, the moment of decision. God or the devil," Tangata said, stripping away all the covers and getting to the crux of what he was driving toward.

"Actually, there was a great argument in my head. When I was living with the Burke's we watched cartoons. There was this one with Donald Duck. He had a little devil sitting on one shoulder telling him, yes, go ahead and do something bad, and a little angel on the other shoulder saying, no. Those two were in my head yelling, No. Yes. No. Yes. No."

"And yes won."

Philippe lowered his head and admitted painfully, "I listened to yes. I tried to do what was right. Yes was just too loud. When she touched me everything went so fast from that moment. I wanted to fight, not to commit another mortal sin. Ha! Fat chance. I jumped in with both feet and exploded like a bloody volcano."

"Then what?"

"I never thought to feel that way. A warm, relaxed feeling overcame me, as if floating. It was wonderful. Master Yamamoto said such feelings could be achieved through meditation. I never experienced it, or thought I hadn't."

"But you had."

"Yes, just not so intense. Then, as I lay there in her bed, the memory came back of that time on the beach with my friend. I held back at first, fighting with myself over whether it was right or wrong. When we stepped into the ocean to clean off, my head was spinning. It felt like a balloon filled with helium. I spread my arms and lay back onto the surf. I was flying. Free. The waves washed me to shore and I lay there, flying. Then it was like my mind separated and floated up to look down. I was lying on my back, arms and legs spread. I was smiling."

"You enjoyed it."

"Yeah . . ., and when Father Josteu unloaded on me I understood I was being punished not so much for the sin . . ."

"As for enjoying it!"

"Yes."

"And when you lay with Christie? When it was over?"

"She lay next to me, playing a finger over my lips and smiled. I smiled back. I didn't resist. Instead, I plummet headlong down another path of sin. I knew better, I failed to resist, and worst yet . . ., damn! I enjoyed it. Now what'll happen? I should have seen a priest and confessed before we left, but I'm scared, Tangata. Will God forgive me a second time?" Philippe looked panicked.

"Well, here we are, safe, sound, and no one's died. It's a war, Philippe, between good and evil. Calling "King's-X" to one's killers isn't part of the game. There is no free card allowing one to pass death and go directly to a church.

"Any time evil can blur or confuse good it wins a victory. You need to determine what is good and what is evil. Take killing those two men who were going to use you as a shark biscuit, for instance. In one setting God says killing another is a sin, in another He will sanction it. You have been as much a victim of man's ideologies as when you were being tossed upon Triton's waves in that little boat. You have to map out what is good and what is evil, and figure out how to wage the war."

"Who do I talk to to learn the differences, or do I have to struggle through life to find it one piece at a time?"

Tangata reached down and hefted a rather sizable book. Unlike all the others in his library that were hard bound or paperback, this was covered in soft leather. He handed it to the young man.

"The Bible?"

"The Bible."

"But you said . . ."

"What I said was that niggling men attempt to control the masses, spouting gibberish while waving that book in the air and claiming what they say comes from God. And just how many people read it, I mean really read it without preconceived coloring, to see if what they have been told is true? God gave that book to Moses. It contains the words God dictated to His prophets. Look what God has to say for yourself instead of listening to someone else's interpretation. It won't be easy. It will take time and effort, but you will gradually come to have an understanding of God . . . and with God."

Philippe stared at the book in his hands.

Tangata continued. "You're concerned God will condemn you for enjoying the pleasures of a woman outside the marriage covenant. I can tell you what God has said on that, but it's my interpretation and would be no different than all the others who spout religion. You study up and see what God has to say about that. If it's okay, your free and clear. If not, find out what it's going to take to make amends.

"Oh, and another thing. Your parents gave you the greatest tool to understanding what you hold in your hands—prayer. Read, try to understand what is said, then talk to God about it. None of that formalized poppycock. Talk to Him as if you were talking to me."

Philippe stared at Tangata. Never once had the man indicated religious beliefs. Not once. Was this the same person?

Tangata cleared his throat and began softly, "When my wife and son were killed, I put the blame on myself because of something I did. I was pretty indoctrinated like you. I was distraught and ready to join them. Then a good friend intervened and set me straight. I grieve their loss, but they died because of a mistake I made in the line of duty, not because God willed it in retaliation for my having committed a sin. I hate people because of what they did to me at the time —their stares, their whispers, their condescending, empty, accusing words.

"Life is a learning experience. It was Fred Burke, in fact, who told me we learn line upon line, precept upon precept. That's how we grow and understand what this thing we call life is really all about, and how to navigate through it. In that book you will learn what things God has asked us to do . . ., and refrain from doing, and more importantly, why. God is not some white-whiskered dude in a toga ready to throw lightning bolts. He's someone with incredible love and patience and when we screw up, He's ready to show us how to get back on the right track. That's what Father James in Spokane was getting at."

Philippe startled. "How did you know his name. I never mentioned that priest's name."

"Father James and I shared some lengthy philosophical discussions over a few bottles of wine before he decided to go off the deep end into professional religion."

"You've arranged for people to just kind of pop into my life. Did you take me to Spokane so Father James could set me straight about how I view myself and my parents' death?"

"That actually was an accident. I wasn't aware Jimmy moved there, but truthfully? . . . I would have found someone to have that discussion. When I decided to get involved in your life, I wanted opportunity to come knocking at your door. It's what I would have done for my own son," Tangata revealed.

"So you arranged for Master Michael to be my bodyguard."

"You needed a bodyguard and to continue your education. There simply wasn't anyone else qualified, other than myself."

"But you left me on my own in Laramie."

"Not entirely."

"Oh. Just out of curiosity who was it . . . No! Not . . ."

"Yes."

"But she was just a college student like me."

"Sandy is twenty-seven years-old. Shaping out to be a pretty good operative."

"A pretty good actress, too." Philippe began to sound sour.

"It wasn't all acting. She was a sports therapist and she did need some training in International politics. Like I said, the best education is often where you least expect it. As for your relationship, you're easy to like. If you'd been a couple years older and she hadn't been so focused on becoming an operative, you would have lost your virginity a lot sooner."

"And the Burkes?"

"I knew Fred Burke in the old days. He was a crutch after my family died. After what happened, he wanted out, but one doesn't really leave the agency."

"He's an agent, like you?"

"No. He is an analyst. They run a safe house, on the side."

"And I couldn't go on a road trip with just anyone, so Clarence, too?

"Yes."

Philippe calmed. "Did you know I was coming

here."

"Yes."

"How? You didn't put a thing in me like they do in the movies to track my movements?"

"In you? No." When Tangata stopped chuckling he said, "Not in you . . . on you."

"On me? Of course, Father's watch."

"Nope." Tangata looked at the young man's feet.

"The friendship bracket? It's a tracking devise?"

"Pretty neat, 'ey? Light weight, totally innocent looking, and only needs a battery change twice-a-year. Get caught, they might take the watch, but a friendship bracelet . . .? Never notice it."

"I almost screwed up everything you've done. Guess I was pretty lucky getting cornered in that bordello?"

"Philippe, you had a shadow from the time I left you in Salt Lake City. Your computer and phone were monitored, so we knew when you booked the flight, and there was someone with you all the way here. When things went south, taking you to Eve's was no coincidence. It was the only place to hide you. Because of Master Yamamoto's training, I knew how you'd react and had all the doors barred except that one leading into Evelien's."

"Don't tell me Aunty Eve's an agent."

Tangata smiled.

"What if I had gone into another room? Would any of them had hid me?"

"Oh, hell, Philippe, you might as well know. Everyone in the brothel are agents. Do you know a better way to get information? To my notion, Christie just happens to be the brightest . . . and prettiest one there."

"I feel like having been a marionette."

"When I discovered that disk, it was enough the

authorities needed to start bringing your uncle down. You weren't necessary for the world to continue, but like I said, you're a likable kid. I took on the job of keeping you alive, and believe me, it hasn't been easy."

"So, where were you the whole time I was running from uncle's men?"

Tangata handed him a hundred dollar bill. "Driving your taxi."

Philippe's jaw unhinged.

Chapter 14

Revelations

As the calender marked the footsteps of man's history in countdown fashion from the time of Adam and Eve, it suddenly did a flip-flop to begin moving upward into the A.D.'s and toward the future. It was at that momentous occasion a Roman military commander, naturalist, and author named Gaius Plinius Secundus expressed something Philippe completely understood. "Home is where the heart is." Seated cross-legged on the bow of the *Adrianne* the young man stared forward, waiting to glimpse the place he felt in his breast to be home.

Born and raised on a small island in the Coral Sea somewhat east-northeast of New Caledonia, that should have been home. No longer. There were a few memories of those times, bits and pieces, and things told him. Those childhood years should have been treasured for a lifetime. Instead, they were blotchy and he understood why. Thanks to other people's warped philosophies he had been lead to believe his actions responsible for the death of his parents, a nightmare that invaded his mind whether the sun shown or not. He learned that wasn't true, but once a person has been cut that deeply, a scar remains.

In truth, whenever Philippe thought of that tropical paradise it resurrected the heart-searing memory of his parents' death, thus the island became a hated place and he wanted nothing to do with it—a place to be forgotten. Sustaining a blow to the head, his mind grasped the opportunity to respond to that wish and bury the nightmare. Unfortunately, a lot of good disappeared when the vault was sealed.

For Philippe, life began upon awaking on a remote, volcanic island. The hermit who pulled him from the raging sea and nursed him back to physical health attempted to help regain those memories. Some returned, while others remained hidden in the deep recesses of his mind, not because those mental pictures hadn't escaped captivity, Philippe didn't want to remember them. The island of his birth would never be referred to as home again. His heart resided about as far from everything except, perhaps, that place one dropped off the earth.

Residing at the University of Wyoming in Laramie, Philippe consoled himself to the cold, colder and coldest, snow, snowier and a half meter of the white stuff overnight! Bundled to the hilt, he literally plowed the knee-deep powder on the way to classes. Every time he looked out the dormitory door, just before launching into the frigid, windy blasts, he thought of the towering, volcanic peak cloaked with an emerald garland, the turquoise lagoon, and gentle, warm breezes. The seeds of homesickness awaited the time and good soil in which to sprout into full bloom.

Philippe came to enjoy and appreciate Wyoming, Utah was milder and marginally better, but only Tangata's occasional visits made life at those places tolerable. When that contact stretched so thin that it might break, homesickness flourished, reason became a weed. Philippe just had to return home, to breathe the wonderful, salty air, walk barefoot on the pink sand beach, feel the invigorating warmth of the sun, and slap a few mosquitoes. That impulsive decision almost proved his demise, but that was the only course for what ailed him. Now looking out at the dots of emerald islands set upon an azure canvas, he knew the events of the last few days had been worth it.

During that five-year absence, he changed physically inside and out. So had the man to whom he owed so much. From the first day he awoke on the volcanic island after literally tossed ashore, their interactions were interesting. The man had sought to be a recluse, disdain for people vocal. At first, he spoke little. When he did, the conversation tended to be short and to the point. No wasted words. True feelings were expressed through action. During that absence, Tangata also changed in that aspect, at least with Philippe.

While one took their turn piloting the *Angelina,* the other sat atop the cabin so to talk. The man asked all sorts of questions about school and trips taken during vacations. Tangata needn't have asked. He already knew the answers, but because Philippe had shown a penchant and ability to write poetry, the questions were framed to elicit feelings and impressions that had not occurred to the young man at the time.

Over time, centimeter by centimeter, Philippe learned a few things about this man who had yet to share his true identity. Islanders called him Tangata Aiwaiwee, man of mystery. A few, very few, called him Jimmy. That was actually part of a pen name, James Tuskin Elam, but who was he really? Keeping that identity secret seemed to be a game to protect cherished privacy, a way of "fooling and confusing the obnoxiously nosy." There was more, a good deal more.

After orchestrating Philippe's disappearance, the question was not so much who was this man as what. In some way, Tangata must be involved with the American CIA. What else could account for the seemingly endless resources and connections, and things he could conjure?

Philippe learned to appreciate solitude, too. Achieving that special time was first learned when Master Yamamoto taught him the art of meditation, especially following an intensive martial arts workout. The noise and hubbub of humanity could be blocked out as the inner world of serenity and reflection eased to the forefront. Philippe went to the University gym at least three times a week, working up a cascading sweat before retreating to a corner to meditate. In those moments it felt as if his mind rose above the temporal body to see and thus understand more clearly what had been encased in the blur of activity ever swirling about a person's life.

When the snow began to clear from Pole Mountain east of Laramie, he loaded a backpack with books, paper, and pen. Mounting the Marauder, he'd find a place with no more distractions than a bird, squirrel, or passing deer. Within a couple hours, he could study and internalize school lessons. Seated on the yacht's bow, gently bobbing across the water afforded a similar opportunity.

The rhythmic, almost hypnotic up and down motion, the panoramic feast of water, clouds, and islands helped clear Philippe's mind. Memories resurfaced, mostly ones already restored, but occasionally something new appeared from a childhood lost. Those were not shunned, simply relegated to another doorless vault labeled "Nice to know." This time, however, Philippe's thoughts focused on the man at the helm. How many times had he asked, 'Who is he? Really. A hermit? A writer? CIA?' Yes, but a nagging feeling said there was something more, much more.

The man who would not reveal his true name remained one very large question mark. For someone professing to dislike, even despise people, he certainly knew a lot of folk among the islands and abroad, reputable and less so. The way they so easily collaborated was mystifying. The way Philippe's first disappearance was orchestrated from his uncle's omnipotent eyes, so complex, so many facets smoothly coming together as if having unlimited resources at his command. That seemed beyond the CIA myth.

And this time! Once again, this man tapped into those vast resources. Could the unthinkably impossible be true? Could the stories he wrote be fact, not fiction? There was little doubt this man was some kind of secret agent, something more than CIA. The prospects were titillating, the complexity almost maddening. Philippe walked back to the stern, sat on the compartment, dangling his feet, and stared at him.

"You want to know who I really am," the man said. That was another aspect of this enigma, the ability to read minds, just like the Aborigine chauffeur in Brisbane. "Okay, conjure up some sandwiches and I'll tell you a bedtime story . . . And don't forget the beer," he called out, as Philippe was half way to the galley.

Ten minutes later Philippe set a stack of sandwiches between them and several bottles of Tasmanian Cascade stout. Tangata took a big bite out of a sandwich and chewed while checking the compass and sail. Finally, he said, "Okay, this is a story about a kid I knew. For reasons that will become obvious, his name was Nebraska."

Chapter 15

The Creed

I am a more elite soldier.
I will not fail my comrades.
I will meet the enemies of my country.
I will fight on and complete the mission,
though I be the lone survivor.'

Snatches of the Ranger Creed whirled through Nebraska's mind as bullets whizzed past it. *Though I be the lone survivor. Well, that could be a distinct possibility,* he thought, squeezing off a three round burst from his M4 carbine. Not a random shot. The target was running forward. It fell and rolled to a stop. A trailing comrade joined the first with a second burst. Nebraska's cool accuracy even in the dim light of a nighttime fire was almost legendary.

"Lone survivor, hell!" he muttered to himself

while turning the corner of another bombed-out building to be met head on by another attacker.

Nebraska operated on instinct honed by intensive training. He was an Army Ranger and that's how they survive. The rifle butt lashed out, the contact slamming the attacker against a wall to crumple lifeless upon the ground.

"What the hell are kids doing carrying guns?" he growled, moving on.

School, in particular high school, had been dismal; the fire of earlier achievements doused with the death his father at the ripe age of thirty-eight of Deep Vein Thrombosis, doctoreze for a blood clot. His dad played flag football with him and some cousins on a wonderful, fall, Sunday afternoon. Late the next morning he was taken from work by ambulance to the hospital. A month later he was dead. Nebraska was all of fourteen.

Life spiraled downhill from that point. Nearing graduation, a school counselor tried a last-ditched effort to help. "You're a bright kid, but you're headed to a dead end with your attitude," he warned.

The kid slouched in the straight back, wood chair. He always slouched before authority now. The only answer was the shrug of his shoulders. All that interested him in school were sports—football, track, swimming. The only reason he achieved a 2.5 grade point? That was the minimum required to participate in sports.

"Normally I encourage kids with your brains to go onto college. I don't think that's your desire."

Nebraska lifted his head, briefly glaring at the counselor as if to say, You got that right.

The man pushed a brochure across the desk. "Maybe you should consider going into the military. Recruiters will be here day after tomorrow."

Ensign Myers, the Navy's smoothing talking recruiter, aroused some interest in a military career. However, it was necessary to go to the MEPS center in Omaha. That's military jargon for Military Entrance Processing Station. Taking a bus to the center in the next town the evening before, he and a large group from heartland America congregated in a hotel. Not the Hilton, but it wasn't bad. Typically withdrawn, he planned to spend the evening watching TV until an effervescent girl coaxed him into a game of chess.

"I better warn you, I'm the chess champ in my school," she teased.

He liked her smile and easy-going manner, and hated beating her so quickly. The look of surprise on her face was like a precious gem, so pure. So was her contrived pout.

"You're pretty good," she said. "Wanna try that again?"

"Not mad?" he asked.

"It's only a game."

He beat her again and then offered to buy a Coke. A hallow gesture. The stuff was free. So they sat in the lounge talking. That was his first ever date with a girl, if one stretched the idea of a date far enough.

"Where'd you learn to play like that?" she asked.

"I play a lot of computer games. Strategy games mostly."

"Are you going into the Navy?

"Don't know. Haven't decided."

"Know what you want to focus on?"

"No." Nebraska's only focus was winning, whatever game was being played.

"I want to be a nurse. Can't afford school so I'll do it through the back door."

"I'd like to be your first patient." He felt so at ease with this girl it was like talking to a sister.

"Well take your time getting shot. It'll take me a couple years to be of any use to you."

The following morning started early, really early. The line of recruits stumbled into the mess hall for a hearty breakfast. He'd never had more than a piece of toast and glass of milk in years, but the facility director said to eat hearty, they'd have a tough day ahead. She was right.

First thing on the agenda was the ASVAB test. (Armed Services Vocational Aptitude Battery) Oh, how the military loves acronyms. Then it was on to the physical. Most of the guys were his age. The city kids were singularly soft, tending to flabby, and universally out of shape. The farm kids were a lot healthier looking. Nebraska was thankful for sports, more than just looking fit.

After the ASVAB came the job search as representatives from the various military branches pitched their service. He initially considered the Navy, but they only offered to teach him about electronics and put him in a sub. Captain Donovich from the Army took the recruit aside during a break.

"What do you think so far, recruit?"

"I don't know," he answered.

"Hey, I just saw your test scores. You got a ninety-eight! A ninety-eight for cryin' out loud. I know generals that couldn't pass near that high. We need guys like you in the Army."

"Does a ninety-eight mean I won't be sent to the front lines and used for target practice?" Nebraska had this deliberately sarcastic streak.

"You scared of going to war?"

"No. Kinda hard to avoid these days. I'd just like, well, do something more meaningful than being gun fodder."

The Captain chuckled softly and stroked the corners of his generous mouth with one hand. He was salivating like a hungry wolf about to corner a tasty morsel. "Tell you what. You're not there yet. I think you can be. We'll see how basic goes, but you appear to have what it takes to be a Ranger."

A tingling sensation pulsed through the kid's breast while taking the oath and signing delayed enlistment papers. Four months after graduating somewhere below the middle of his class, Nebraska was dropped into boot camp at Ft. Sill, Oklahoma, a lovely corner in the Garden of Hell. Several weeks from graduation the Company Commander called him in.

"You are a damn fine recruit, son. I see you've expressed an interest in the Ranger program. Think you're good enough?"

"Yes, sir," he was pretty confident in himself by this time. Boot camp can do that . . . or break you.

"So do I. So do I," the captain said.

Ranger program! Yes! When his father died the fire in Nebraska's heart had died, too, except for a tiny spark the Army found and fanned back to life. From basic he went directly to Ft. Benning, Georgia and the Army Basic Airborne school. If anyone thought basic was tough, this proved it to have been a cakewalk.

First, a person has to demonstrate how smart they are to get into the program. They weren't taking just anybody. In basic, a person had to prove how tough they were physically. That's where all those flabby recruits were turned into muscled jocks. After a battery of brainteasers came the APFT (Army Physical Fitness Test). Everyone passed as far as he heard. Some not great, but they passed.

That test requires push-ups, sit-ups, and a two-mile run in that order with ten minutes rest between tests. To pass, a recruit has to do a minimum of thirty-five push-ups in two minutes. Pretty pathetic after all those weeks of practice in boot camp. Likewise, the minimum sit-ups in two minutes is forty-seven. The two-mile run only requires a finish time of sixteen minutes thirty-six seconds, practically a walk.

Nebraska lifted the eyebrows of the testers. That was part of what the Company Commander alluded to. He did ninety push-ups, eight-one sit-ups, and ran the course in twelve minutes fifty-four seconds. That put his composite score twenty-three points over a perfect 300, thirty-six hours after being down with a flu bug.

At 175 pounds with a thirty-two inch waist, he carried thirteen percent body fat. Other factors came into play as well. Nebraska was not just strong, but mentally agile, and by this time focused. Perfect Ranger material.

However, there were more hurdles to overcome. The first was AIT (Advanced Individual Training). He set sights on Counterintelligence. Of course, they slipped in more physical tests, like swimming fifteen meters fully clothed, with boots, pack, and rifle, and running five miles in under forty minutes. High school sports provided the foundation to succeed. Don't get the idea this kid was some kind of superman. He was one in a class of supermen.

Next was Airborne School at Ft. Benning, Georgia. He wondered what it would be like jumping from a perfectly good airplane. The first time was scary, evidenced on everyone's face, but like ants, they followed the leader. Touching ground that first time, he stood, jumped up and down like a little kid yelling, "Yes!" at the top of his lungs. He was addicted.

The move to Ranger School was a matter of hauling his gear to a different part of the base. That included three weeks in the thick forests of central Georgia, three weeks of mountaineering, and tactics. Three weeks in the swamps of Florida was the closest thing to real hell imaginable. Mosquitoes, humidity, and a menagerie of nightmarish critters seen eyeball to eyeball was par for the course. You've never experience real thrill until a Coral snake slithers across your rifle barrel while lying flat in six inches of swamp grass.

The physical toll during these nine weeks was intense with high levels of fight-or-flight stress, sleep deprivation, and unending physical strain. The body could not recover naturally from such physical and mental abuse. What could? Dehydration, heatstroke, fractures, ligament, tendon and muscles tears, swollen hands and feet, cuts, and insect, spider, and wildlife bites, not to mention an entire medical text of other things. However, he and others endured and survived. He not only survived, but did so at the top of the class earning him the rank of E-5, Sergeant.

The first day of school, the lead instructor told the class, "Search your heart and your psyche. Rangers are warriors. Rangers are trained to face highly dangerous and stressful combat actions. Ranger training requires the utmost in courage, physical stamina, and self-discipline." That's what he said, and he was right. Oh, how he was right! And Nebraska loved every moment.

Perhaps that's why a brief respite at home after graduating left him feeling uneasy and eager to get back to his unit and their first assignment in Afghanistan. Two weeks after arriving, his company was assigned an outpost near the Pakistan boarder. It had been a relatively quiet area. Too quiet. They were to stir around and see what was really happening. The Taliban didn't wait.

Nebraska's Delta Company arrived at the remnants of a mud-brick village near an anemic, dirty-looking river late in the afternoon to reinforce Bravo Company and a company of Afghan soldiers. Nebraska's squad was to take the mid watch on the south perimeter. That allowed time to catch a quick nap. Curling up in the dark corner of what had been a house before the roof and one wall were blown out during fighting a year earlier, his team mate finished tidying up his mess kit.

Slipping quickly into a foggy haze, his mind settled on a training incident at Ft. Benning. The instructors went to great pains to re-create realism as grenades exploded and live bullets flew overhead. The dreamtime was so real he actually thought to hear the whine of bullets, thud of grenades, and shouts of soldiers.

"We're under attack!"

Of course we're under attack you idiot. That's . . ., he thought, then came full awake. It was a real attack! At that moment, Corporal Jackson grunted and toppled back against the one good wall as two, black forms entered the doorway. Nebraska saw the flash of their weapons. They hadn't seen him. They wouldn't as his 9 mm pistol greeted their arrival.

A quick check confirmed Jackson was dead. Without a second thought, Nebraska snatched up his carbine, extra ammo belt, helmet and leapt through a hole in the back of the wall and into the fight.

During tactics, training the instructor told them a story about this ancient Hebrew guy, Abraham. When some kings kidnapped his nephew, Abraham went on a rescue mission. Badly outnumbered, Abraham launched a night attack, something totally new at the time. It was successful because in the confusion the enemy took their own as attackers and began killing one another. That was exactly the problem here. It was black as pitch except for some growing fires as a couple structures began burning. The trick was to kill the enemy, not your own, and not get killed the process.

His first concern was for the members of his squad. They gathered in seconds after the attack. A quick count revealed two wounded, including their lieutenant who was bad off, and Corporal Jackson who was dead. Blue Squad joined them, carrying the platoon sergeant who was unconscious with a head wound. With one command, Nebraska began welding the soldiers into a fighting unit.

"Circle up!" he called out. Although one of the youngest Rangers, the others in his company had great respect for his abilities and sprang into a defensive circle.

If the Taliban had thought to scatter the troops, they were sadly mistaken. The Afghan soldiers were disoriented with the loss of leaders, but not the Rangers. Nebraska's group swelled as friendlies joined the circle. The initial wave that had penetrated the perimeter was quickly beaten down, but he spotted a much larger force preparing for an assault.

Up to this time, the firefight had taken twenty minutes. Apparently, their strategy was a quick attack, kill however many you could, and wait for the Americans to cluster into a defense. A mass assault would be easier than trying to ferret them out scattered all over the sprawling village. But that was their undoing. Twenty minutes was enough time.

"Choppers coming in!" his radioman announced over the gunfire. "Wanna know where the enemy's located."

Taliban recon had failed to notice Black Hawk helicopters had taken up station on a level plateau eight kilometers from the village. They were reinforcements for an impending action. The distant thump of rotors was a welcome sound to the embattled soldiers.

"I'll mark the spot," he called back and slammed a flare into the tube of the 40 mm launcher attached to the underside of his carbine.

Crouching, he aimed the weapon, not into the air, but for a direct hit on the enemy. The flare arced low, just clearing the rooftops to explode in the rocks and trees a hundred meters distant. The intent was accomplished. It marked the spot, set some trees and a few Taliban on fire, and created havoc among their ranks. Within seconds came the put-put-put of machine gun fire, then the roar of three Black Hawks overhead.

A number of attackers had taken position in the building Nebraska originally occupied providing them good cover while firing on the Ranger's position. He judged there to be four of five. The only approach was straight on. Suicide. Even if successful they could slip out the back as he had done.

While motioning for his left and right ends to spread out, one of them cut loose a burst of automatic fire. An Afghan next to him cried out. They returned fire, but it was ineffective against the thick walls.

"Sorry, Clint," he said while slamming a grenade into the launcher. He didn't like the thought of mutilating his friend's body, but there wasn't much choice.

The grenade arced through the door and seconds later erupted into a yellow ball of flame as the rest of the walls toppled outward.

"Alright, let's get our perimeter back," he called out. The men instantly began moving through the village, clearing out insurgents until re-gaining the outer edge of the village. Meanwhile, other groups moved to face the enemy as the choppers held them at bay with machine gun and rockets.

Still, the Taliban were intent on attacking despite casualties. Nebraska figured it was a suicide mission, and he was more than willing to help any of them to whatever afterlife they were destined. When the main attack came, he had thirty-seven Rangers and Afghans to face them. To make things easier, a couple flares lite up the field.

Often in the fall, Nebraska's dad, his uncle, and two cousins went duck hunting, sequestered in a blind as a large flock circled in for a landing. Five shotguns blasted the flock. The Taliban were just like those ducks.

Through the night and into late morning Nebraska and a core of Rangers rallied the Afghans soldiers and held off repeated attacks until reinforcements arrived. The Taliban scattered and disappeared into the mountains, their surprise thwarted, but not without cost—to them and the defenders. Seven soldiers died, sixteen wounded, including himself. Nineteen Afghan soldiers also died and twenty-three wounded. Of the enemy they counted forty-seven bodies. They guessed at least twice that left wounded. The boy he had encountered at the outset was not the only teenager who died that night. That bothered him. Someone forgot to mention he'd be warring with children.

Had he neither planned nor expected what would happen next. Sitting in a wheelchair, anxious to get back to his platoon, he looked up to see the Battalion Commander and aids walking across the grassy, medical grounds straight for him.

"You needn't get up, Sergeant," the short, ram-rod-straight officer said. He did anyway and stood at attention.

"How's the wound?" he asked.

"I'm ready for action, sir. These doctors are slow with the paperwork."

"That's alright. You'll be released this afternoon. I wanted to personally thank you for what you did during that attack."

"It's what I was taught, sir."

"Yes, I know, but worth some recognition. I signed the papers recommending you for the Bronze Star to go along with a Purple Heart."

He was speechless as evident when his jaw dropped, but recovered quickly. "Sir, I was only doing my duty the way I was taught. There were others . . ."

"Yes, there were others, but it was your actions in light of the loss of your commanding officer that rallied the troops, significantly reduced casualties, thwarted the enemy, and brought about their defeat. You're a hero, Sergeant. We need heroes in this war."

After a long silence, Nebraska saluted and replied, "Thank you, sir."

A month later, the nineteen-year-old was ordered to report to command.

"You wanted to see me, sir?"

"Come in Sergeant," Captain Pearson said.

The officer was of average build, a college grad and lifer. He'd been a Ranger for seven years. Pushing thirty-five, he was still a force to be respected.

"I've got a job for you, if interested." He was standing bent over a makeshift table studying a map.

"Yes, sir, anything. I've had my fill of sitting around polishing my carbine for the millionth time."

"We got word the Taliban and al-Qaida have set up a training camp in this area," he said, pointing to a spot within Pakistan territory. "The Pakistanis know about it, but can't, or more likely won't do anything about it. I'd like you to take a squad in there and eliminate it."

The Bronze Star wasn't a fluke. They didn't completely eliminate the camp's personnel, but it was useless for further training. When they ran into a Pakistani patrol he had orders. No witnesses. Sufficient evidence left behind implicated the Taliba. From there it was off to Iraq. The scenery was different, but not the job. Then came a shock when he was called before the Company Commander. The man was short and to the point as always.

"Nebraska, you're being reassigned."

"Yes, sir," he said. It wasn't not, I am? or Why? or Where to now? It was, okay, let's get going.

"The Brass feels your skills are better served by transferring you to the 4th Battalion at Ft. Benning."

"Ft. Benning?" Now that took him by surprise.

"Yes. You'll be an instructor."

Normally a fighting soldier would protest, but he gathered himself up, saluted, and replied, "Yes, sir."

"Hey, Nebraska, it's not that bad. I happen to know you'll be training graduates in recon and surveillance, and you'll be doing it as a Warrant Officer-1. Congratulations, son."

A Warrant Officer is a direct representative of the president of the United States, deriving authority from the same source as commissioned officers. The difference is that they are specialists, whereas commissioned officers are generalists.

The adjustment to less stress took time, but he enjoyed the work, even if his students didn't. He expected perfection, the same as he expected from himself. It was in the third month at Ft. Benning that he met a girl, a supply Lieutenant. He found her attractive, despite the hair pulled back into a bun and no makeup, but her personality was "cold as Antarctica," according to other soldiers on base. He didn't think so, nor did she find the young instructor as fearsome as he looked.

The first date was at the PX, an accidental meeting while shopping individually. They paused long enough to have a root beer and talk. Three months later they were engaged and seven months later married. That was also the time he finished officer school, and transferred again, this time to Ft. Belvoir, Virginia and Army Intelligence.

He had nightmares this might be a paper-pushing job, but not so. Within weeks he found himself in Chicago, Illinois leading a counter-terrorist unit. He was fighting a deadlier war on the soil of his own country. He approached the assignment the same as if in Afghanistan or Iraq. The local cops were miffed when they found a warehouse full of arms, munitions, and bomb material, and a bunch of dead guys shot to pieces.

That was Nebraska's life . . . until . . ." Tangata said and stopped.

"Are you telling me, you're Army Intelligence, not CIA?" Philippe said.

"I am part of a secret Counter-terrorist group. Our assignment is to go around the world doing what the CIA can't. There are too many eyes on them and we can crawl under the radar."

"So, you moved to the island to write books?"

"It gives me something to do."

"But you're not retired."

Tangata's casual shrugged of his shoulder sent a chill down Philippe's back. That hazy, translucent response was enough. He needn't dig further.

"I've been a pain in your backside. I'm sorry. Really."

Tangata laughed. "You have had your moments, but I don't think I would have traded them for anything in the world." Suddenly he became somber. "Maybe not everything."

"Your family? I saw the photos you tried to hide back home, in the desk with that pistol. And the one you keep below deck."

"Yes."

"That little boy in the pictures, is that your son?"

Tangata took in a deep breath and let it out, but didn't answer as a great pain shrouded his face. Philippe regretted the question as soon as it cleared his lips.

A very long silence separated the two as Philippe could see Tangata's eyes glaze over, looking into the past. A hurting past.

"The picture below was taken a week before the . . . It wasn't an accident. I . . . I made a mistake. That cost my wife and son their lives."

"I'm sorry. I shouldn't have asked," Philippe said remorsefully.

"His name was Philip, too. Philip James," Tangata continued barely above a whisper. "He was six. My wife's name was Adrianne."

Philippe turned away. If ever someone needed space and time, it was now. Both of them. Returning to the bow, he stared out at the panorama ahead, but didn't see it. What he saw for the very first time was the death of his parents, the murderous machinations of his uncle directed at him, then a boy and dog on a small boat on a very big ocean in an even bigger storm. Ellie pulling him ashore. A man tenderly caring for his broken body and spirit. In his own, distant way, the man of mystery had loved and cared for an orphan and nurtured him back to the living. Philippe walked back to the helm, tears trickling down his not quite so brown cheeks and sat across from Tangata at the second helm.

"It occurs to me we have something in common," Philippe said.

"What?"

"We each believe we made a mistake that cost the lives of those we loved most."

There was a huge silence as Tangata stared back.

"If God really does care, maybe we were thrown together for a reason. I've never said thank you," Philippe said, his voice cracking with emotion.

"And I've never said thank you," Tangata replied.

Yes, life had changed, for both men on that boat making its way home. Each had become freer, and that brought them closer together.

Chapter 16

Time Travel

Rousseau wanted his brother's lucrative resort and would have it no matter what. Calling it a "hostile takeover," he laughed while giving the go-ahead to the murder of his brother, sister-in-law, and their only child. As he said, "That their spawn lived is a minor inconvenience easily remedied." The crime lord's arrogance failed to understand the boy's will to live and incredible luck, as if some powerful guardian angel or gaggle of angels hovered over him.

The sprawling villa along the southeast coast of New Caledonia was the center of Rousseau's activities and the large patio heavily used to administer the expanding business. As a result, it frequently became cluttered with drinking glasses, dishes of partially consumed food, and towels. When the person who doubled as waiter/busboy and pool area maintenance quit, Tomas hired a Lau Island boy about the same age as Philippe. Napo had several qualities Tomas liked; he was quick, efficient, and silent, an unobtrusive shadow flitting about tending to work.

As the name implied, the boy was a wave, long legs constantly in motion. A flaring nose and huge smile exposing a dentist's dream of perfect, white teeth dominated a slightly elongated face. The thick, coal black hair lay fuzzy and close-cropped. His equally black eyes sparkled with enthusiasm, at least for the first couple days after arriving. Like Philippe, the boy's dark chocolate skin was a hairless pallet displaying several tattoos on shoulders and thighs, a combination of bands with intertwining designs and dragons.

The first day on duty he wore a white shirt, mid-calf length sulu vaka taga, the traditional island wrap similar to the lava-lava Philippe wore, and sandals. Rousseau was working at a large table beneath an umbrella, attired in his usual Lycra swimming shorts. He worked that way so whenever desiring a break he could simply jump into the Olympic-size pool and swim three or four laps, thus maintaining his trim, athletic figure and work off the constant supply of snacks and booze. Upon exiting, Napo stood ready with an over-sized towel which Rousseau used and dropped on the ground when finished.

Philippe always maintained a distance from his uncle, never venturing to the expansive patio when he was there. Instead, the boy busied himself on the beach out of sight of the patio or sailing one of the smaller boats, always accompanied by one of Tomas' men. The second day after arriving, Napo was wearing a wrap barely coming mid-thigh, no shirt, and no sandals at Rousseau's orders. The third day, the island boy's smile and happy eyes were gone, as well.

The fifth morning Rousseau left for meetings in Sydney. Philippe appeared on the patio just as Napo finished vacuuming the pool. Tomas was seated at the patio bar eating breakfast.

"Good morning, Philippe. Have you had breakfast?"

"No."

Philippe didn't like his uncle's men because he knew what they were about. He had overhead his father and mother talking about Rousseau's business several times. However, Tomas stirred different feelings. On the surface, he didn't like the man, but something deeper inside wasn't as hateful or fearful.

When Napo saw Philippe sit at the bar, he immediately laid the cleaning hose aside and trotted up.

"Napo, you two haven't been introduced. This is Monsieur Rousseau's nephew. He came to live with us when his parents . . . disappeared." Philippe detected an unsettled tone in the man's voice as he paused to select a word to describe his parent's death, apparently not wanting to bring any hurt to the boy. "Napo comes from southern Lau Island. Philippe is partial to eggs Benedict, two slices of bacon, and wheat toast. And while you are about it, make some for yourself and join us."

"Sir?"

"I want you and Philippe to get to know one another, an added responsibility. In the absence of Monsieur Rousseau you will be Philippe's companion. That will relieve my men from having to be at his side when he goes swimming or boating or whatever he decides to do to relieve the boredom."

"Yes, sir." Napo didn't smile, but there was a return of some joy in his expressive eyes.

"Also, it is not necessary for you to wear that loincloth. What you wore the first day here is perfectly acceptable in Monsieur Rousseau's absence."

"Yes, sir. Thank you."

When Napo brought breakfast fifteen minutes later, Philippe was seated alone at one of the smaller, umbrellaed tables. Tomas had moved inside to his office overlooking the patio. Occasionally he glanced up from the modest desk to see the boys talking, and smiled before resuming work. An hour later Philippe knocked and entered the open door.

"Napo has finished cleaning the pool and breakfast dishes. I'd like to go sailing for a little while, if that is alright."

"The weather is perfect. Have Napo prepare a lunch and stay out as long as you like."

"Thank you."

"And Philippe, use the *Catherine*."

"The *Catherine*?"

"She is a bit larger than you've been using, but exceptional in open water and would be more comfortable for long outings. Just be back before dark."

"Thank you, Tomas. We will."

"Another thing. Be safe."

To Rousseau, owning the *Catherine* was like having a 1939 Jaguar in his car collection. The crime lord had a several substantial-sized yachts and a fleet of smaller sailboats, but the *Catherine* was special. American-built in 1966, her kind continued to mesmerize sailing enthusiasts with the forty-foot length and eleven foot beam according to American dimensions. The wood-fiberglass hull was designed for speed and stability in the open seas. Below, the cabin provided cruising comfort. With consistent racing wins, it attained a place in boating halls of fame. Tomas' suggestion, or more like insistence, that Philippe take her out, and for a day-long trip, was a surprise.

Philippe was a little nervous piloting the racer as she cut through the protected harbor away from Quinné. He'd handled others this size, but just because of who owned her caused some concern, but an hour out and he was totally one with the boat as she clipped along under full sail at over fifteen knots. Napo was obviously uptight as well, but not about the trip. He'd grown up sailing outriggers, a toothpick compared to this boat. Once in open water he came up from below, having shucked shirt and sandals.

"Where are we headed?" he asked, handing Philippe a soda.

"Let's see how fast we can cross over to Lifou. It's only 115 kilometers. With this wind we should be back well before sunset."

After a long silence Napo said, "I am sorry to hear about your parents. You are very lucky to have your uncle take you in."

Philippe stared at him, anger building, but did he dare speak his mind? He could contain himself no longer. "I don't like him. He is a bad man. One day I am going to leave and go as far from him as possible."

That seemed to put Napo at ease. "I do not like him as well." There was an anger in his eyes that seemed to burn hot.

Suddenly Philippe felt very uncomfortable, beginning to suspect something happened. That first day the boy smiled and was cheerful. After that, he became withdrawn and sullen. He had to ask.

"Did something happen between you and my uncle?"

"I would rather not talk about it," Napo said, turning away to look forward.

Nearly an hour passed this way until the Islander turned back to look at Philippe. "He called me to his bedroom. He wanted something to eat. He . . . he . . . made me stay." Philippe's dislike for his uncle became compounded. "I will leave."

"Have you spoken to Tomas?"

"Before you came for breakfast this morning I told him I wanted to leave. He is good man. He was sorry for what happened, but said it was important I stay a little longer, at least until your uncle returns, then he will help me to leave. As long as your uncle is not here, it will be all right. When he returns, I leave."

The boys returned in time for the evening meal. Tomas looked up from his desk as they came onto the patio laughing. As planned, they had bonded, and with Rousseau away, and life in the villa quiet, the boys spent all their time together, mostly talking whether playing Monopoly, sailing, and kicking a soccer ball.

Following several weeks tending business in Australia, Philippe's uncle was to return the following morning. Being the last quiet day at the mansion, the two boys played soccer together on the expansive lawn. Tomas watched as some of his men joined the game. After lunch Napo cleaned up while Philippe went to the bathroom. Returning, he spotted Tomas and Napo talking. It appeared serious and secretive. After that the Islander was very quiet, returning to the somber withdrawal of earlier times. They played Monopoly, but Napo's mind was not on the game. It was obvious he wanted to say something, but not until Tomas' men were not where they could hear.

"You are leaving?" Philippe asked when Tomas called the men to do something elsewhere.

"Mr. Tomas says I shall not be here tomorrow when your uncle returns," Napo said, leaning forward and speaking very softly. "Philippe, I . . . I . . . overheard talk. When your uncle returns tomorrow you are not to be here also."

"Where am I going?"

"There is a big storm coming. Big typhoon. Some men are to take you out in a boat and kill you. They will blame your death on the storm. You must get away, Philippe, before they come for you."

Philippe's world suddenly went berserk, spinning in all directions, unable to focus until hearing the gentle, but firm voice of his Budō teacher inwardly guiding him to regain control. He began to focus.

"Did you hear, Philippe?" Napo asked.

"Huh? Yes. I heard. Thank you."

"There's something else. I heard that your uncle keeps money in his private safe behind the picture of a sailboat, in case he has to leave in big hurry. It's in a bag. The combination is under the top, right drawer. I saw it while cleaning up paper dots that spilled from a punch."

"When are they to take me?"

"Sometime this afternoon."

"You're a good friend, Napo. I hope someday we'll meet again."

As the Islander left to vacuum the pool, Philippe turned to leave, running into Tomas.

"You look very pale, Philippe. Are you not feeling well?"

Tomas had always been friendly toward him. Philippe wondered if that had been faked. Did he know? Of course he did. It would be his men who did the dirty work.

"I'm going to lay down for a bit."

Tomas felt Philippe's forehead.

"Maybe that would be good. If you need anything, call my cell. I'll see you are not disturbed. I'll check on you at dinner time."

That would give Philippe a five-hour head start. Entering his room, he grabbed a backpack and looked around. What to take? There wasn't much, just a few clothes. All his things were still at the resort. He'd have to travel fast and light. While stuffing a change of clothes inside the pack, Ellie, his uncle's Golden Retriever, padded into the room. From the first day, Philippe had become her boy, seldom leaving his side, apparently sensing the hurt and loneliness. That irked Rousseau.

Normally Tomas' men wondered about, patrolling the sprawling compound, but at this moment they were engaged in a card game on the patio with their boss. Philippe and Ellie worked along a side veranda, circumventing the house and down to the first level where Rousseau's office was located. Standing on the patio outside the office, Philippe stopped and looked around.

Seeing no one, he told Ellie, "Sit, stay." Well trained, she would remain in that spot almost forever. Then he gave the command, "Guard." Her lips seemed to curl into a smile as she sat, panting expectantly for the next command. "Guard" meant she would bark once if anyone approached.

Slipping through the patio doors, the boy went directly to the desk and opened the top right drawer. There was a small pistol inside. Ignoring it, he looked at the underside. There was the combination. Closing the drawer, he went to the picture, swung it out, and began dialing the numbers. The thick door opened smoothly. Grabbing a brown, cloth bag, he quickly untied the cord fastener and peeked inside. Sure enough, money, lots of it. Needing nothing else, Philippe closed the bag, stuffed it into his backpack, and returned everything as it had been.

Rejoining Ellie, the two headed for the only possible way to escape the villa—by boat. He knew what he needed. Rousseau's fleet at dock ranged in size from three to forty meters, both sail and power boats. He picked the *Catharine*. Thanks to Tomas, he had sailed her almost every day his uncle was gone. It was something manageable alone, fast, and built for the rough seas he could expect before making land just ahead of the approaching storm.

"Well, hello," one of Tomas' men said, stepping from a small service building. Another man was right behind him. "We were just coming to find you. Thought you might like to help us move some of these boats to a safer location. Big blow coming our way."

"Yeah, I heard. I was coming down to see if I could help. But, can we move the *Catherine* first? I'd like to take her out for maybe an hour."

The two goons looked at each other, not believing their stroke of luck. "Sure. We got time. Let's go."

Someone always accompanied Philippe, therefore, it might have raised suspicion if he tried to leave them behind. These two were the dimmest bulbs in Tomas' cadre, and neither was any kind of a sailor, therefore of little help as the boy set the sail, and began tacking through the bay, pointing the bow seaward. Ellie took her favorite spot on the bow, tongue happily dangling from her mouth. From all appearances, the boy was having a great time as the two men sat amidships. They were talking so not to be heard, giggling, and casting furtive glances in the boy's direction. They were obviously planning their next move. So was Philippe.

From his position, keeping an eye on the two assassins was easy. He watched the sails to keep them full and the bow on a northerly course that would take him between Ouvéa and Lifou islands and on to the northern most of the Vanuatu islands. By his calculations, he would arrive just ahead of the storm. The question was how to handle them when they made their move. If they came at him with guns, he might not have much chance and his uncle would be a happy man. It might be possible to swing the boom and knock them overboard, but if they approached on opposite sides of the boat, he'd only be able to get one.

Thirty minutes under sail the brisk breeze propelled the boat fifteen kilometers into open water at which point the men stood and came, one either side of the cabin.

"I think we've gone out far enough," the leader said.

"I suppose. Do you know how to handle a boat like this?" Philippe asked.

"We're no experts like you, but we'll manage," he said, pulling out a long knife.

"Uncle wants me killed?" Philippe said, sounding calm, while his mind and body quaked with fear. He tried to control his breathing. How many times Master Yamamoto prepared him for exactly this sort of situation. Before, it had been a training exercise, a game. This was not going to have a peaceful conclusion, and no appreciative bowing when the combat was over. Someone was going to be dead. *Not me!* rang loudly in his head. "So how is this supposed to happen? Toss me overboard?"

"No. Your uncle was very specific. You have too much luck. There is always the chance you could swim back, though I seriously doubt that," the thinner one on the left said, on the verge of being giddy.

"Or tread water until some boat happens by," the nearest one on the right added. "This will be quick, although not altogether painless."

"Yeah, not painless," the giddy one chimed in.

"I'll open you up so you don't bloat and float ashore. That will also help attract sharks."

"Is that what Tomas said?"

"My orders come direct from your loving uncle. Tomas doesn't know anything about this."

"But you work for Tomas. He's the one you take orders from."

"Yeah, but not in this case. Your uncle thinks Tomas may like you too much."

"You are looking forward to this, aren't you?"

"Oh, yeah. It is what I enjoy," the knife man answered with a cold, lopsided grin.

Philippe stood.

"Don't think of jumping overboard. We got a whole chest full of bloody fish to drop over to attract the sharkies," the thin one said. "Tell him how you"re going to do it, Zack." He was shivering with excitement.

"Do you want me to face you or turn my back?"

"I'd prefer you facing me," he said, advancing with the diver's knife held hip high.

"I guess if I am to die, struggling will only make it worse," Philippe said, his heart racing faster than the wind of any typhoon. He held his hands out to the side, opening himself up.

The question must have circulated through their little-used brains, Why is this kid cooperating? The leader found out as he stepped within range. A front snap kick caught the average-size thug in the groin.

An interesting physiological effect occurs when a man receives a blow to that area. The body reacts to the searing pain before it completely registers in the brain. The result is that the body instantly freezes, eyes bulge, and mouth opens preparatory to the ensuing scream, which becomes choked off to an agonized groan. Before reaching that stage, a roundhouse caught him alongside the head. The thin man was taken totally by surprise as he watched his companion fly from the boat. When he looked up Philippe was advancing. The pistol on his hip was half drawn when Ellie struck from behind throwing him forward, off balance into another roundhouse kick.

As the boat sailed on Philippe watched the two men treading water, waiving and yelling. That wasn't a concern. One of the other boats sailing for cover might pick them up, although the boy thought the chances of that were slim. Everyone was too concerned finding safe harbor and the water was getting choppy. But no, that wouldn't do. As his uncle didn't want to leave anything to chance, neither did Philippe. He needed time to put as much distance between him and his uncle's killers as possible. Now arose the dilemma. Knocking them from the boat was self-defense. Leaving them to drown was murder. God forbid murder. Turning, the boat made a wide circle that would put the men on the bow. Bringing them back aboard would put him in peril again. Not to was murder. Yet, their orders were to murder him and they would try again. His only hope of continuing to live was going as far from Uncle Rousseau's tentacles as possible. Running them down would not be sufficient. One or both might survive. Leaving them afforded a chance they might be rescued. He could throw them life preservers. But did cold-blooded murderers like these deserve to live? The war waged in his head. Yes. No. Yes. No. As the *Catherine* passed, Philippe jettisoned the slashed bait fish, a cooler full, the cocktail intended to accompany his demise.

The men's screams quickly faded as the boy raced north under a stiffening wind propelling the *Catherine* ever faster toward Vanuatu. After waiting out the storm, he must push beyond that, to where he had no idea, but not close. Perhaps the Solomans further north. No, his uncle reached there. No, he would have to leave his beloved Pacific altogether. That decision would have to wait until after the typhoon passed. He turned up the radio to listen to the weather forecast.

"This is a navigational weather warning issued by the Southwest Pacific Tracking Center for the islands in and around New Caledonia and Vanuatu. A class 5, tropical typhoon with sustained wind speeds at 112 knots is presently located 585 kilometers west of Suva, Fiji traveling at 110 degrees. It's present speed is 22 kilometers per hour, however, the storm appears to be accelerating. On the present course, the eye of storm is expected to pass between New Caledonia and the Vanuatu islands. Waves are running in excess of eight meters ahead of the storm. A

storm surge is predicted to be ten to twelve meters in some locations accompanied by torrential rain. These conditions can be expected between now and passage of the storm's eye in 24 hours and last for 18 to 24 hours. Owners and operators of large and small water craft are urged to . . ."

Philippe didn't need to hear any more. He was trying to head for safe portage—safe from the storm and safe from his uncle. Despite the weather, the *Catherine's* sails gathered all of the wind to slice the swells building ahead of the storm. That would give him enough time to find safe port.

Standing on the veranda overlooking the private marina, Tomas saw Philippe join the two assigned to lose the boy at sea. He watched as the boat sailed out into the Coral Sea toward Lifu. Their orders were to go out about ten to fifteen kilometers. After 30 minutes Tomas judged they were about that far when his attention was needed elsewhere, and went into the house, assured all would go as planned. He had done everything he could.

Rousseau's return was delayed because of the storm, but was pleased. Two of Tomas' men had taken the boy on a boat ride just ahead of the storm. A radio message was received that they were taking refuge at Lifu as the approaching storm pushed high seas ahead of it. Tomas admitted they were good assassins, just not that good with a sailboat in such weather. When the storm finally passed and no word received from the men, Tomas reported to his boss who wasn't immediately concerned. It would be another forty-eight hours before it was determined something might be wrong. There was no sign of the

Catherine at any of the islands.

"Maybe they all drown," Rousseau said, sounding a little irritated. "I liked that boat."

It was the crime boss's faithful, careful, right hand, Tomas, who made the suggestion, "Perhaps we should make a discrete search, just on the outside chance they made port, perhaps a fishing village, and the boy is still alive."

"You may be right. The brat has more lives than a cat," Rousseau said while opening the safe. The next sound was heard throughout the house. "I've been robbed!" He flailed about the contents of the safe. "The money and computer disk! They're gone! It was that kid! He stole it! Tomas, find that little bastard. If he's alive bring him back to me. I will personally carve him up and feed him to the sharks! Do you understand? Find that kid!"

♦   ♦   ♦

Philippe repeatedly checked the charts, listened to weather updates about the approaching storm building ominous, black clouds behind him, calculating how long until arriving at a safe port. The swells increased, forcing him to slow. He wasn't making the progress he had hoped. The storm was catching up. Vanuatu was still hours away and darkness closing in fast. There was no way to make safe land until morning when he could see, otherwise the *Catherine* would be smashed on the rocky shoreline. A quick calculation suggested he would be near the north end of Vanuatu by morning. He would have to turn to the east side of the island. There was a huge bay and fishing villages there. That would work, but as the little light allowed to filter through the thick clouds reveled that morning, the winds and waves ahead of the storm had pushed him pass the island. He was a good sailor, but conditions rapidly deteriorated way beyond his abilities. Left to the mercy of the storm, all that remained was a prayer that he'd find land or ride out the storm. Prayer was out. After all he had done, the cause of his parent's death and the murder of those two men, God obviously had turned his back on him. Despite the *Catherine*'s great design he gravely doubted the ability to ride out the storm. He wanted to cry, but there was too much to do as he fought to stay alive with the last of waning strength. That's when the volcanic peak and lagoon rose out of the black, churning waters directly ahead.

The boy's incredible luck continued as a storm surge carried him beyond the reef's teeth. Thanks to faithful Ellie he was spared a watery death, and nursed back to health by a mysterious man who lived in an old volcano. He had learned martial arts, thanks to dotting parents. When Tomas and his uncle's henchmen found him, Philippe escaped death again, thanks to a man turned creature. The boy over-powered Tomas, the lone survivor, and sent him away. Tomas did not know the man who nursed and cared for him stood in the jungle watching, ready to step forward, but wise enough to let the boy do it himself. Philippe knew, but he took charge of his own destiny.

What followed was a whirlwind of deception as numerous misdirections so confused Rousseau's men to drive the crime lord mad. Frothing at the mouth like Lewis Carroll's Queen of Hearts, he screamed for just about everyone's head. His nephew and whoever helped him at the top of the list. However, the computer disc Philippe unintentionally stole survived to wrought havoc upon the crime empire.

Tomas had said it contained more incriminating data in a protected file, and Philippe knew the password. That was another reason Rousseau wanted him so badly. At the time, the boy had no idea what the man was talking about. Still, there was enough information that political influence cowered and shriveled. People began cutting deals with prosecutors. Philippe had wrought a typhoon the little man could not weather unscathed.

♦   ♦   ♦

Things change over time and are never as one remembers, but not here. Nothing changed on his volcano home. Standing on the overlook, Philippe gazed out upon the adjacent island as turquoise swells played leapfrog over the reef. Like a gangling teenager attempting the long jump for the first time, the waves failed miserably, reduced to white-flecked swells rolling more gently onto the lagoon's shores. The wind, like an old aunt, tousled his hair. Still a nudist by birth and at heart, civilization had tempered life, but upon taking up his old room the first thing to go were the clothes, traded for a bright, blue lava-lava, a gift from Aunty Eve made from the old dress he had liked so much and she could no longer wear.

Before going to America, Philippe explored the cave and the southern half of the island with its steep, volcanic cliffs and black and pink coral sand beaches. He particularly enjoyed the long, idyllic shore facing the sister island, and swimming in the lagoon. There was no desire to return to that place on the other side. The time had come to let its ghosts sleep. For whatever reason, there didn't seem to be much desire to venture toward the bulk of the island to the north, or interest visiting the single village at the far tip. No interest, that is, until one morning while standing in this very same spot above the old, ruptured caldera, he felt drawn toward an opened area off to the west. Tangata said it was occasionally used as a helicopter pad, although he had never seen one land.

He remembered that particular day. It felt like a long time ago. A cool, southerly breeze had been blowing for several days, buffering the hot sun, its mediating puffs a delightful respite as he ventured down the trail. The shading canopy was open enough to allow the breeze to penetrate, but upon entering the clearing, the sun's full force came to bear. The seldom-used trail abruptly ended at the clearing, except something haunted Philippe that there was more.

Much of the small plateau dropped precariously into dense jungle, but the northwestern side was more inclined, albeit steep. Walking along the perimeter, he noticed two parallel lines of small rocks a meter apart disappear into the jungle. Looking back toward the rising volcanic cone, it felt strange not to have Ellie at his side, but she injured a paw several days before and was staying with Tangata to recuperate. Pushing the vegetation aside, he uncovered the thin residue of a trail skirting the base of the mountain. Forcing himself into the brush, Philippe was rewarded by instant relief from the direct sunlight and set out upon the remnants of the trail, badly overgrown, but still negotiable.

The pencil-thin line marked by small stones dove into a steep, zigzag descent. The further he traveled the denser the over story became until neither sunlight nor wind could penetrate. It was steamy inside this jungle vault, difficult to breathe as sweat gushed from every pore to cascade down his body in rivulets. Even the ever-present roar of the ocean became muted, creating an eerie silence. The constant chirps of insects and buzz of mosquitos only added to give this place an unnerving, haunted feel. High above, birds fluttered through the tree tops, afraid to penetrate to where a smörgåsbord abound. Instead, they seemed to chirp a warning—go back.

Further down the base of the hill, the ground turned marshy, but the trail continued to hug the mountain just above the muck and impenetrable growth. Traveling northward along the west shore, he eventually came to a wide stream tumbling off the mountain. The trail swung right to follow the watery gorge upstream for fifty or so meters.

To his amazement, the remains of a short suspension bridge span the stream's deep, sheer walls, apparently something leftover by the Japanese soldiers sixty years previous. He wondered what lay ahead that they would have gone to so much trouble to build a trail and bridge. That afternoon he returned with a length of durable polypropylene rope. By scaling an old, gnarled tree, he was able to secure one end of the rope. Placing a large knot on the free end, he then swung across the gorge.

Once over, he resumed exploration along the trail as it turned left, back along the stream, then right, to resume skirting the hillside just above the swamp. Eventually, some of the jungle cleared so he could both see and hear the surf. The marsh yielded to rockier ground and a long, smooth beach facing an expanse of open ocean dotted with a smattering of small, coral islands, some with only one or two trees.

A small stream bisected the path, which divided

at this point, one section continuing northward, one upstream toward a cliff, and one downstream to the beach. Easily jumping across, Philippe followed the trail down until coming to a point overlooking a full stretch of beach. There was a concrete pillbox, its machine gun encrusted in a thick layer of rust, forever silenced.

"So, a reason for this trail, but what of the others?" he asked himself.

Returning to the fork, Philippe studied the ground for a moment, making an interesting observation. The trail coming in from the north seemed more traveled as was the one heading up stream. The one back to the helicopter pad not at all. Philippe suspected the northward trail went to the village, but what was so important about the cliff? He proceeded upstream until coming to the sheer wall where the stream poured through a fissure just wide enough for a body to pass. The trail seemed to stop at this point, but indications pointed to it continuing into the fissure. Working into its depths, Philippe came to a sharp bend. From beyond came the recognizable sound of a waterfall. Pushing on, the young man wasn't ready for the unsullied sight as the fissure fanned out. It was like standing in the bottom of a huge coffee cup and looking up as the liquid is poured in.

The stream plunged nearly twenty meters into a deep, clear pool taking up three-quarters of the bowl. The craggy wall sheared some of the water into a mist that filled and cooled the sun-bathed area.

Having learned a valuable lesson in the cave, he tested the water with a toe. With delight, it was comfortably warm. Tossing the sweat-soaked lava-lava aside, he dove into the crystalline pool to loll about like a sea otter, rolling, diving, floating in complete delight before lounging on a broad, flat rock overhanging the pool. The other trails obviously met defensive needs, but this branch was answer enough why the soldiers spent so much effort getting here.

Returning after a near seven year hiatus, Philippe found the swing rope still serviceable and the hidden pool exactly as remembered. Sitting on a large, flat rock overhanging the pool, he once again imagined hearing the soldiers' youthful laughter during a much too brief respite from a bitter and murderous war.

"How hard it must have been for them, too,' he wrote in a journal. *"The machinations of politicians and warmongers to inflame and destroy— destroy not only the way of life of another, but ultimately that of their own people. Here boys no older than I found a few minutes respite from insanity."*

Once again Philippe tossed his lava-lava aside, dove in, and paddled lazily about before allowing himself to stretch out to dry in the sun, feeling the last vestiges of cold upon his bone marrow finally melt. When a low rumbling rose up from his stomach, he decided to venture back down the trail to where wild mangoes grew. Garment in-hand he headed toward the beach, exiting the crevice to come face to face with a young girl.

Both were startled at seeing another human, so much so neither moved, staring at one another opened-mouthed. She was an Islander, tall as

Philippe, slender, with unblemished, milk chocolate brown skin, hair so black it cast a bluish tint. Wide, expressive eyes narrowed and slowly looked the young man up and down. Despite living his formative years a nudist he suddenly felt naked and quickly wrapped the cloth about his loins.

"Uh, hello," he said lamely.

"What are you doing here?" she challenged.

"I live here," he stammered.

"So do I. I have never seen you before."

"I live on the south end."

"Only the hermit lives on that part of the island."

"I live with him."

"I spoke with only two days ago and he said nothing about someone being with him."

"No one is supposed to know I am here."

"Are you that boy the men looked for?"

His heart quickened. "When was this?"

"I was just a child, but remember some men came looking for a boy. They were rude."

"I was the one."

"Have you been hiding in the mountain all this time?"

"I went away, to America so those men would not find me. I just returned."

Her voice softened. "You must be special to live with such a man as the hermit. My name is Mira. What is your name?"

"Philippe."

"That is a pretty name. How did you come here without passing through my village?"

"I found a trail when I first lived here. The Japanese soldiers built it during the big war. I think they came here to get away from all that, at least for a little while. This is my first time back."

"I come often, to get away."

"Get away from what?" he asked, looking over her shoulder to see if anyone else was present.

"Men. I am of marrying age now so they all chase after me, but I don't care for them. They are arrogant, loud-mouthed bores. I come here to have peace. Are you leaving?"

"I was just going to find something to eat."

"Here," she said, reaching into a bag draped over one shoulder and fishing out some fruit.

Returning to the pool, the two sat on the flat rock facing the waterfall, eating, and talking as young people do when first meeting. Exchanging snippets of their lives, the walls of newness gradually pushed aside, but he was carefull to avoid mentioning his uncle. Mira was an only daughter, the youngest of three, and spoiled by her parents.

"I want to swim," she finally said, standing up.

Philippe watched as her slender body arced through the air and knife into the water, barely disturbing the surface. She was very beautiful, but something about her eyes and the way she smiled stirred feelings in his breast very different than that experienced in Brisbane. It was confusing. Slowly he rose, pulled the low ends of the lava-lava up to form a diaper to free his legs, and then dove into the water. Soon they splashed water, giggled, playing like little children, eventually returning to a small stretch of sand in the shade of the diving rock, and quietly talk.

"Did you meet many girls at the school in America?"

"Yes, but no one like you," he replied spontaneously, then chided himself for making such an obvious pass, but that was part of the unusual feelings. It was as he had known this girl all his life.

A dark blush tinted her brown cheeks as she

averted her eyes.

"I'm sorry. I didn't mean to embarrass you," he said quickly, feeling the heat rise to his own face.

She giggled softly.

Each day for the next week, Philippe rose early, finishing his chores before hurrying to the waterfall. Sometimes Mira was waiting, other times she came later. Those times before her arrival he spent in quiet meditation, but it was hard to focus as his mind seemed to race in all directions.

"I think I'm in love," Philippe blurted one afternoon.

"Who is the girl," Mira responded, a panicked twinge in her voice.

He swallowed before answering, "You. Whenever we are together I feel alive and whole, and at peace, but when we are apart . . . there is a void inside that makes me very sad."

"Me, too," she whispered, lowering her eyes.

Philippe slowly stretched forth his hand, lifting her chin with two fingers. Gazing into each others eyes their lips drifted together until kissing—slowly, tenderly, quietly passionate. Parting, they stared again into one another's eyes, understanding their true feelings. Leaning forward they kissed again, their arms encircled one another. He relished the soft warmth of her body pressed close, the feel of her slender fingers coursing over his back. With a slight nudge, he lay back, not losing the kiss as she lay beside him, her hand stroking his side along the hip until coming to the upraised knee. That was what Christie did the night he would forever remember.

The tiny voices inside Philippe's head began their argument as her hand began to slide along the top edge of his lava-lava, the motion frozen when a male voice echoed off the basalt walls, "Mira, where are you?"

"They have followed me!" she squealed, panic in her voice as she leapt to her feet. "If they find you here with me they will hurt you! Quickly, follow me!" Without another word she dove into the pool.

Philippe had no fear of intruders, but her flight was so quick there was no time to calm them. He followed to where she hid behind the curtain of water.

"Take a very deep breathe and follow me," she said, gulping in a huge lung-full of air and slipping beneath the surface.

Philippe complied, following into the depths of the pool to an underwater passage and through the rock wall. When lungs felt about to burst, she arched suddenly upward breaking the surface into a hidden cave. He gasped for air as his head broke the surface, wishing he'd not been in such a hurry and inhaled better. Following hand signs to be silent, he came up behind the girl as she peered through a fissure looking out through the waterfall to where they had been seated moments earlier. Three men stood there now.

"Mira, where are you?" the largest called out.

"Come out. Your future husband wants you," the smallest called through hands cupped around his mouth. They laughed.

"Mira, I know you are here, but with who? Come out and show yourselves!" the biggest bellowed angrily.

The men began searching the many crevices among the crumbled rocks in which one could hide. The angle of the sun reflected a glare off the water hiding their underwater retreat, but one of the men apparently knew of the cave, too, and dove into the pool surfacing in the cavern, however could not see them secreted among the rocks as Mira and Philippe watched from less than ten meters away, afraid even to breathe.

"I know you have met someone here," the biggest called out, holding up the food left behind. "I bought you. You are mine. I order you to come out."

"No way, you fat-bellied pig," she mumbled softly.

"All right. We return to the village and say to your father you have met a man here. You will be disgraced, and when Malo find him, Malo will tear him into many pieces."

"Yeah, you and who else?" Philippe said softly. The two giggled.

Receiving no reply, Malo stalked out through the narrow entrance, his anger resonating with each heavy footstep. The others followed close behind, casting about, obviously wondering where their quarry could be hiding.

"They will wait just outside the rock for us to appear," Philippe whispered. "We must stay here until certain they are gone."

"We do not have to go that way," Mira said, moving deeper into the cave before nimbly climbing upward.

Presently a light appeared, a small opening large enough to allow them out atop the cliff. Without a word Mira worked along the ridge, careful of the sharp rocks as they were bare footed. Heated by the sun, the black rock burned their feet until reaching the jungle where the ground was moist and cool. Running some distance, they finally stopped to regain their breath.

"Where does this go?" Philippe asked.

"I do not know. I only found that way out a couple months ago. I have never come this far."

"So, who are those guys?"

"The ugly one is Malo. My father says I must marry the pig. I will jump off a cliff first. The other two are my stupid brothers. They follow him like women."

"You're engaged to that?"

"Not as far as I am concerned. Because I have not chosen a man yet, my father made a deal with him when he showed up with some goats."

"Your people still do that?"

"Girls my age have found men to marry. The men in my village are blowfish. I will not marry any of them. I will be nineteen in a few months and getting old. Father is worried I will not marry and give him grandchildren."

"Well, why don't we go to your village and tell your father we want to marry?"

Mira stopped and stared at Philippe. They had felt love grow between them, but hadn't spoken of marriage. With a squeal of delight, the girl threw her arms around Philippe's neck and kissed him. They might have parted, but the moment was too wonderful. They made it last.

Philippe felt as if melting as passion surged up like a big wave. Suddenly he heard the voices, "Yes." "No." Warm, moist lips, the soft, smoothness of her skin pressing against his, her hands playing across his broad shoulders, Philippe was becoming aroused.

"No!" he said suddenly, backing away and holding Mira at bay by the arms.

"What is wrong?" she asked, her breathing coming in short gulps.

"In my culture, people are not to lie with one another before becoming married. Many do anyway," he said, having to be honest.

"So it is with my people."

"But I have been taught that . . . that coming together as man and wife before marriage is not right," Philippe said.

"That is strange. In my village young men and women come together whenever they like. That is how they learn to please one another and find who they like."

"You have done this?"

"A few times. Not for many years now because I do not like the men of my village. You have not done this?"

"Well . . ." He could not lie. "I did spend a night with a woman."

"Did you like it?"

". . . Yes."

"Did you not like this woman?"

"I liked her very much, but not to marry."

"Then we could do this."

"I cannot. I love and respect you too much. Please, let's wait until we are married."

Mira's expression was one of wonder and surprise until changing to a brilliant, vivacious smile that almost destroyed Philippe's resolve.

"You are a beautiful person, Philippe," she cooed and kissed him on the cheek.

Philippe looked around to get his bearings. They seemed to be about mid-island. Mira's half lay to the north, his towering fortress home rose ominously to the south.

"The trail connecting our two homes can't be far. Once finding it we should be able to reach your village in an hour or so."

"We cannot go there," she said, the panic rising in her voice. "If Malo does not kill you, my brothers, or father will. They must to save face."

"I need to tell you something . . ."

"No! We cannot go back," she said. "Please."

"Okay. Then we will go to the mountain, but eventually we have to break the news to your father and that Malo guy."

The jungle was not kind as they pushed through the heavy undergrowth. Blazing a trail through the jungle, they could have become hopelessly lost except for the mountain to their right. The island was not wide, but their journey seemed to take an eternity, and Mira worried they might have somehow gotten turned around until unexpectedly breaking out into the trail. Continuing uphill, the two waifs finally arrived at the back entrance to Philippe's volcanic home.

"What shall we tell your guardian?" Mira asked as they stepped to the cave's entrance.

"The truth would be nice," a voice seemed to boomed from inside the black interior as it was amplified by an echo. Mira loosed a small scream and jumped while Philippe went into a defensive stance. "Sorry. I didn't mean to frighten you kids," Tangata said, stepping into the gray light just inside the entrance. "What happened? You two look like you've been whipped."

Philippe quickly explained their escape through the jungle.

"That Malo fella should have an interesting story to tell your father, Mira. Running off to a secret place, obviously to meet a lover, then vanishing. Well, Adam and Eve, I suggest you come inside so we can find something more suitable than those shredded fig leaves."

Scratches medicated and clothes replaced, the three sat in the study, Tangata in a wood rocking chair, girl and boy crossed legged next to one another on the floor facing him. Ellie curled peacefully next to Mira as she scratched the dog's ears.

"So, let me get this straight. You two have been meeting covertly for nearly two weeks. I suspected something afoot when you kept disappearing. You've declared love for one another and you, Philippe, have gone off and proposed. And you, Mire, accepted?"

"Yes."

"And you've sealed the proposal with a handshake?"

Boy and girl looked at each other a moment. She bowed her head as Philippe looked straight at Tangata.

"No handshake," he said. "I read the book. It was a promise and only a kiss."

Tangata's lips moved slightly to an imperceptible smile. "It's going to be difficult for you to return home, Mira. When they learn Philippe was with you and you're betrothed to one another over your father's agreement, it will be very hard for both of you."

"We will leave the island," Mira said.

"Running away solves nothing. You have to think of your mother and father. They love you. Running off will only cause them great hurt."

"But if we go back they will hurt Philippe. Malo is very strong and has great anger. He has hurt some of the other boys very much."

Tangata scoffed. "Malo is not the problem. You need to salvage the respect of your parents and the people of your village. Those boys have already returned to your village and spread their story. Do you think your father will listen to your side when you show up to explain that you have fallen in love with this boy, especially after having been gone overnight? It's too dark to return to your village."

"No." Tears now began to trickle down her cheeks.

"That's the way gossip works. It colors people's mind against the truth," Tangata said.

"What can we do?" Philippe asked, seriously concerned for the girl's welfare.

"I guess the only thing left is to get you both married."

The man just stared at the two as they looked startled, first at him, then at each other.

"But . . ., but," Philippe started to protest.

"For Pete's sake, what is the big headline here, Philippe? You've gone and pledged yourselves to one another. In centuries past, they didn't use clergy. All it took was an exchange of a promise to become husband and wife. In today's world an official ceremony is the next step, or were you just going to live together? Well, I'm off to bed. It's been a busy day, and I suspect you two are tired as well, what with your adventure." Tangata stood, stretched arms wide and yawned. "Mira can use one of the spare rooms." He then disappeared, leaving the two young people alone with Ellie.

"He is right," Mira said softly after a very long silence.

"That we get married? But . . . but," Philippe began stammering. "It's all happening so fast, like being caught in a waterspout."

"You do want to marry me?"

Philippe took both of the girl's hands and looked into her eyes. "Yes. More than anything. It will be difficult to explain this to your father, but we will find away."

Mira smiled as they kissed, then backed away,

but not letting loose of his hands said, "Will you show me to my sleeping room?"

The two padded silently down the corridor to a vacant room near Philippe's. Standing in the doorway, she took both of Philippe's hands into hers once again, staring at him through soft, black pools.

"I do love you," she said, then quickly placed a kiss on his cheek, but he held fast, pulling her back. They kissed longer.

"I love you, too," he whispered tenderly.

Philippe sat motionless for an a long time on the edge his bed before lying back, but sleep would not come as his body churned with excitement and apprehension. The next morning Tangata seemed to brood as Mira whisked about the kitchen preparing breakfast, Philippe hovering close to help.

"Why do you seem so angry today, Tangata?" Philippe asked bluntly as that is how the man had taught him to be—honest and straightforward.

"I came here to get away from people, now I have a veritable village budding under my nose."

"We will leave. We can make our home on the other island," Mira replied.

"Nonsense! How could I hold the babies except to take time from my work to paddle all the way over there every day?"

The girl blushed as Philippe protested, "Babies?"

"A very natural circumstance arising from marriage."

"But . . ., but . . ,"

"Oh, stop fooling yourself. You are in love with each other. You have made a pledge, and gone off and sealed it with a kiss. Next is marriage. Then what follows? Babies, of course. That was Johnny's dream, remember? Get married and have lots of babies. The way I hear it six, and still counting. You'll have to make up for lost time."

Philippe saw the twinkle in Tangata's eyes.

Mira blushed and turned to hide a giggle.

"And just how am I going to support a family? I don't have a job."

"Amazing, isn't it? Kids run off into a fit of love, throw reason to the wind, and seldom consider the basics like how they intend to build and provision a home. At least here you can fish. Hunt, maybe. Garden. Tie some poles and palm leaves together to make a hut then lie around, and have lots of babies."

"You are obsessed with babies!" Philippe shouted.

Tangata's laughter began as a soft chuckle swelling into a rolling laugh, as a renewed joy entered into the tone of his life. Ellie joined with happy barks.

"I always loved children. Wanted children, but that was canceled out, until you were tossed into my lap. It will be kind of nice to hear the patter of little feet, and the laughter . . ., and cries in this mausoleum. Not so sure about the diaper smell.

"As for an income, I took care of that years ago. Your uncle attempted to destroy your father's will, but we found a copy at the French Consulate on New Caledonia registered about the time you were born. That blocked your uncle from having any legal claim or control of your parent's assets. As for the resort, it is in the hands of a reputable management company your uncle can't leverage. It's being run at the same, quality level your father ran it and continues to be a lucrative cash cow. Coupled with the insurance monies, and a bank account your parents had, and a savings account they set up for you, and other investments your father had, you've got somewhere around 200 mil in cash, bonds, and stocks. That doesn't count the resort and several other properties scattered around the islands. Those are valued at roughly another 250 million or so on today's market."

Philippe's lower jaw went slack, dangling in disbelief.

"We believe there is more, but the information was encoded and placed in a computer storage system. The coding looks very much like the one your uncle used on the CD you stole, a long list of names, all of which are characters in a novel."

Philippe's brow furrowed as another memory slipped into place. "Are those characters from The Three Musketeers by Alexandre Dumas?"

"As a matter of fact, yes. There is a well-read copy on your father's bookshelf, but we haven't found a connection other than the names are all underlined. It has driven our cryptographers crazy trying to figure it out."

"All for one and one for all," Philippe said, sounding remote.

"Care to explain?"

"After what you have said, all for one means all those names, or files, are for one person, me. Papa said that growing up, it was he and his brother's most favorite story, and that had been their motto . . . until one became too greedy."

If you insert another name anywhere in that list and press the enter key, that will open the files. For my father's files, that name would be my mother. The code name for my uncle's files would be the only person he ever loved, other than money, power, and himself – my Aunt Catherine."

"Okay," Tangata said, let's get back to the issue facing you two."

Swallowing a sudden lump in his throat,

Philippe said, "The wedding. So how do I go about it? We really should include Mira's family."

"Oh, yes. That's why we're going to her village today and break the news."

That suddenly tied a knot in the young man's stomach. "That over-weight Malo character is not going to take kindly to the idea." he said.

"That's not the real problem. It's meeting and winning approval from Mira's father." Tangata said.

The sudden appearance of the hermit walking into the village with the two in tow garnered lots of shouting as people began flocking in from all directions.

"Mira! Where have you been? Sleeping with this . . . this . . .?

"His name is Philippe, father, and we have pledged to marry," she said resolutely, a huge effort considering children are brought up to obey their elders.

"No!" her father bellowed like a wounded buffalo. "Malo bought you!"

"I am not for sale, especially to that . . . that pig!"

"You will do as I say!"

Mira clutched more tightly to Philippe's arm.

"We seem to have a problem," Tangata said calmly.

"You stay out of this. This is my daughter."

"And Philippe is my son."

Mira's father's dark face darkened with rage, and her mother began to cry as the brothers stepped forward.

"Then this . . . this one must fight us," her oldest brother said. While shorter than Malo, they were still pretty stout boys.

Malo now stepped up. "I bought Mira. She belong to me."

"I belong to no one, especially you! You sorry excuse for a . . .,"

"Mira, I accepted his offer," her father said.

"I'm not marrying that ugly, boar-snouted bully!"

"You will do as I say."

The village chief, who had been standing on the edge of the verbal war, stepped through the crowd. "It is the custom of our ancestors, if Tangata's son desires Mira, he must fight."

Malo and her brothers laughed "I accept that," Malo announced, raising his Popeye-sized fist to Philippe.

"Okay, eel lips, let's get on with it," Philippe answered.

"No!" Mira protested.

Taking her hand, Philippe looked in her dark eyes and said, "It will be alright. Really. Trust me."

Battle was an old custom. Usually no one got hurt, but Mira knew in this instance Malo was intent on killing Philippe, yet he didn't seem at all worried.

"Malo, you, and Mira's brothers prepare yourselves. When you are ready, meet on the beach," the chief said, then turned to say something to Philippe and Tangata, but another villager, a man about Tangata's age stepped forward.

"Mira's young man can prepare in my home."

The chief nodded approval.

"It has been too long since you came to visit, Tangata," the man said as he lead them through the village. He walked with a decided limp.

"Yes, but there are still a few who would rather I were not here," Tangata said. "Philippe, this is Ponui Atiu. He's a friend. About the only one in these parts."

Philippe sensed there was a story behind this that neither was about to share at this moment as they stepped inside the thatched home.

"I have things from the old days. They don't fit any more," he said, patting his pot belly.

"Ponui is a warrior . . .," Tangata began.

"Was. I am long past that. Remove your cloth," Ponui said as he rummaged through a woven chest and began removing items.

First was a long piece of coarse cloth. This was placed between Philippe's legs and wrapped around his waist, both ends to hang to mid-thigh front and back forming a loincloth. Once tied in place, Ponui encircled the boy's hips with a wide belt of woven palm leaves and cloth, tying it securely behind. Disappearing outside a moment, he returned with a stick that had obviously been in a fire. Using a knife, he scraped charcoal into a small bowl, added a bit of spit and began painting it on Philippe's face using one finger. From there he painted decorations on the young man's arms and thighs.

"What do you think?" he asked Tangata.

"Not bad. You still do tattoos?"

"Yes. I would love to work on this young warrior. Such nice, smooth skin. I could make him very beautiful and fearsome."

"Alright, Philippe, I better lay this out. Malo has a lot to prove. For him, this will be a fight to the death. Mira's brother, too"

"I can't kill them," Philippe protested.

"Malo won't give you much choice. The brothers may not be all that dedicated, but must put on a good show."

"But . . ."

"Remember what I said about that awhile back? Between now and when you get to the beach I suggest you have a plan because that character Malo has one . . . to separate your head from your shoulders and put it on a shelf for Mira to look at all her life."

Ponui tied a bright red clothe around Philippe's head. "I hear big mouth calling. Time to go."

Stepping out of the tree line, Philippe saw Malo and Mira's brothers standing on the beach about thirty meters away. Like him, they were decorated with black soot except they also had tattoos, especially Malo who had one that curled from the left pect over the shoulder and wrap around the left bicep. There was another running the outside of both legs from hip to ankle. Tattoos were big among Polynesian, both men and women. Something permanent never appealed to Phillipe. All three were similarly attired, free for serious fighting. They also had long spears, clubs, and long, blade-like sticks.

"Weapons?" Philippe hadn't considered weapons. In fact, he hadn't considered much of anything.

"Yes," Ponui said, handing him a spear and weapon that looked like a wooden version of a long Samurai sword except that it had a much longer handle. "Don't let them get in close. They are good wrestlers. Malo likes to hear his victims scream just before breaking their bones."

"Oh, great."

Tangata then spoke quietly. "This is no different than what Master Yamamoto talked about during training. Focus. And Philippe . . .?"

"Yes?"

"Keep your head."

Philippe stepped further onto the beach, a weapon in each hand, the biggest issue, the argument inside his head. Are you willing to kill one or all of these guys? Taking a side-facing stance he watched as the three began the ritualistic dance, making grotesque faces, their guttural chants filling the air.

"Ha, he, hu! Ha, he, hu! Ha, he, hu!"

Occasionally they'd make sudden faints forward. It was their way to call out for their ancestors to help, to build up for the attack, to frighten their opponent. He'd seen this before when dancers came to entertain guests at his father's resort. In response, Philippe stood his ground, watching each movement closely until Malo's bulging eyes and extended tongue struck a funny chord. Philippe began to laugh.

The three stopped. That simple act stripped away all their frenzied buildup. Mira's younger brother looked at the others, took two hops forward, and launched a spear. Mira gasped as the long, feathered shaft arced through the air heading straight for her love. Philippe didn't move. Had he not seen it? It buried in the sand a foot to the side of him. He didn't flinch.

Seeming to take no notice of the spear, Philippe began walking toward them, gauging the distance. Mira's oldest brother jumped forward to launch his spear. As it arced in, its intended victim continued to move forward, doing a pirouette at the last minute, using the wooden sword to knock the shaft harmlessly aside and resumed the advance. At ten meters, Philippe launched his spear. The brothers dove sideways in opposite directions just in time as the shaft flew between them. It wouldn't have hit either, but they didn't know that.

Malo had a club, a two foot piece of wood with a ball on the end, stuck through his wide belt, and a sword similar to Philippe's. The brothers also had clubs, nasty, curved boogers embedded with shark teeth. Philippe continued to advance as they picked themselves off the sand, then with guttural cries, charged. Their victim continued walking as if on a Sunday stroll of the beach. When they arrived, weapons overhead, he wheeled into action, stepping to the outside of the older brother.

The last second move was too quick for the Islanders to react. The flat of Philippe's bamboo sword caught older brother across the right shin, ripping the leg from under and sending him face first into the sand. The younger brother came to a sliding stop, but Philippe landed the flat of the blade against his side, then against the back of the knee. He went down in howling pain, rolling on the sand, clutching the leg. Two spinning steps and his blade lay across the shoulders of the older brother, driving his face back into the sand, rendering him unconscious.

With two companions so quickly taken out of action, Malo looked around for more help. It wasn't coming. He charged, but was no match for an obvious swordsman as Philippe whipped around him like a water spout, landing blow after blow on his chest, back, and legs until Malo brought his own weapon down with tremendous force, burying the end in the sand. Philippe's side kick splintered the wood and knocked it from the man's hand. Pulling the balled club free, it barely cleared the belt when it dropped after Philippe's sword struck the wrist. Had it been a lesser person, the bone would have fractured.

The young man went into automatic as his sword swung around and struck Malo along the right shoulder knocking him sideways. Around again, smacking the left thigh with a loud crack, around again, the flat side striking the back of the knee. He went down.

By this time, Mira's older brother recovered and stumbled to rescue his friend. He should have stayed down. A side kick caught him in the chest, a roundhouse alongside the head sent him down for the count. Now, with opposition out of the way, he concentrated on Malo.

The Islander was big. He may have developed a gut, but his shoulders were wide as a canoe is long and rippled with muscle. They afforded him nothing. Kick, strike, kick, punch, Philippe methodically took him apart. There was no defense offered. Tangata became worried. It looked as if the boy was going to kill the man, piece by piece, until Philippe stopped and stood in front of Malo.

Grabbing him by the hair, he jerked the head back. The man's eyes were glazed, but knew he could still hear him. "I will not kill you this time, Malo, for Mira's sake, but stay out of our way, or I will do things you could never imagine," Philippe said just loud enough only they could hear, then stepping back, laid a roundhouse kick alongside the man's head, throwing him sideways onto the sand, unconscious.

Walking past the older brother sitting with knees pulled up, head in hands, Philippe went to the younger writhing on the beach, holding his knee. He stopped crying, eyes wide with fear as the victor approached. Kneeling by the leg, Philippe took it in both hands, and felt around the injury. Then, with a sudden movement, did something that elicited another excruciating howl of pain from the boy.

"Enough!" the village chief who had been standing on the sidelines shouted.

Philippe stood and walked back to where Tangata was standing. The villagers stood in mute silence after what had just happened. Some went to the aid of their relatives, but the younger brother waived off any help as he stood on his own. The leg was tender, but he could walk. The people suddenly realized the young man who wanted to marry one of their daughters was not only a warrior to be feared, but a healer.

The chief came up to where Philippe and Tangata stood with Ponui, pulling Mira along by the hand, her father, head bowed, trailing behind.

"I decide that this boy will be a proper husband. We will plan the ceremony," he said, placing the girl's hand into Philippe's.

That was it.

Heads clearing and limping, Mira's brothers briefly consoled one another before sheepishly coming up to Philippe.

"No one has ever beaten Malo." the older brother testified as he came up to where the betrothed stood.

"Never," the younger added.

"We are sorry."

Philippe extended his hand and one by one, they shook hands and embraced.

"It will be good to have a brother such as you in the family," the older said.

Sharing tears of joy, Mira hugged both brothers before they limped off for further attention to their wounds.

It was now time for Mira's father. He was stunned, embarrassed, unsure what to say. Philippe extended his hand in friendship. That was enough as the older man tried to smile while nodding, yes.

"The ceremony will be held in three days."

As Tangata and Philippe walked alone back to the mountain, the young man asked, "Son?"

"Ah-h, kind of a spontaneous adoption. Don't take it seriously."

"But I do. You've been every bit of a father to me."

"What about your real father?"

"He gave birth and raised a boy. You saved a boy and raised him to be a man. I am the most fortunate person on earth to have two wonderful fathers."

Tangata put a hand across Philippe's shoulder as they continued in silence. After a time he said, "Tradition says that the groom's family sponsors the marriage, providing a wedding dress, and throwing a party after which the bride leaves her home to go to live with her husband's family. In this situation, that would appear a little difficult."

"Perhaps there is something we can do." Philippe had total confidence Tangata would pull something out his bag of tricks. The problem for him was that Mira would stay with her family until preparations were made.

The next morning, Tangata lead his charge to the underground marina. Passing the *Adrianne*, Philippe was stunned. The first time they came here, he thought to have seen something low in the water just beyond the light. It was a submarine.

"Has its uses," Tangata said when Philippe stopped to stare.

Painted a dark gray, it was small.

"Patterned somewhat on the Japanese M24 used during World War II. It's half as long at 12 meters thanks to new technology. Has two tubes and carries six-arm-length torpedoes. Like its predecessor, it can run twelve hours submerged on batteries before needing a recharge. Modern technology has reduced the size and number of them allowing more room for two, but one person can operate it. It's a lot more stable than the M24, too."

"What do you use such a boat for?" Philippe asked.

Tangata didn't answer as he continued walking into the dark. Philippe vaguely remembered something about a ship carrying drugs sending an SOS, but all anyone found was some debris and an oil slick. Authorities presumed there had been an explosion aboard and it sank. Whatever happened must have been catastrophic and quick. There were no survivors. Recalling an earlier conversation, there may have been one survivor. Philippe remember that his father seemed delighted. Something about the ship belonging to his brother. At the time, Philippe thought it strange his father would be happy about his brother's loss, but knowing now what Rousseau was about, he understood. Beyond the sub they came to an outrigger, long, clean, beautiful, floating silently on the perfectly still water.

"I want you to paddle this around to the other side and present it to Mira's father. The nets, too. It's your payment. Tell him we will return tomorrow evening for the ceremony. Bring a couple sturdy lads when you return to carry some things back for the party. That canvas bundle inside belongs to Ponui, for his help."

Philippe was too stunned to answer. Once in the boat, however, he said, "Will you open the mountain for me to leave, or is there another way?"

Tangata handed him a small, black box. A remote. "Just open it enough to get out. Works like a garage door." He then walked back toward the single spotlight that shown on the yacht, his body silhouetted.

Late the following afternoon the two walked into

the village, Philippe in a bright blue lava-lava, red headband whose ends hung behind his right ear, and leather sandals. His mother's pendant hung proudly on his bare chest. Tangata was wearing a black lava-lava, white shirt, and sandals. They proceeded directly to Ponui's home where the man sat on the ground mending a net.

"All is ready. Mira's father should be back soon. He's been out sailing that fine boat all day and using the nets. Sent the goat back. Really thinks he's gotten a better deal."

"And you?" Tangata said.

"Oh, yes, my friend. Not really necessary, you know."

Tangata shrugged.

After Ponui's daughters decorated the groom's hair with flowers, and laid a woven, green wreath about his neck, they headed for the beach, intercepted by the chief and his entourage.

"As you are to become one with us, you should have a new name," the elderly man said. "From this day forth, you shall be known among the people of the islands as Oro-I-Te-Tea-Moe."

Philippe looked at his guardian, the question in his eyes.

"Oro is the god of war. Oro-I-Te-Tea-Moe means Oro with spear tip down, a man of peace. But that could change."

"Thank you," Philippe said. "Let's always keep the tip down."

With the chief proudly in the lead, the procession continued to the beach and a setting sun.

Standing side by side before the village shaman, the old man smiled. The boy in front of him was handsome. The girl, in a beautiful red and blue, floral dress and adorned with flowers, could cause a war and actually did. The chief felt fortunate not having permanently lost three men, although one he would like to see on another island.

"Oro-I-Te-Tea-Moe, will you provide a home and food for this woman?"

"Yes," Philippe answered.

"Mira, will you provide a home and food for this man?"

"Yes," she answered, casting a smile toward the man at her side.

Taking their hands, the shaman brought them together. "May you live long, happy lives . . ., and have many babies."

Philippe would have rolled his eyes at that last comment, but was too busy kissing his wife as she nearly knocked him over with enthusiasm. However, that was short-lived as family and friends jumped in to congratulate the newly joined couple. Still limping and sore, Mira's brothers were almost the last to congratulate the couple only because everyone else pushed them aside and they were still moving slowly.

As the sun slipped into the ocean, the party went into full swing. With the pig roasted and a barrel of salted pork opened, a keg of a freshly made kava-kava appeared. Seated on a white cloth, the two ate and watched as the people sang and danced. From a hut further back in the trees, Malo lay alone on a sleeping mat still unable to move from the beating he'd taken, knowing he wouldn't be welcomed even if he were able. He'd have to find someone else for his goat. Maybe on one of the other islands.

The party was over by late the next morning, most of the men unable to rise from where they collapsed from too much food, drink, and partying. Oro and Mira weren't allowed to rest, either. As the sun reached its zenith, she hugged weeping parents and said goodbye. The walk to their home in the mountain was quiet as all they needed to say passed through their hands.

That evening, as a huge, yellow moon rose above Kahuna's teeth, Philippe stood on the beach gazing out at the lagoon and island beyond, but this time he stood with a wife snuggled next to him. Indeed, courtship, marriage, and the ensuing celebration seemed like being swept into a whirlwind, but now they stood alone, wrapped securely in each other's arms.

"This is where I was tossed ashore," Philippe said softly.

"The ocean gave birth to you here."

"Did you notice? Babies. That's all everyone talked about."

"The place of your birth would be a good place to start," Mira said.

Chapter 17

Closure

ᛏomas stood alone on the patio outside
Rousseau's office. The financial data on the stolen CD
had caused his boss a great many problems. When
Interpol used the secret code accessing other
information on the disk, Philippe's uncle had far too
many worries to think about the boy. He avoided jail
for three years thanks to legal maneuvering, but like
a sea surge, the law rose up to crash down on the
balding, little man and his empire, a fragile house of
cards.

Temporarily released from jail on yet another
technicality, Rousseau returned to his villa at the
head of Quinné bay overlooking the ocean caressing
New Caledonia's eastern shore. No sooner had he
taken a seat behind the big desk than the phone
rang. Faithful Tomas sat on the other side. He knew
what the call was about and smiled secretly.

Philippe's uncle placed the call on speaker phone.

"Mr. Rousseau, this is Andrew Sullivan." It was the lead barrister handling the fast-aging Rousseau's legal problems. "I was just visited by the solicitor general. A new development has arisen in the charges against you. It seems new evidence in the form of a deposition and confession is in their possession linking you directly to the death of your brother and his wife."

The crime lord's face turned ashen. He said nothing.

"It is most damaging evidence coming from the man who planted the bomb. It says the order came directly from you."

"That's a lie! You're smart enough to break a phony confession."

"It was a dying declaration, Mr. Rousseau. Coupled with substantial evidence collaborating that declaration, there's not much we can do. I suggest you turn yourself into the authorities in Neumea."

"I pay you a lot of money. Handle it."

"That's another issue, Mr. Rousseau. The last check you wrote was refused by the bank."

"What!"

"Insufficient funds."

"There are millions in that account and the police have no access to it."

"That account, like all the others, appears to be empty. Under the circumstances, it is the considered opinion of those in this office that further representation is withdrawn. Good day, sir."

The click on the speaker phone ending the call seemed particularly final. Rousseau looked up at Tomas who now stood at the sliding glass door. The gang lord's expression was that of a broken man about to sink beneath the waves for the third time.

"How, Tomas? How could my Swiss account be empty? Very convenient that bastard confessed then died. Find a way to discredit it. You are good at that."

"I don't believe that will be possible," Tomas answered.

"Why?"

"Perhaps you should look at your laptop, specifically a message sent just before you returned this afternoon."

Philippe's uncle turned to the computer on his desk, tapped a couple keys, and began to read.

> *To Mr. Tuskin, United States of America Embassy, Canberra, Australia.*
>
> *My dear Friend,*
>   *As you have contact with the young man, please forward this to Philippe. Thank you.*
> *Your servant,*
> *Tomas Bonnell.*
>
> *Dear Philippe,*
>   *As painful as this may be, the time has come that you know the full story of your parents' death.*
>   *Their death was at the hands of your uncle as surely as if he placed the bomb himself. He personally ordered it. Your father's brother is a greedy man. He wanted the resort to further plans to expand drug trafficking and other illegal activities in this part of the Pacific. Your father stood against staggering offers. That resort was like a precious child to him, second only to*

you.

   I was not involved in the murder of your parents and argued strongly against it. I thought to have dissuaded your uncle from such a horrible and cowardly action. I was deceived. As soon I became aware that the plan was being implemented, I tried to warn your father, but my call came after the plane departed.

   I loved your mother deeply. She and I were childhood sweethearts and we would have married. Because of the life I chose, that could not be. I would not subject her to a life of disgrace and humiliation. It was I who introduced her to your father, a much better man. I could not have been more happy for her as the day I stood at your father's side during the wedding, with the possible exception when I became your god-father. No one except your parents and Madam Evelien knew of this. I had the greatest respect for your father and watched you from afar, as if you had been my own son.

   As for my actions against you on that little island upon which you found refuge, I was in a very difficult position and those actions could easily be misunderstood. I am very sorry my attempts to protect your mother and father and you failed.

   When I learned what was planned against you, I used the Island boy to pass that information along and cleared *the way for you to escape, including stealing the money from your uncle's safe. I was careful to plant the computer disk in the bottom so you would not see it. When some of the information on that CD surfaced, I knew that you survived the storm, something that must be credited to your guardian angels.*

Your uncle continued to press for your death in retaliation for betrayal, as he so misunderstands the word. I personally lead the hunt to find you, having a plan to deliver you to a safe haven, a plan not unlike that which Monsieur Tuskin skillfully executed. That poor devil on the island did a great service eliminating the others. That charitable act would have greatly aided my plan, but you took charge of your own fate. That obviously has been the right course and can only credit your guardian angels once again for your outstanding, good fortune. May they continue to guide and protect you.

I only regret that my attempts in your behalf were so feeble. One cannot serve two masters. Always listen to your heart. It will not lead you wrongly. My hope now is that perhaps someday you will find it in your heart to understand and forgive me. The day will come that I must face God and confess my sins. With Him, I expect no forgiveness, which is only justice.

I know that you have more than

enough for a comfortable life and no need or desire for ill-gotten money. However, the information I give below is to an off-shore bank account in the Caribbean Ocean. These are funds amassed by your uncle, taken from honest people. He will not have need of it. Perhaps it could be dispersed through charitable organizations under your direction. Politicians would only squander it as readily as your uncle would have.

I am told that you have taken a very nice, young woman to wife and now have beautiful twin children, a girl and a boy. May God continue to bless you and your wife with many more children and a long and prosperous life.

Incidentally, you play Black Jack quite well for a beginner. Contacts could never hide your mother's eyes.

Your friend, Tomas.

No man could have appeared so pale with horror as Rousseau Bonnét. As realization settled in at what had been happening behind his back his complexion began to darken.

"Tomas? You? You stole my money?"

Jerking a side drawer open the man started to reach inside, stopped, and stared into the empty drawer before slowly turning to face Tomas.

"You have no need for this," Tomas said, holding a nickel, .32 cal. Beretta subcompact.

"But why? I trusted you!" Rousseau began to whine.

"You would have continued to have my devotion and trust if you had not killed Charles and Danielle, and tried to kill Philippe. My e-mail is sufficient explanation. You are the last threat to the boy, something he shall not have to live with."

◆　　◆　　◆

Philippe stared at the computer screen, re-reading the message from Tomas several times. Two days later, a news article appeared on Brisbane's, The Courier Mail, website.

Gang Lord Dead
Australian Associated Press

Noumea, New Caledonia. *Convicted crime boss, Rousseau Bonnét, was found dead at his New Caledonia mansion Thursday, an apparent suicide.*

Bonnét, founded of a crime syndicate that stretched throughout the SW Pacific with ties to criminal organizations in Asia. Police became successful in their battle eight years ago when financial information on the organization was uncovered. Since that time, Bonnét has been in and out of both the courts and jail. He was recently released from jail on a technicality.

In a new development, police received conclusive evidence that Bonnét personally ordered the murder of his brother, Charles Bonnét, a highly respected businessman in the Pacific region. Police went to his mansion located on the east coast of New Caledonia to effect an arrest where they found his body seated at a desk with one bullet wound to the head.

No one else was found at the sprawling mansion. It is believed that all those involved in his organization abandoned him to his troubles. The whereabouts of Bonnet's only known relative, Philippe Bonnét, son of Charles Bonnét, who disappeared several years ago is still unknown. Financial records indicate Rousseau Bonnét died a pauper and unless someone steps forward, he will be interred in a pauper's grave.

Philippe turned off the computer and walked out into the sunlight where his wife and Ellie sat playing as they waited for him. Looking out over the lagoon, the other island, and blue ocean beyond, he took in a deep breath and let it out.

"The children's grandfather is watching them while they nap. Let's go for a swim," he said, taking Mira's hand and heading down the trail.

He could now walk in the open without listening for the sound of aircraft or worry about a white yacht prowling the island's shoreline. He could go anywhere in the world now, without looking over his shoulder.

◆   ◆   ◆

Most times, going back is not possible because people and places change, never being quite the same as remembered. Philippe realized this and had no desire to return to his childhood home, instead keeping the best of returning memories of those days close to his heart, sharing them with his children as they sat high on their mountain home overlooking the tranquil lagoon below, the past put behind as the boy, now a man, focused on the future.

Sean Patrick O'Morda

is a product of the American west, growing up in Laramie, Wyoming. He began a writing career in 1962 as a newspaper reporter, later serving as a special page editor. He is the contributing author to several history tomes of the American west, and author of numerous articles for police journals and other publications. In addition he has published numerous short stories, several of which have earned awards. He publishes a weekly post, sharing insights to writing learned over his long experience. *Man With No Name* was first published in 2011 as his sixth novel.

Sean can be found at:

https://celtic-publications.com/
or
celtic.publications.of.arizona@gmail.com

www.ingramcontent.com/pod-product-compliance
Lightning Source LLC
Chambersburg PA
CBHW062035170626
46813CB00001B/343